Eureka College Alumni association

A History of Eureka College

with biographical sketches and reminiscences

Eureka College Alumni association

A History of Eureka College
with biographical sketches and reminiscences

ISBN/EAN: 9783337388706

Printed in Europe, USA, Canada, Australia, Japan

Cover: Foto ©Andreas Hilbeck / pixelio.de

More available books at **www.hansebooks.com**

A HISTORY

OF

EUREKA COLLEGE

WITH

Biographical Sketches and Reminiscences.

ILLUSTRATED.

St. Louis :
CHRISTIAN PUBLISHING COMPANY,
1894.

EXPLANATORY.

At their annual reunion, June 16, 1892, the Alumni Association of Eureka College decided to publish a history of their Alma Mater. The work was placed in charge of a committee, consisting of Benjamin J. Radford, Clara S. Davidson, Carl Johann, Oliver W. Stewart, with Elmira J. Dickinson as chairman.

The chairman of the committee was chosen editor of the book. Asa S. Fisher, the first teacher of the school that developed into Eureka College, who was associated with it nearly forty years, and who is the only survivor of those who were prominent in starting the enterprise, was appointed historian for the period extending from the beginning of it to the time of his leaving Eureka in 1886. From that time to the date of publication, Carl Johann was more fully associated with all the interests of the institution than any other person, and was therefore chosen to prepare the record of that period.

Faithful effort has been made to procure photographs of all who have been regular teachers in the

(3)

institution, with biographical sketches of them; and, although success in this has not been complete, it has been fairly good.

It was hoped that the work might be brought out by Commencement, 1893, and the committee strove hard to do this; but in the preparation difficulties were encountered that made it quite impossible except at the sacrifice of merit. Therefore longer time has been taken and better work done.

Hoping that the volume may receive a cordial welcome from the present friends of the college, and be a means of winning for it many others, without further preface it is offered to its readers.

TABLE OF CONTENTS.

HISTORICAL.

CHAPTER I.

(5)

REMINISCENCES.

MISCELLANEOUS.

DIVISIONS.

HISTORICAL.
BIOGRAPHICAL.
REMINISCENCES.
MISCELLANEOUS.

HISTORICAL.

HISTORY OF EUREKA COLLEGE.

CHAPTER I.

WALNUT GROVE.

The community known as Walnut Grove, Woodford county, Illinois, had its origin in the early 20's, while Central Illinois was practically a vast wilderness. It was rapidly promoted by emigrants from the adjoining States, most of them hailing from *Old Kentucky*, bringing with them characteristics of that noble people, and soon the community became widely and favorably known for its hospitality and other social distinctions.

THE OLD SPRING.

At or near the head of a ravine, and not forty rods south of the present site of Eureka College, the early pioneers found a sparkling fountain

(13)

gurgling up through broken strata and supplying the water of a rill winding its way over the roots and pebbles, leaves, twigs and other impediments to the creek near by. An excavation was here made which was walled up with fragments of rocks found in the vicinity, and the origin of the little rill soon came to be known as "The Spring." Here pedestrians and teamsters, those on horseback and others, often halted to drink of the limpid water and to rest beneath the cool shade of the primeval forest. Near the spring, also the early pioneers were wont to assemble beneath the noble forest trees in religious convocations, for the Fourth of July celebrations and for other purposes.

But the "Old Spring" is no longer a prominent feature of Walnut Grove. Since cultivated fields and pastures have occupied the tracts formerly covered by dense forests and the luxuriant growth of the wild meadows of the prairies, the strata that formerly produced the famous little fountain have been so far modified by the evaporating power of the sun and other causes, that the sparkling liquid no longer comes forth, and the famous "Old Spring" exists only in history.

THE "BURGOO."

The early inhabitants of Walnut Grove were free from all caste distinction. They all moved on the same social plane. Religiously, they were generally communicants of the Christian Church, and habitually addressed one another as brother or sister. Annually they convened near the "Old Spring" to enjoy the rites of a popular feast known in the locality as the "Burgoo."* It was a feast peculiar to that people ; was introduced by Elder John T. Jones, formerly from Pennsylvania, and was held in the springtime, or early summer, when young squirrels were abundant.

When all the surroundings appeared propitious, some of the recognized leaders would proclaim a day for the feast, when a general invitation would be circulated.

In the morning of the appointed day, the old men and women, the young maidens and children would start for the "Spring," some going on foot, some on horseback, and others in wagons, all aiming to reach the place of rendezvous by nine o'clock of the forenoon.

The young men and experts at hunting would traverse the forests in search of suitable game for the festival. Squirrels being numerous, the hunters invariably secured an abundance on their way to the "Spring."

It was always assumed that Elder Elijah Dickinson—they called him "Uncle 'Lijah"—would

---

*Probably a corruption of the French word *Ragout*, meaning a meat stew.

provide kettles and the necessary condiments.
The good old patriarch was sure to be at the place
of rendezvous at an early hour, when he would
diligently proceed to kindle the needed fire, provide for the suspension of his kettles and adjust
other essential preliminaries before the arrival of
the bouyant hunters with their respective trophies
of success.

On arriving with their game, the exulting and
jubilant hunters, while narrating their many and
assumed important feats of the morning raid,
would speedily and neatly prepare the same for
cooking, and turn it over to Uncle 'Lijah, who,
assisted by some good sisters, would quietly proceed to complete preparations for the social
dinner.

While these preparations were in progress, all
others were at liberty to spend the hours in any
way most congenial to their respective tastes. The
fathers and mothers might be seen in groups, on
chairs and other improvised seats, in shady nooks,
discussing economic questions pertaining to the
future improvements of the new country. Some of
the young men engaged in sundry athletic sports,
running foot races, jumping and wrestling. Others of the young people might be seen congregated
beneath the boughs of the noble forest trees,
"chasing dull care away" by gleeful songs and
romping plays.

THE SCHOOL HOUSE — 1846

Meanwhile Uncle 'Lijah and his volunteer helps kept diligent watch over the contents of the boiling kettles, seasoning them from time to time with cayenne pepper and other condiments, until the whole was brought to a degree of palatable perfection assumed by the manager to be good and *very* good. Although the process was somewhat tedious, yet the sun would only have passed the noon-day meridian ere Uncle 'Lijah would announce "Dinner ready." At this announcement, conversations and all sports would promptly be suspended; and in a quiet, orderly manner all would proceed to examine their respective baskets and boxes for bowls, spoons, plates, knives and forks and bread. Uncle 'Lijah, with dipper in hand, stood guard over the savory contents of his capacious kettles, and in his accustomed pleasant mood would bountifully supply every one with soup or meat as bowl or plate would be presented.

The social dinner of *so many courses*, enlivened by anecdote, story-telling, wit and repartee, being over, conversations, discussions, athletic sports and romping plays would be resumed and continued until the rapidly lengthening shadows "told the hour for retiring," when all would depart for their respective homes, delighted with the adventures of the day.

2

ELDER JOHN T. JONES OPENS A SCHOOL.

About the year 1847, Elder B. Major, E. B. Myers, Elder Wm. Davenport, David Deweese, A. M. Myers, B. J. Radford, Sr., Elder E. Dickinson, Elder John T. Jones, Wm. P. Atterberry and R. M. Clark were the prominent and leading citizens of the community, the major part of them immigrants from Kentucky, and all were members of the Christian Church. They were all men of advanced views on the subject of education, and recognized the establishment of schools of a high order an essential in the great work of developing the resources of the Prairie State.

Elder John T. Jones, an evangelist of distinction in Central Illinois, was induced to open a select school for the education of girls, in the autumn of 1847, upon his own premises, where now is the residence of Elder W. H. Boles, within a few hundred yards of the present site of Eureka College. In this school his wife—known in the community as "Aunt Emily"—a woman of superior education for that time, and his daughter, Miss Susan E. Jones, who was educated at Jacksonville, Illinois, were the principal teachers.

The school was liberally patronized, and the outlook for the near future was very flattering. But an unforeseen calamity blasted the buoyant hopes of the projectors. In the winter of 1847–8,

1 W. P. Atteberry.
2 David Downose.
3 B. J. Radford, Sr.
4 R. M. Clark.

5 E. B. Myers.
6 A. M. Myers.
7 H. D. Palmer.
8 Wm. Davenport.

a malignant form of the measles became epidemic in the community. Many of the students suffered from attacks of the disease. In the panic ensuing the institution was suspended, the students returning to their several homes. The community was greatly scourged and the school was never revived.

WALNUT GROVE SEMINARY.

In August, 1848, A. S. Fisher, a student from Bethany College, appeared in the community and made application for a school, proposing to teach all the common English branches, the higher mathematics, natural philosophy, chemistry, rhetoric, logic, etc., etc. He was employed to teach a school for ten months, Elder B. Major, E. B. Myers, Elder E. Dickinson, B. J. Radford, Sr., and others guaranteeing his salary. On the tenth day of September, 1848, the school was opened in a small frame building, modestly provided with seats, desks and other furniture, and located near the northeast corner of the present Eureka Cemetery.

THE GREAT HENDERSON MEETING.

Soon after the opening of the school, Elder D. P. Henderson, an eminent Christian evangelist from Jacksonville, Illinois, commenced a series of meetings in the community, which was protracted for many days, producing a wonderful revival among the inhabitants of Walnut Grove.

There had been at Walnut Grove a Church of Christ for many years, one having been organized in the early 30's. In this church the widely-known and popular Christian evangelist, Elder William Davenport, had his membership.

Elder Davenport, James Robeson of Panther Creek, A. Pealer of White Oak Grove, James A. Lindsey of Tazewell county, and other pioneer Christian preachers, had long been teaching the people the true doctrine of the Bible. Elder H. D. Palmer, the aged patriarch of Marshall county, had often, by his earnest exhortations from the pulpit, and by his exemplary course when mingling with the people in their daily avocations, urged them to forsake sinful ways and unite with the Christian army. And the great Alexander Campbell, influenced by his knowledge as to the cherished design of Elder B. Major and others to establish a seat of learning in Walnut Grove, had made that community a prominent feature in more than one of his western tours.

Whatever may have been the contributory causes during the protracted effort the membership of the Church of Christ at Walnut Grove was increased by nearly one hundred additions. The occasion was long remembered and referred to as *"The great Henderson meeting of 1848."*

THE SEMINARY.

SCHOOL WORK RESUMED.

During the progress of the protracted meeting, the school work had been suspended. At the termination of the meeting the work was resumed, and continued with but slight interruption to the end of the session, July 4th, 1849.

Elder Major and his coadjutors, in an interview with the young teacher, urged him to continue with them and conduct the school another session. Upon the following conditions he promised to comply with the request:

1. That an addition properly furnished with seats, desks, and other appliances be made to the school-house.

2. That he be permitted to employ an assistant to aid him in the primary teaching.

3. That adequate provision be made for boarding all students from other localities.

4. That he be allowed the net income from tuition fees as his salary.

The preliminaries for the ensuing year having been arranged, the contracting parties proceeded diligently to prepare for the fulfillment of their respective parts of the agreement, each party providing " ways and means " of its own, " without let or hindrance " from the other.

The said A. S. Fisher had been negotiating with a certain party of Marshall county concerning the formation of a co-partnership wherein the relation of the parties is expressed by the correlative terms, husband and wife. The pending negotiations having resulted in a mutual agreement, *ratifications were exchanged* at the residence of Elder H. D. Palmer, on the 25th day of July, 1849.

During the summer of 1849, the first printed announcement of the school was put in circulation. It read as follows:

WALNUT GROVE SEMINARY.

The second session of this Institution will commence on the First Monday of September next. The directors hope to have their new building completed, and ample boarding accommodations will be provided for all students attending the Seminary from other localities.

The course of instruction will include Reading, Penmanship, Arithmetic, Geography, English Grammar, History, Algebra, Geometry, Trigonometry, Surveying, Rhetoric, Logic, English Composition, Chemistry and Natural Philosophy.

TERMS.

The academic year will close on the 4th day of July, 1850. The price of tuition will range from eight to fifteen dollars per session, according to the branches studied. Those attending from other localities can obtain boarding, fuel and lights included, at from one dollar to one dollar and twenty-five cents per week.

SITUATION.

The Walnut Grove Seminary is located in Walnut Grove, Woodford County, Illinois, about twenty miles east of Peoria. For health of climate, beautiful scenery, intelligence and morality among the people, the community is not surpassed by any locality of the State.   A. S. FISHER, *Principal*.

E. B. MYERS,
E. DICKINSON, } *Directors*.
R. BARD,

The Principal employed Miss Sue E. Jones, a graduate from Jacksonville and a young lady of superior ability and tact as a teacher, to assist him in conducting the primary classes. The capacity of the school had been increased, and consisted of two rooms well supplied with the school furniture of that time — "home-made" blackboards, seats and desks.

In accordance with the printed circular, the second session was opened on the first Monday of September. The number of students in attendance was very encouraging, and the weekly applications for admittance soon impressed Elder Major and others that additional room would be requisite in the near future. Accordingly, in the autumn of 1849 the promoters of the school were called together for the purpose of considering the erection of a more commodious building.

At this meeting Elder Major insisted that an effort should be made to erect a two story brick building at a cost of twenty-five hundred dollars. Many of those present expressed very grave doubts as to the probability of raising a sum of money so large. Mr. Major listened patiently to the discussion, but kept silent till *called out.* Some one said, " Brother Major, let us hear from you." " Brother Major!" " Brother Major!" was earnestly called out from various parts of the audience. In response Mr. Major said, " Brethren, this is a matter very dear to my heart. You all know that I have long entertained the hope of witnessing an institution of high order established in our midst. Perhaps I am too sanguine, but I believe we can raise the money." "Tell us how, Brother Major," said some one, "what is your plan?" Said he, "I'll tell you." After a pause he continued, "Let Brother David Deweese, Brother E. B. Myers and myself open the subscription, each writing $150 opposite his name, and appoint Brother William Davenport to act as our solicitor to canvass this community and others near us." Messrs. Myers and Deweese, being both present, readily agreed to the proposition. Elder Davenport was appointed solicitor, who, by his earnest and eloquent efforts, obtained the requisite amount of pledges in a few weeks.

WALNUT GROVE ACADEMY.

In December, 1849, the school was incorporated as Walnut Grove Academy, under the management of twelve trustees—Elder John T. Jones being president, and A. S. Fisher, secretary.

The following interview between Elder B. Major, the recognized founder of Eureka College, and A. S. Fisher, who spent thirty-eight years as a teacher and earnest promoter of that institution, may serve to indicate that the development of the College from the humble seminary of 1849 was not a for-

THE ACADEMY

THE OLD MEETING HOUSE.

tuitous accident, but was the legitimate outgrowth of an ideal entertained by the original promoters. The interview was in the early spring of 1850.

The two brethren were walking along the road leading eastward from the Seminary building, and, as usual, conversation was in relation to the school. As they neared the edge of the Grove, at the suggestion of Elder Major they stopped and turned about, facing the gentle elevation on which Walnut Grove Academy was subsequently erected—the lot just west of the one on which the gentlemen's boarding halls now stand. It was then dense woods. Elder Major remarked, "On that rise we intend to build a college, and we want you to be the president." Mr. Fisher replied, "I am not ambitious for such a position, and possibly have not the requisite qualifications, but I am strongly in sympathy with the enterprise, and to the extent of my power will aid the brethren to push forward the noble work they have so generously undertaken. I am without pecuniary wealth; but if the brethren of the Grove will furnish money to erect the necessary buildings, to provide suitable furniture, a library, etc., I will utilize my humble ability as an organizer and instructor to assist in making the pending enterprise successful." Said Elder Major, "We will most certainly succeed, and you shall always hold a prominent place on the Board of Instruction."

ELDER JOHN LINDSEY.

To provide for the accommodation of students wishing to study the ancient classics of Greece and Rome, Elder John Lindsey, a young evangelist of great promise, a graduate of Bethany College—class of '48—was elected a member of the Board of Instruction. He accepted the appointment, and promptly appeared in September, 1850, to assist in the school under its new name.

The new building was not completed till the following December. In the meantime the Seminary building was utilized as a substitute.

WALNUT GROVE LITERARY INSTITUTE.

While waiting for the completion of the new building, a literary society was organized by the students, which they christened "Walnut Grove Literary Institute." The society held weekly sessions, at which the regular performances were reading original essays, declamations, orations, debates and miscellaneous business. It was a useful and important auxiliary of the Academy. Many years after it was incorporated as The Edmund Burke Society.

It has had an uninterrupted existence since its first organization, although soon after the Academy was merged into Eureka College the original name was dropped for that of The Edmund Burke Society. Under its auspices hundreds of students have received a training in the rules of parliamentary usage that has contributed largely to make them valuable citizens in the many localities where they have respectively located since leaving their Alma Mater.

Under the supervision and fostering care of the college authorities it has ever been an important and useful organ of the general college work.

PHILOSOPHICAL AND CHEMICAL APPARATUS.

During the session of 1850-1, the Board of Trustees made an appropriation for the purchase of apparatus needed by the teachers in illustrating and demonstrating the laws of Physical Science.

The money was transmitted to Professor Ray, of Cincinnati, Ohio, who was appointed a special agent, and instructed to select, purchase and forward to Peoria such apparatus as he might deem most useful to the school. He made a most excellent selection, which he forwarded to Peoria during the summer vacation of 1851. It was there received by A. S. Fisher, conveyed by wagon to the Academy, unpacked, tested, and placed in the apparatus room for future use.

AN APPEAL TO THE MISSIONARY CONVENTION.

The Annual Missionary Convention of the Church of Christ in Illinois for 1851 was held in

Walnut Grove. The Board of Trustees of the
Academy explained to that convention the nature
and design of their incorporation ; that they were
endeavoring to establish an institution of learning where the young people of both sexes might
receive the advantages of a liberal education
under the care and influence of Christian teachers,
entirely free from all sectarian prejudices.

While the Convention, informally, were quite
liberal in expressing their hearty approval of the
movement, and, in many ways, commended the
work of the original promoters, and strongly urged
the Trustees to persevere in their work, yet they
neglected to make any appropriation to aid in the
future development. There was no formal refusal
to endorse the Academy and to give it *"substantial aid and comfort,"* but immediate action was
postponed by the appointment of a committee on
Education, with instructions to report at the next
annual convention, to be held at Abingdon.

CHAPTER II.

CHOLERA EPIDEMIC.

Near the close of the fourth session, the institution was interrupted by the sudden appearance of the Asiatic cholera in the community. One of the victims was Elder B. Major, President of the Board of Trustees. In his death the academy suffered the loss of its most zealous promoter, the church its leading elder and the community its most influential citizen.

Soon after his death, at a call meeting of the Board, the following preamble and resolutions were unanimously adopted:

WHEREAS, in the dispensation of Divine Providence, it has pleased the Heavenly Father to remove from among us our beloved president, the founder of this institution, Elder Ben Major, therefore,

Be it Resolved by the Board of Trustees of Walnut Grove Academy, that in the death of Bro. Ben Major we recognize the loss of an able counselor and faithful presiding officer, that we deeply sympathize with his affectionate consort and family in

(29)

their sudden and sorrowful bereavement, and with the whole community in their irreparable loss.

Resolved, That this preamble and these resolutions be spread upon our record, and that a copy of them be delivered to Sister Major, widow of the deceased.

E. DICKINSON, President.

A. S. FISHER, Secretary.

Upon the death of Elder Major, Elder E. Dickinson was unanimously elected president of the corporation, and for ten eventful years, up to the time of his death without an opposing vote, he was annually re-elected. He was a man of incorruptible integrity, a devoted friend of the school, a beloved officer of the church and an honorable citizen of the community.

The epidemic was of short duration, but the students became greatly alarmed and promptly departed for their respective homes. No effort was made to recall them, and thus the session was abruptly closed about one month before the stipulated time, being the only serious interruption to the institution from its first organization, in 1848.

RESIGNATION OF ELDER LINDSEY.

During the summer of 1852, soon after the cholera crisis, it became known that Elder Lindsey contemplated resigning his place on the Board of Instruction. Notwithstanding the managers of the school earnestly labored to prevent such a step, fearing it would be disastrous, yet the resignation was placed at the disposal of the Trustees, who very reluctantly accepted it, knowing his ability as an instructor and his great influence over the students.

Professor John H. Neville, a graduate of Bethany College, class of '49, a young man of excellent literary attainments, was elected to fill the vacancy. He accepted the appointment, with the proviso that he should be professor of higher mathematics and the Greek and Latin languages.

At the opening of the session in September, 1852, Elder Lindsey assembled with the students to bid them a formal farewell as one of their teachers, and, in a brief way, alluded to the cholera episode of the previous session. He spoke very tenderly of the great loss sustained by the academy in the death of the lamented Elder Major, and to the vacant place among the students created by the death of Joseph Davenport, a young nephew of Elder Major. Said Joseph was a young man of superior natural ability. He was a great favorite in the community, and was a recognized leader among his fellow-students. He was modest, a hard student and an earnest promoter of any exercise among his fellow-students that seemed to be for the general good. He was, therefore, a prominent worker in the Walnut Grove Literary Institute. But "death is no respecter of persons." He was stricken down by the dread disease, notwithstanding the earnest efforts of school-fellows and other friends to save his young life.

PROFESSOR JOHN H. NEVILLE.

Professor Neville assumed his place in the academy as the successor of Elder John Lindsey, and soon became a popular teacher. All classes allotted to his management were conducted into the labyrinths of literature in a way that developed within his students an insatiable desire for thorough investigation, and accordingly all his pupils became ardent workers, and ambitious to excel as proficients. He had an inoffensive way of impressing all his classes that a master mind was at the helm, and that their success and their best interests required an unchallenged and cheerful compliance with all his requisitions as their teacher.

THE ABINGDON MISSIONARY CONVENTION.

In September, 1852, the Missionary Society of the Church of Christ in Illinois assembled at Abingdon. The Committee on Education, appointed at the Convention in Walnut Grove, in 1851, submitted a report recommending the appointment of an Educational Board to prepare a plan of operation and report to the next convention. The report was adopted, and Elder William Davenport, Elder John Lindsey, A. S. Fisher, Elder George W.

Minier, Elder Jonathan Atkinson, Elder T. J. Matlock and Elder A. J. Kane were appointed said committee.

All who are acquainted with the early history of the Reformation urged by A. Campbell and others, know that the original promoters were obliged to depend very largely for evangelists upon men possessing only limited academical training; and, although those were generally men of undoubted Christian integrity, very zealous in the Master's work and very successful in attacks upon the strongholds of infidelity and sectarianism, yet they were often made to feel the want of that preparation secured only by extended training, in early life, at institutions under the control of cultured men. Although many schools of learning were then in existence, yet not one of them was conducted by a faculty acknowledging the important principles of the current Reformation.

It was the want of such an institution that led to the organization of Bethany College, in Virginia. And the Christian congregations of Illinois thought the work in which they were engaged required a school of high order in their own State.

The congregation at Walnut Grove, Woodford county, having organized a school in accordance with what they understood to be the general desire of the congregations in the State, were anxious for a concentration of effort to assist in pushing for-

3

ward their enterprise to a state of more general
usefulness. The subject was called up at the
Abingdon Convention, subsequent to the creation
of the Educational Board, by Elder D. P. Henderson, of Jacksonville, in the following preamble and
resolution, which were adopted:

WHEREAS, Walnut Grove Academy, now under the control of
a Board of Trustees, organized under the general law of Illinois,
which has been in successful operation for the last four years,
taught by A. S. Fisher, Principal of the department of mathematics, and John Lindsey, Principal of languages; and which is
the only regularly organized Institution of learning controlled by
our brethren in the State; and WHEREAS said institution proposes
to educate young men for the ministry "free of tuition fees,"

Therefore, *Resolved*, that we commend to our brethren in Illinois this institution, and urge upon them to foster it by sending
their sons and daughters, and donating to its library and appar-
ratus, and raising such means as may enable the Trustees to place
it upon a sure and permanent basis, and be recognized as the
Institution for the brethren of this State.

ELDERS LINDSEY AND DAVENPORT APPOINTED CANVASSERS.

Encouraged by the foregoing action of the Abingdon Convention, the Trustees of Walnut Grove
Academy appointed Elders John Lindsey and
William Davenport solicitors to canvass various
localities and explain to the people of the congregations the nature of the school at Walnut Grove,
the action of the Missionary Convention in relation
to it, and solicit the patronage and funds recommended in the Abingdon endorsement.

Many localities were visited by the two representatives of the academy, and they were liberally rewarded by promises of future patronage and by donations in money, and pledges for the future, as indicated by the catalogue of students for the session of 1852-3, and by the treasurer's report of those years. Students were in attendance from more than twenty localities within the State, and some from the adjacent States of Indiana and Missouri.

THE POSTOFFICE.

At the origin of the school, and for three or four subsequent years, the nearest postoffice was Washington, in Tazewell county, eight miles away. Friends of the institution, and especially students in attendance from other localities, were greatly annoyed by the consequent tardy mail service. The Board of Trustees recognized the situation and realized that the evil was destined soon to become a serious obstacle in the development of many inportant interests. But an adequate remedy was not under their immediate control. It could only be effected through officials of the general Government. The work was inaugurated, however. The officials at the nearest postoffices were interviewed, and through them correspondence was opened up with parties at Washington, D. C. As the result, a postoffice was established near the academy, at the residence of Professor A. S. Fisher, who was the first postmaster. For a time the office was supplied weekly from Metamora.

THE FIRST BEQUEST.

The first bequest to this institution was made by Jonathan Tressler, a native of Pennsylvania, who came to Walnut Grove early in 1838. He was a carpenter, a young man of quiet ways, warm heart and earnest life, and soon became identified with the community in all benevolent, educational and Christian work. He had but little means, but steadily plied his trade, and gradually accumulated a fair amount of property.

He was a devoted friend of the academy from its beginning. The only bequest it ever received was from him. It consisted of a quarter section of land about three miles northeast of Eureka, and eighty acres directly west and southwest of the cemetery.

He died February 4, 1853, and his body rests near the center of Eureka cemetery.

He it was that built the little frame Schoolhouse and The Seminary pictured in this volume; also the academy building, and "The Old Meeting House," and nearly all the farm houses, barns, etc., that were built in the community about that time.

ORGANIZATION OF THE BOARD OF EDUCATION.

As provided in a resolution by the Abingdon Missionary Convention in September, 1852, the Board of Education assembled in the city of Springfield on the 28th day of December, 1852, the following members being present: William Davenport, A. J. Kane, Geo. W. Minier, A. S. Fisher.

Elder William Davenport was appointed temporary chairman, and Elder Geo. W. Minier secretary. The following preamble and resolutions were adopted :

WHEREAS, our Lord and Saviour imposed upon his followers to teach the principles of his kingdom to all nations; and, WHEREAS, the brethren of the Church of Christ in Illinois, in annual convention, recognizing education an important agent in the spread of Christianity, appointed a Board of Education to assemble in Springfield and organize for the purpose of reporting ways and means for the establishment of academies in various parts of the State; and, WHEREAS, a majority of said Board are now present, therefore,

Resolved, that the following be adopted as our platform for deliberation:

1. This association shall be known as "The Board of Education of the Christian Missionary Society of Illinois."

2. The object of this association shall be to provide for the promotion of primitive Christianity by urging the Churches of Christ in Illinois to establish schools under their exclusive management.

3. The officers of the association shall be a president, vice-president, treasurer and secretary, whose duties shall be the same as those of similar organizations.

Elder William Davenport was chosen president,

Elder John Lindsey, vice-president; Elder Geo. W. Minier, treasurer, and A. S. Fisher, secretary.

The Board then adjourned to three o'clock in the afternoon.

AFTERNOON SESSION.

The Board asembled pursuant to adjournment. The following was adopted :

Resolved, That every member of the Board be requested to prepare an essay in relation to the number of academies that ought to be established, and suggestions as to the best method of securing the means necessary for the erection of buildings, purchasing libraries, apparatus, etc.; and that the essays be forwarded to our secretary by the 4th day of July next, who shall from the various suggestions prepare a report for consideration at our next meeting to be held at Jacksonville, in September, 1853.

*   *   *   *   *   *   *   *

Resolved, That Professor John H. Neville be requested to fill the vacancy created by the removal of Elder T. J. Matlock from our State.

Thereupon the Board adjourned to meet in Jacksonville, in September, 1853.   WM. DAVENPORT, President.

A. S. FISHER, Secretary.

SESSION 1853-4.

At the Annual Meeting of the Trustees, in June, 1853, it was resolved that the increase of students during the past session and the prospective further increase for the next, make it necessary to employ a stronger force of instruction. They, however, declined to take further action without conferring with the present Board of Instruction.

Professors Fisher and Neville recommended that provision be made for assistance in conducting the primary classes, and signified their preference for Miss Sarah Fisher and Miss Elmira J. Dickinson, two young ladies, students of the Academy. These were accordingly employed.

BOARD OF INSTRUCTION.
Session 1853-4.

A. S. FISHER,
Of Natural Sciences, Mathematics, and Principal of the Preparatory School.

JOHN H. NEVILLE,
Of Higher Mathematics, Greek and Latin.

SARAH FISHER AND ELMIRA J. DICKINSON,
Assistants in Preparatory School.

To provide additional boarding accommodations, a canvass for means to erect a boarding house was inaugurated. This resulted favorably, enabling the Trustees to erect and complete a commodious building during the spring and summer of 1854, arranged to accommodate about fifty students. It was placed under the management of the affable Christian gentleman, R. M. Clark, one of the Trustees and an ardent friend of the Academy. The house was opened for the reception of students in September, 1854, and while presided over by Mr. Clark and his amiable wife was a pleasant home for the numerous occupants.

REPORT FROM THE BOARD OF EDUCATION made to

the Missionary Convention assembled in Ja·kson-
ville, September, 1853.

The Board met in Jacksonville, pursuant to adjournment, and instructed the secretary to present
to the Convention there assembled the following as
the result of their deliberations:

Before submitting any plan for a combined effort by the
brethren in the establishment of schools, the Board would call
attention to what has already been done. At the Annual Convention held in Woodford county, in August, 1851, it was
resolved that our true interest as a Christian community requires
an institution of such character that the brethren may endow
their sons and daughters with a liberal education under the
immediate control of Christian teachers. At the next Annual
Convention, which was held at Abingdon, Walnut Grove Academy was recognized as the institution of the brethren, and they
were called upon to foster it by sending their sons and daughters,
and making such an amount of donations as would enable the
founders to place it upon a sure and permanent basis.

In October following the Convention at Abingdon, the Trustees of Walnut Grove Academy appointed Elders Davenport and
Lindsey to canvass the State for students and the means recommended.

All these had been done, or were in progress, when the
Board of Education assembled in the city of Springfield for the
purpose of organizing.

While we have great confidence in the liberality of our brethren, yet we fear the draft upon them at the present for means to
establish a State Institution of the contemplated grade, may
prove to be somewhat burdensome, as they are now contemplat-
ing the endowment of a chair in Bethany College. We, therefore, limit our report to the creation of academies in the various
missionary districts, in which the course of instruction shall
include Reading, Writing, Arithmetic, Geography, Grammar,
History, Natural Philosophy, Algebra, Geometry and First Lessons in Greek and Latin.

In order to establish an academy in any given district, the brethren thereof should be called together, and the principles of education and their legitimate effects upon a community should be fully unfolded to them, and the strong obligation of all Christians to donate of the means entrusted to their respective stewardships for its promotion.

If an academy should be voted for, the whole matter should be referred to a Board of Trustees, comprising one or more members from every congregation.

*   *   *   *   *   *   *   *

Impressions during childhood being most enduring, and wrong impressions always difficult to remove, the matter of primary education is of paramount importance, and all our brethren should be strongly urged to make use of all laudable efforts to secure competent Christian teachers in all our common schools.

On the subject of text-books, the Board would recommend that none be used in any of our schools that are at all tainted with the withering principles of sectarianism. Use only those that, in all their suggestions to the young mind, tend towards building up a high order of moral character. The Bible should have a conspicuous place in the daily exercises of every school. Having been prepared by the Author of the human mind, it is superior to all human productions in developing morality among any people.

As Christians, it is our inalienable duty to develop the great plan of salvation in its ancient simplicity, and it is the unchallenged testimony of all Christendom that only an educated mind is competent to disengage the simple facts of Christianity from the many false dogmas with which they have become entangled through many centuries of false teachings and interpretations; hence a well organized system of schools is a matter of the first magnitude.

Brethren, shall we have such schools among us and under our control? We have the necessary talent and wealth. Shall we appropriate them to so noble a purpose? Or shall we be lured into the general vortex of speculation and " strive to accumulate more money, to buy more land, to make larger farms, to gro r more corn, to secure more money." In such a circle the children of mammon always move. But having tasted of the good things of eternal life, we should direct our energies in a channel whose plane is far above the accumulating of worldly wealth.

The realization of the system proposed will require many years of toil and wasting anxiety. But is not the end proposed worthy of the required effort? "There is no excellence without great labor." Let us, therefore, push forward the begun work with firm reliance on Him who is the head of all principalities and powers.   A. S. FISHER, Secretary.

It was thought appropriate to narrate, thus minutely, the doings of the Board of Education, and to call attention to the resolutions by the Missionary conventions at Walnut Grove, Abingdon and Jacksonville, because they all resulted from repeated attempts by the friends of Walnut Grove Academy to cause a co-operation of the Christian congregations in Illinois in building up an institution of high order. It is believed that the prominent brethren of the State were favorable to the work, and the commendatory preamble and resolution at Abingdon clearly indicates that Walnut Grove Academy was their preference.

The matter was presented to the convention in 1851, and decisive action was postponed by the appointment of a Committee on Education instructed to take the subject under advisement and report at the next annual convention to assemble at Abingdon, in September, 1852. At Abingdon the Board of Education was appointed, which seemed to put off definite action another year, but the resolution introduced by Elder D. P. Henderson placed a different phase on the outlook, inviting the trustees of Walnut Grove Academy to canvass among the congregations without further delay.

RECEIVED BUT NOT ADOPTED.

The report of the Board of Education to the Jacksonville Convention was received by that body, but its recommendations were never adopted. The purpose for which the committee of seven had been called into existence had been at least partially effected, and for many years immediately succeeding that period, all questions concerning the establishing of schools were totally banished from the annual conventions of the Illinois Missionary Society. Just why that organization would not permit the discussion of such topics was never formally promulgated, and it would perhaps be unproductive of good results to attempt, at this late day, an explanation of the strange feature. We will only suggest that other regularly organized institutions of learning, under the control of Christian trustees, were started up in certain localities, which became applicants for general assistance.

CHAPTER III.

THE MUSIC DEPARTMENT.

During the summer of 1855, the Board of Instrution organized a department of music, employing Miss Ellen F. True of Mt. Vernon, Ohio, as the teacher. The department was opened for the reception of pupils at the beginning of the first session under the college charter, in September, 1855.

THE COLLEGE CHARTER.

The trustees of the Academy made application to the Legislature, at its session of 1854–5, for a Special College Charter, and the following liberal provisions were unanimously granted:

(44)

AN ACT

To Incorporate Eureka College.

Section 1. *Be it enacted by the people of the State of Illinois, represented in the General Assembly,* That Elijah Dickinson, William Davenport, Elias B. Myers, John Darst, John Lindsey, Abishai M. Myers, John Major, William H. Davenport, Benjamin J. Radford, David Deweese, Robert M. Clark, William Atterberry, William T. Major, Sr., Christopher O. Neville, John Bennett, William M. Brown, John T. Jones, William S. Pickrell, George McManus, Bushrod W. Henry, Stephen T. Logan, Peter C. Redding, Henry Grove and John W. Taylor and their successors be, and they hereby are, created a body politic and corporate, by the name and style of "The Trustees of Eureka College," and by that style and name to remain and have perpetual succession. The number of trustees shall not exceed twenty-four, exclusive of the president or presiding officer of the college, who shall be *ex officio* a member of the Board of Trustees, any seven of whom shall constitute a quorum.

§2. Eureka College shall be at or near the place where the Walnut Grove Academy is now situated, in Woodford county.

§3. Said corporation shall have power to sue and be sued, plead and be impleaded; to acquire, hold and convey property, real and personal or mixed, in all lawful ways; to have, use and alter at pleasure a common seal; to fill all and every vacancy or vacancies occasioned in their body by death or resignation or otherwise.

§4. Said trustees shall have power to make, alter, and establish from time to time, such constitutions, rules, by-laws and regulations as they may deem necessary for the good government of said corporation and the proper management of the institution under their control: *Provided* such constitutions, rules, by-laws or regulations be not inconsistent with the constitution or laws of this State or of the United States.

§5. The trustees of Eureka College shall have authority from time to time to prescribe and regulate the course of studies to be pursued in said college and in the preparatory department attached thereto; to fix the rates of tuition, room rent and other necessary expenses; to appoint instructors and such other officers and agents as may be needful in the management of the institution; to define their powers, duties and employments, to fix their compensation, to displace or remove either of the instructors, officers or agents, or all of them, as said trustees shall deem the interest of said college requires; to fill all vacancies among said instructors, officers and agents; to erect suitable buildings; to purchase chemical and philosophical apparatus and other suitable means of instruction; to put into operation all proper and suitable means for the health, comfort, and advancement of the students in the various branches of a literary and scientific education, and to make rules for the general management of the affairs of the institution and for the regulation of the conduct of the students.

§6. The trustees shall faithfully apply all funds collected by them according to the best of their judgment in erecting suitable buildings, in supporting the necessary instructors, officers and agents, the procuring books, maps, charts, globes and all philosophical and chemical apparatus to aid and promote sound learning in the institution: *Provided*, that in case any donation, devise or bequest shall be made for particular purposes accordant with the objects of the institution, and the trustees shall accept the same, every such donation, devise or bequest shall be applied in conformity with the express condition of the donor or devisor; *Provided, also*, that if the donation be in real estate the lands be sold within ten years from the date of said donation, and the value thereof be applied as specified by the donor.

§7. The president of said college, by and with the consent of said trustees, shall have power from time to time to ordain, regulate and establish the course and mode of instruction and education to be pursued in said college, and, together with such professors, instructors and tutors as the corporation may designate, shall be styled "The Faculty of Eureka College," and shall have power to adopt and enforce such rules as may be deemed expedient for the good government of the institution; which rules and regulations shall not be inconsistent with the constitution and laws of this State nor of the United States, nor inconsistent with the laws and ordinances of said corporation, and shall be in full force until disapproved of by the trustees, or a quorum of them, and no longer.

§8. The said trustees shall have power to establish departments for the study of any and all of the learned and liberal professions and to confer such degrees as are usually conferred in similar institutions in the United States in the learned arts and sciences. The trustees may also attach to said college an academical or preparatory department; and when a common school department shall be in operation agreeably to the common school law of this State, the trustees shall be entitled to draw their proportion of the township, school, college and seminary fund for such scholars as live in the township where said college is located.

§9. The trustees, or a quorum of them, shall have authority to meet at such times as they shall deem necessary for the examination of candidates for literary degrees; and they are hereby authorized and empowered, upon recommendation of the faculty, to confer such degrees on such persons as in their judgments shall merit the same in as ample a manner as any similar institution can do, and under their common seal to grant testimonials thereof, signed by the faculty of the college.

§10. The trustees, or a quorum of them, shall elect a treasurer (whom they may remove at pleasure) who shall give bonds, with approved security, payable to the trustees by their names aforesaid, and their successors, faithfully to discharge the duties of his said office, and shall render an account of all moneys, goods and chattels received and expended by him on account of, and for the use of, said college, and on failure or refusal to do so, shall be subject to like proceedings as are prescribed by law in cases of county treasurers of the State: *Provided*, that no appropriation, payment or disbursement shall at any time be made by the treasurer but such as shall be in pursuance of the directions or orders of the trustees.

§11. Not less than seven trustees shall form a quorum to do business, but a less number shall be a quorum to fill vacancies in the office of trustees: *Provided*, that on sixty days' notice, published in the nearest newspaper, a full quorum cannot be obtained.

§12. Whenever the trustees of the Walnut Grove Academy, or a quorum of them, shall execute and deliver to the clerk of the circuit court of Woodford county, their written consent to this act and the same has been duly recorded, all the property, real and personal, and all debts due to said Walnut Grove Academy shall be vested in the corporation hereby created; and all the acts of the said trustees of Walnut Grove Academy are hereby declared to be legal and valid, notwithstanding any irregularity therein.

§13. The tract of land now owned by the trustees of Walnut Grove Academy shall, when transferred to the corporation hereby established, together with the library, apparatus and other property of said corporation, be exempt from all State and county taxes.

§14. The said trustees, or a full quorum of them, shall have power to remove or suspend the president or any of the professors, instructors or tutors at any time; and when there shall be a vacancy in said Board of Trustees, occasioned by death, removal, resignation, or refusal to act, the remaining trustees, or a quorum of them, shall supply the vacancy. The president, with concurrence of two of the trustees, or any three of the trustees, shall have power to call special meetings of the board.

§15. Whenever any trustee shall absent himself for three successive annual meetings of the board, without assigning a sufficient reason at the fourth, the trustees of the college, or a quorum of them, shall have power, by entry on their minutes, to declare his seat vacant, and may elect a new trustee to supply such vacancy.

§16. There shall be an annual meeting of said trustees, the day of meeting to be fixed by themselves.

§17. That the said Board of Trustees shall never be less than twelve (12) nor more than twenty-four (24).

APPROVED, Feb. 6, 1855.

AN ACT

To Amend the Act Incorporating Eureka College.

Section 1. *Be it enacted by the people of the State of Illinois, represented in the General Assembly,* That so much of section eight as entitles the trustees to draw their proportion of the township, school, college and seminary funds, to be distributed, in proportion, for such scholars as live in the township where such college is located, be and the same is hereby repealed.

§2. The trustees of said college shall be entitled to draw their proportion of the township, school, college and seminary fund for each scholar residing in the district and adjoining district where such college is located, and attending school therein.

§3. That the word "tract," in section thirteen (13), of the act to which this is an amendment, be amended so as to read " tracts."

Approved Feb. 9, 1855.

FIRST SESSION UNDER THE CHARTER.

The school was continued as Walnut Grove Academy to the close of the session 1854-5. In September, 1855, it was opened as Eureka College, having the following Faculty:

Elder William M. Brown,
President.

A. S. Fisher,
Professor of Mathematics, and Principal of Preparatory.

John H. Neville,
Professor of Greek and Latin Languages and Literature.

O. A. Burgess,
Professor of Natural Sciences, of Mental and Moral Philosophy, and Lecturer of Sacred Literature.

Richard A. Conover,
Teacher in Preparatory School.

4

Mrs. Sarah F. Conover,
Teacher in the Female Department.

Miss Ellen F. True,
Teacher of Instrumental and Vocal Music.

Elder William M. Brown and Elder William Davenport were appointed Solicitors of the college. They were instructed to visit various localities in Illinois and adjoining States for the purpose of making known the scope and aim of the college, to canvass for students and procure donations.

THE COLLEGE CAMPUS.

Among the first acts of the new Board of Trustees was a movement to secure a commodious campus on which to erect a suitable building for the Institution. The tract secured contained about fifteen acres, magnificently adorned by noble specimens of the primeval forest trees, the black walnut species predominating. The natural undergrowth having been removed, in a few years the whole campus was adorned by the spontaneous appearance of a beautiful blue grass sward.

A large part of the campus was donated to the college by Elias B. Myers, one of the original promoters of the school, and Elder James Conover, who identified himself with the community soon after the academy was merged into Eureka College.

BURGESS MEMORIAL HALL.   ORIGINAL COLLEGE BUILDING.   CHAPEL.

ENDOWMENT FUND.

The Financial agents were instructed to canvass for donations payable in ten equal annual installments, bearing interest at the rate of six per cent per annum, payable annually, all donors being allowed a rebate of four per cent, payable in tuition at Eureka College, on demand. And any donor having paid up all his installments, according to the terms of his obligation, was to receive a certificate showing the amount of his donation, and obligating the college to pay him six per cent per annum in tuition upon the amount donated.

The first third of all money thus donated was set apart as a building fund, the balance to be a permanent endowment.

The conditions upon which donations were asked greatly assisted the college financiers in their canvass, and, in a few months, they reported over $60,000 secured by notes bearing six per cent interest.

A COLLEGE BUILDING ERECTED.

Presuming upon the convertibility of the endowment notes at maturity, and relying upon the future liberality of college friends, Messrs. John Darst, E. B. Myers and William H. Davenport kindly offered their respective individual responsibilities to aid the Trustees in procuring a loan that would enable them to erect the contemplated building without delay. The generous offer was accepted, and the contract for the building was let in the spring of 1857, and it was completed during the summer of 1858.

FAILURE OF THE ENDOWMENT.

The financial depression that came on in the fall of 1857 affected the ability of many donors to such a degree as to render their pledges of but little value, many of them being worth less; and a large percentage of all others could only be made available by allowing ruinous discounts, the result being that of all the many thousands of dollars pledged to the college, very little more than sufficient to defray the expense incurred by the building committee in erecting the new edifice and supplying it with needed furniture was ever collected.

PROFESSOR C. L. LOOS ACCEPTS THE PRESIDENCY.

In the summer of 1856, Professor O. A. Burgess resigned, to accept a position offered him by the church at Washington, leaving the college with no one in the faculty to conduct the department of Sacred Literature.

Soon after the opening of the ensuing session, in September, 1856, the Trustees sent a committee, composed of John Darst and E. B. Myers, to Cincinnati, Ohio, to confer with Professor C. L. Loos, a graduate of Bethany College and an ex-professor in the Primary School of that institution.

The committee called on the professor at his humble home in Cincinnati, made known to him their mission, explained the character of the college, its origin, some of the more important obstacles encountered in its development up to that period, and their design to make it, ultimately, an important auxiliary in the work of urging forward the current reformation, led by A. Campbell and others. They closed the interview by inviting him to remove to Illinois, and locate in Walnut Grove, promising him a prominent place on the Faculty of the college. The professor's reply was somewhat diplomatic; he neither accepted nor rejected the proposition, promising to take the matter under careful advisement, and to communicate with them in the near future.

On their return to Illinois the committee submitted a report of their conference, and advised the Board of Trustees to take immediate action. Professor Loos was promptly elected President of the Faculty by a unanimous vote. A short correspondence ensued. Professor Loos at once accepted the position, and soon thereafter removed with his family to Walnut Grove, entering the college as President in January, 1857.

Having had the advantages, during many years

of his student life of training under the direction
of the great Alexander Campbell, and having been
conducted through the intricacies of sacred literature by that eminent divine, he was abundantly
prepared to conduct the Bible Department of the
college.

He continued his work with the Institution until
the summer of 1858, being much admired for his
ability as a scholar, and for his executive resources
exhibited in the skill with which he performed his
perplexing duties as president of the institution.

RESIGNATION OF PRESIDENT LOOS.

The new building was nearing completion,
patronage had greatly increased, and a brilliant
future for the college was predicted by its numerous friends and promoters. Such was the attitude
of affairs when the students dispersed for their
respective homes at the close of the session of
1857-8, and the several members of the Faculty
made their respective arrangements to spend the
annual summer vacation.

President Loos took a tour into northern Ohio,
where he was met by certain parties from Bethany
College, who induced him to accept an appointment on the Faculty of his Alma Mater.

This unexpected movement left the Faculty of
Eureka College without a presiding officer and
without any one to conduct the Bible Department,

and the existence of the chasm thus created was not communicated to the Board of Trustees until a few days prior to the opening of the next session. But notwithstanding the awkward phase, the chasm was promptly bridged, and the session was opened by the following Faculty :

GEORGE CALLENDER,
President.

B. W. JOHNSON,
Professor of Ancient Languages.

A. S. FISHER,
Professor of Mathematics and Natural Philosophy.

J. M. ALLEN,
Professor of Chemistry and Belles-Lettres.

MISS SUE S. SMITH,
Teacher of Music.

A. S. FISHER,
Principal of Preparatory School.

MISS E. J. DICKINSON,
First Assistant in Preparatory School.

MISS JANE EWING,
Second Assistant in Preparatory School.

RESIGNATION OF PROFESSOR NEVILLE.

In the summer of 1857, Professor John H. Neville resigned his position on the Faculty of Eureka College and accepted an appointment on the Faculty of Christian University, at Canton, Missouri. He had been identified with the Educational move-ment in Walnut Grove since September, 1852, and had proven himself eminently prepared for his chosen profession. He left the college admired by the Trustees, members of the Faculty, the students, and by all who knew him. Having remained at Canton during one session, he resigned, and in the fall of 1859, accepted an appointment in Bowman University, at Harrodsburg, Kentucky.

B. W. JOHNSON.

Upon the resignation of Professor Neville, B. W. Johnson was elected to a professorship. He was a graduate of Bethany College, and had conducted a private school in the city of Bloomington. When it became known in that city that he had accepted a professorship in Eureka College, many of his former pupils applied for matriculation permits.

Professor Johnson was a member of the Faculty when President Loos resigned, and was asked to assume the Presidency ; this, however, he declined; but consented to act as Vice-President and to lecture daily upon sacred and secular history.

PERICLESIAN SOCIETY.

During the session 1855-6, another literary society was organized, and was incorporated as The Periclesian Society. The weekly performances consisted of reading original essays, orations, declamations and debates. All its sessions were governed by parliamentary rules, and the numerous members, therefore, received a training that gave them great power for usefulness in subsequent life when aiding to promote the best interests of organized society.

MATHESIAN SOCIETY.

About the year 1857 a literary religious society was organized for the benefit of those intending to enter the Christian ministry. They had weekly performances, also, consisting of Scripture recitations, sermons and discussions of religious questions. It was known as the Mathesian Society.

EXCELSIOR SOCIETY.

During the session of 1857-8 the young ladies of the college organized an association known as The Excelsior Society. It at once assumed an influential rank, and for many years was an important feature of the college. It was never incorporated, and when the Edmund Burke Society and the Periclesian Society altered their respective organic laws so as to make females eligible to membership, the Excelsiors found their membership gradually decreasing in numbers from term to term, and soon the weekly meetings were abandoned, and ultimately the Excelsior Society became *non est*, having died of starvation for want of members.

A CONTRACTION AND ITS CAUSE.

From the beginning of the institution in 1848, down to and including the session of 1857-8, the patronage had been constantly on the increase, the matriculations of 1857-8 numbering two hundred and seventy-six. But the financial depression that commenced in the fall of 1857, and swept over the entire country as a withering blight, caused a temporary check upon its further expansion in the immediate future, and even produced a great decline in the number of annual matriculations.

THE FIRST GRADUATE.

E. W. Dickinson, a young man of exemplary habits, was the first graduate of the college. Having completed the prescribed course of studies, the Trustees, upon the recommendation of the Faculty, conferred on him the degree of A. B. at their annual meeting in 1860.

FACULTY OF 1860-1.

GEORGE CALLENDER, A. M.,
President.

B. W. JOHNSON, A. B.,
Professor of Greek Language and Literature, and Lecturer on Sacred and
Secular History.

A. S. FISHER, B. S.,
Professor of Natural Philosophy.

J. M. ALLEN, M. D.,
Professor of Physiology, and Moral and Mental Philosophy.

R. H. Johnson, A. B.,
Professor of Latin Language and Literature, and Teacher of Natural
History.

J. H. Rowell,
Professor of Mathematics.

Miss Sarah Lanpheare,
Teacher of French, German and Painting.

Miss Sue Smith,
Teacher of Music.

A. S. Fisher.
Principal of Preparatory Department.

Miss Mollie G. Clark,
Teacher in Preparatory Department.

J. M. Allen,
Librarian.

R. H. Johnson,
Curator of Museum.

OFFICERS OF BOARD OF TRUSTEES, SESSION 1860-1.

E. Dickinson, *President.*
George Callender, *Secretary.*
E. B. Myers, *Treasurer.*
A. G. Ewing, *Bursar.*

COMMITTEES OF TRUSTEES, SESSION 1860-1.

John Darst,
E. B. Myers, } *Executive Committee.*
James R. Burton,

A. M. Myers,
R. M. Clark, } *Prudential Committee.*
C. O. Neville,

George Callender,
Wm. H. Davenport, } *Auditing Committee.*
A. M. Myers,

CHAPTER IV.

THE FIRST SECRETARY.

At the organization of the Trustees of Walnut Grove Academy, A. S. Fisher was elected secretary, and he continued to act in that capacity until that school became Eureka College, and was continued in the same office by the Trustees of the college till the close of the session of 1855-6, when he was relieved by Mr. Callender, that he might the more closely attend to the other matters pertaining to the college work.

THE FIRST TREASURER.

At the organization of Walnut Grove Academy, in 1849, E. B. Myers was made treasurer, and he was continued in that capacity, by re-elections, during the existence of that institution; and when the Academy was merged into Eureka College the Trustees retained him in the treasurership until his death, which occurred in 1866, having been treasurer for sixteen years. At no time during his long service was there any intimation of unfaithfulness. Every dollar of money committed to his care as treasurer was faithfully accounted for.

JOHN DARST.

Mr. Darst was elected a trustee of the school about the year 1855. He removed from near Dayton, Ohio, and located near the Academy in the year 1851. From the first he was a devoted friend of the institution. Being a man of great energy and of eminent financial ability, he was placed upon the Executive Committee and kept in that position continuously for more than forty years. Without exaggeration it may truthfully be affirmed, that, financially, he has been the leading promoter of the college. While Elder B. Major must ever be regarded as the *Founder* of the school, Elder John Darst has been, pre-eminently, its great supporter, having on more than one occasion rescued it from impending destruction, when other friends regarded its condition desperate. He was made President of the Board of Trustees at the death of Elder Ewing, in 1873, and still occupies that position.

ATTITUDE IN THE CIVIL WAR.

During the terrible War of the Rebellion the college was eminently loyal. When President Abraham Lincoln issued his first proclamation, calling for volunteers to assist in maintaining the integrity of the nation, many of the students and one member of the Faculty promptly enlisted, and remained in the army during the war.

GEORGE CALLENDER.

Mr. Callender emigrated from Liverpool, England, in the year 1853, and located a short distance northward from Walnut Grove Academy. He was a gentleman of culture, having been liberally educated while in the Old Country. He was of a kindly disposition, benevolent and generous. Very soon after his location in Walnut Grove he united with the Church of Christ in that community, and became a devoted member. He was elected a trustee of the institution, and became one of its best promoters. Upon the resignation of President Loos, in 1858, he was elected president of the college, which position he continued to fill till 1862, when he resigned and was succeeded by B. W. Johnson.

PROFESSOR B. W. JOHNSON.

Mr. Johnson's boyhood home was near Washington, Tazewell county, Illinois. His father was a farmer, and consequently the boy's life was somewhat monotonous. Until verging into manhood his educational advantages were such as could be obtained in the common school of his neighborhood. He was noted for his love of reading, biographies and histories being his favorite books.

In 1851 he became a student of Walnut Grove Academy, where he remained three years, making a splendid record. He then entered Bethany College, presided over at that time by the famous theologian, Alexander Campbell. Being permitted to enter as a junior, he completed the college course in two years, receiving a diploma as a member of the class of 1856.

After leaving college he opened a private school in the city of Bloomington, Illinois, where he remained one year. In the fall of 1857 he accepted a position on the Faculty of Eureka College, and remained a devoted friend and promoter of that school during six years, performing all the duties of the president from the opening of the session 1858-9 to the close of the session 1861-2. He was then elected President, which position he accepted. At the close of the session 1862-3 he resigned, and soon thereafter became Professor of Mathematics in Bethany College, West Virginia, where seven years before he had received the degree of A. B. Subsequently he accepted the presidency of Oskaloosa College, in Iowa, where he remained for a term of years. Being interested in the publication of a religious paper, he removed to Chicago, where he prospered as an editor for a time, when he formed a coalition with a publishing house in St. Louis, and for many years has been one of the editors of the *Christian-Evangelist*, a weekly paper of vast influence among the many congregations of the Church of Christ in the West and South.

DR. J. M. ALLEN.

The Doctor was a Kentuckian. He first appeared in the community as a practicing physician about the year 1854. He was a young, affable, Christian gentleman, and noted for his kindness and generosity. Being of a jovial disposition, witty, possessed with an inexhaustible store of anecdotes, and a good story-teller, he was ever a welcome guest at all the entertainments of the young people.

Having abandoned his profession as a physician, he entered the Christian ministry, and soon became known among the congregations as an earnest evangelist. During the session of

1855-6 he was a student of Eureka College, taking
lessons under the direction of Professor Neville.
In 1856 he was elected Professor of Natural
Sciences in Eureka College, and for more than
thirty years thereafter he was a zealous worker for the college, most of the time as a professor, but frequently he was excused from work
as a teacher that he might serve the college
as financial agent, soliciting among the people
for students and donations. In 1882 he became
President of the Faculty. As president he was
an ardent promoter of the college for seven
years. Resigning his place in the Faculty in
1887, he was retained for a year or two as college solicitor. In 1891 he removed with his
family to the State of Washington, and there continued his work as a Christian evangelist.

THE COLLEGE AID FUND.

The report of the treasurer at the Annual Meeting of 1863 caused a rumor that the college
was about to suspend for lack of funds to meet
current expenses. The citizens of Eureka called
a meeting to inquire as to the degree of the rumored danger. A careful and extended discussion
established the fact that the college needed funds
to prevent an impending collapse. At that meeting a committee was appointed who canvassed
among the people of the village and the surround-

5

ing country and obtained about four thousand
dollars, which was turned over to the college
treasurer to supplement the income from tuition
fees. The treasurer being thus reinforced, the
threatened calamity was avoided, and the college
work continued on as of yore. President Johnson having resigned, the official duties of that
office during 1863-4 were assumed by other members of the Faculty.

H. O. NEWCOMB.

In the summer vacation of 1863, H. O. Newcomb,
of Hiram, Ohio, a graduate of Ann Arbor, Michigan, was elected Professor of the Greek and
German languages and literature. The appointment was accepted and Professor Newcomb entered upon the duties of his chair in September,
1863.

The crisis had been reached and passed without disaster. The number of students was once
more on the increase, and the college was again
prosperous.

H. W. EVEREST.

In 1864, H. W. Everest, a graduate of Oberlin
College, Ohio, and President of Hiram College,
in that State, accepted the presidency of
Eureka College. He was an executive officer of

superior ability, and presided as the head of the institution for many years. During the first three years of his administration the number of students increased from one hundred and twenty-five to two hundred and twenty five.

THE ENDOWMENT.

About 1866 the Trustees resolved to make an effort for an increase of the endowment fund. Dr. J. M. Allen was excused from the Faculty and accepted the place of general financial agent. Many plans of operation were suggested, discussed and discarded. At length the Doctor entered upon the work, taking pledges upon the condition that twelve thousand dollars should be raised in Woodford county. The work was pushed by the Doctor until the pledges amounted in the aggregate to about twenty thousand dollars. A meeting of the Board was called to hear the report of their agent. The amount of pledges gave great satisfaction, but an inspection revealed the fact that the pledges in Woodford county did not amount to twelve thousand dollars, and consequently none of them were binding. A few of the Woodford county donors were prevailed upon to increase their respective pledges, whereupon Mr. George Callender agreed to become responsible for the balance of the twelve thousand dollars necessary to make the many pledges of legal force.

The college now possessed an endowment fund of more than twenty thousand dollars. But there was an unfortunate feature of weakness in the otherwise well-guarded scheme. All donors were dealt with as preferred borrowers, everyone being allowed to retain in his possession as a loan the full amount of his pledge, giving his own note therefor without collateral. As a consequence a large percentage of the endowment became worthless from unexpected failures in business.

A. G. EWING.

Mr. Ewing was a native of Tennessee, but in early life removed to Virginia. He emigrated to Illinois and located in Walnut Grove, near the college, in 1858. He was elected to a trusteeship soon after his arrival. At the death of E. Dickinson, in 1862, Elder A. G. Ewing was elected President of the Board of Trustees, which office he held continuously for more than ten years, and until his death in 1873.

THE CHAPEL.

The building which had been erected in 1858 had abundant room to accommodate all the legitimate wants of the college at that time, but was en-

THE ORIGINAL COLLEGE BUILDING.

THE CHAPEL.

tirely inadequate for the demands of 1867. There was an insufficient number of rooms, the chapel was too small for the increased number of students in attendance, the literary societies were clamoring for larger rooms, and the library and museum needed additional space.

To provide for these pressing demands the Board of Trustees resolved to erect another building on the college campus. The ceremony of laying the corner-stone took place at the close of session 1867-8, and the superstructure was completed in 1869.

The edifice was known as the Chapel. It was a large building of two stories. The whole of the upper story was fitted up for a chapel and lecture room. The lower story was sub-divided into three rooms, one of which was assigned to the Edmund Burke Society, one to the Periclesian Society, while the other was appropriated for the use of library and museum.

THE $12,000 LOAN.

The resources of the college were tuition fees, interest on a small endowment, and donations. But the aggregate of these was insufficient to defray current expenses. Every year there was a deficit and some of the creditors would receive interest-bearing treasury orders. Many of these would be *cashed* by some of the college friends, who would carry them from year to year. But after a few years the amount of such outstanding orders would become so great as to suggest danger.

In 1871 the floating debt had become quite alarming. Fortunately the debt was almost exclusively owned by friends of the college, disposed to aid the institution to the extent of their ability. The owners of the claims were interviewed by college agents, and they canvassed the matter among themselves. As a result, the individual claims were, in numerous instances, surrendered, and thus the floating debt was reduced to an aggregate of about twelve thousand dollars. To provide for this balance a loan was obtained. In this way the Trustees were relieved, temporarily, from the annoyance of overdue debts.

To provide for the semi-annual interest, and for the liquidation of the principal when due, the endowment committee made renewed efforts to increase that fund. They also decided to ask for donations bearing ten per cent interest and payable at the maturity of the loan.

Sundry men of ability were employed and sent into the field of work to make known to the numerous college friends the financial situation and to solicit their co-operation in providing for the emergency.

During 1872-3 Elder W. T. Maupin operated as the traveling financial agent. He visited numerous localities and accomplished many favorable results, by awakening enthusiasm among the people for the ultimate triumph of the college. During the session of 1873-4 Elder W. G. Anderson was employed to occupy the field as financial agent. It was largely by his activity and earnest appeals that such an amount of pledges was obtained as induced the trustees to announce to the people, by publication in the Eureka *Journal*, that the loan was provided for and would be paid at maturity.

RESIGNATION OF PRESIDENT EVEREST.

In 1872 H. W. Everest resigned and accepted a call to preach for the Church of Christ at Springfield, Illinois. He had been a faithful presiding officer of the institution for eight years.

A. M. WESTON.

Upon the resignation of President H. W. Everest A. M. Weston was elected President of the Faculty. He had been called from Ohio two years previously to take a place on the Faculty as Professor of Greek.

B. J. RADFORD.

Mr. Radford was educated at Eureka College. His father, B. J. Radford, Sr., emigrated from Ken-

tucky and located in Walnut Grove many
years before the existence of Walnut Grove
Academy, and was a charter member in the incorporation of that school. B. J. Radford, Jr., was a
student of Eureka College when Abraham Lincoln
made the first call for volunteers to aid in suppress-
ing the rebellion. In company with many others
who were his fellow students, he promptly offered
his services. He subsequently enlisted for three
years and was in the army during the war. After
the war he renewed his connection with the college
and graduated in 1866. Soon after leaving college
he entered the ministry of the Church of Christ.
In 1870 he was elected Professor of Latin. At the
resignation of President A. M. Weston, he was
elected to fill the vacancy. At the expiration of
two years he resigned the presidency and accepted
a call to preach for the church at Des Moines, Ia.
In 1878 he returned to Eureka and was again
placed on the Faculty as Professor of Greek and
Sacred Literature. In 1881 he resigned his professorship to accept a call as pastor of one of the
congregations of the Church of Christ at Cincinnati, Ohio. While in Cincinnati he was appointed
one of the editors of the *Christian Standard*. In
1890 he accepted a call as pastor of the church in
Denver, Colorado, and removed to that city. Finding his health fast declining under the climatic
influences of that mountainous region, in 1892 he

returned to Eureka, Illinois, and was again placed on the Faculty of the college.

CHAPTER V.

H. W. EVEREST AGAIN PRESIDENT.

In 1877 Professor Everest was again elected President of the Faculty. He accepted the appointment and entered upon the duties of his office in September of that year. But in 1881 he again resigned to accept the appointment as President of Butler University, at Irvington, Indiana.

THE BOARDING HOUSE COMPANY.

This was an incorporated company organized in 1878 for the purpose of increasing boarding facilities for the accommodation of students. A boarding hall of two stories was erected in 1878 of such dimensions as to afford ample accommodations for forty-eight young men—two in each room.

APPARATUS REPLENISHED.

Soon after the return of President Everest,

GENTLEMEN'S HALL, NO. 1.

GENTLEMEN'S HALL, NO. 2.

through his earnest representations as to pressing wants of the college, the Board of Trustees appropriated one thousand dollars to be used in the purchase of mathematical and philosophical apparatus. This money was placed in the hands of President Everest, who was authorized to make such purchases as he thought would be for the best interests of the college. Thus instructed, President Everest went to Boston, Massachusetts, where he made a very judicious selection of apparatus.

FACULTY OF 1881-2.

J. M. ALLEN, A. M., President,
Professor of Latin and English Literature.

JAMES KIRK, A. M.,
Professor of Natural Science.

CARL JOHANN, A. M.,
Professor of Modern Languages.

A. S. FISHER, A. M.,
Professor of Mathematics.

ANDREW J. YOUNGBLOOD, A. M.,
Professor of Greek, and Mental and Moral Science.

Professor of the Bible and Sacred Literature.

PROFESSOR J. W. METCALFE,
Honorary Graduate of the Royal Conservatory of Music, Leipsic,
Germany, Director of the School of Music.

MISS SARAH JEANNE GARRETT,
Teacher of Drawing and Painting.

JAMES KIRK,
Curator of Museum.

CARL JOHANN,
Librarian.

The Faculty during the session 1883-4 was the following :

J. M. ALLEN, A. M., President,
Professor of Mental and Moral Philosophy and Sacred History.

B. J. RADFORD, A. M,,
Professor of the Bible and Sacred Literature.

JAMES KIRK, A. M.,
Professor of Physical and Natural Science.

CARL JOHANN, A. M.,
Professor of Modern Languages.

A. S. FISHER, A. M.,
Professor of Mathematics.

ANDREW J. YOUNGBLOOD, A. M.,
Professor of Ancient Languages.

J. V. COOMBS, A. B.,
Professor of English Literature, Elocution and Didactics.

N. S. RICHMOND,
Professor of Penmanship, Bookkeeping, Business Forms and Stenography.

PROFESSOR J. W. METCALFE,
Prize Graduate of Royal Conservatory, Leipsic, Germany, Director
of School of Music.

JOHN DEPUE,
Vocalist and Assistant Teacher of Piano and Organ.

PROFESSOR EDWARD E. BLITZ,
Graduate of National Conservatory, Paris, France, Insructor of Violin.

MISS CLARA J. HATCH,
Instructor of Drawing and Painting.

JAMES KIRK,
Curator of Museum.

CARL JOHANN,
Librarian.

ENDOWMENT.

The promoters of the college from its first organization had realized that an adequate endowment fund is necessary for ultimate success. Accordingly many efforts had been made to procure such a fund and many thousand dollars had been promised, but only a very small percentage had been paid into the treasury—the donors being considered as preferred borrowers and allowed to retain their promised donations as loans, without security, except promissory notes, without endorsements. In numerous instances the unforeseen vicissitudes in the fortunes of men caused such assets to become of small value. But notwithstanding this faulty financiering, persisted in by the endowment committee, the college sessions had been continuous for twenty-nine years without the loss of a week, and hundreds of young men and young women had received valuable training, enabling them to secure honorable and profitable situations in the on-going and rapidly developing departments of business in our vast Mississippi Valley.

Large numbers had completed the college curriculum and had been awarded diplomas as evidence of their faithful work, nor have they failed to reflect honor upon their Alma Mater. They may be found in pulpits, at the bar, in lecture-rooms, as college presidents and professors, in legislatures, in the halls of congress, in places of prominence and trust along the channels of trade and at the centers of commerce.

But deficits in the treasury were not infrequent, and would be provided for by the liberality of college friends, who were at times burdened by such sacrifices in their efforts to temporarily relieve the institution. The Trustees foresaw clearly that such a condition of affairs could not continue indefinitely—that sooner or later a collapse would be the inevitable result.

At a meeting of the Board in January, 1884, the nonresident members proposed to raise $50,000 outside of Woodford county, if the resident members would raise $25,000 within the county, of new permanent endowment bearing six per cent interest.

The Endowment Committee were aroused into a state of activity and zeal above their common plane of effort. In their counsels they carefully considered all the suggestions from buoyant friends and the mutterings of evil from chronic croakers, and were not a little influenced by rumored offers from a distant city. Zealously the work was pushed forward, and largely through the earnest appeals of Professor W. F. Black, the popular Christian orator and college promoter, of Tuscola, Illinois, the commendable attempt was abundantly successful.

At a mass meeting called for the purpose, and held in the Christian church, the Endowment Committee submitted a report from which the following has been taken:

New Endowment Raised in Woodford County—6 per cent. interest-bearing notes - - - -	$25,125.00
New Endowment Raised Without the County, bearing 6 per cent. interest - - - - -	5,750.00
Total New Endowment - - - - - -	$30,875.00

College-Aid Fund in Treasury - - -	$4,375.00	
New Aid Fund Raised in County - -	3,812.55	
		$ 8,169.55
New Bequests - - - - - - -		$ 1,300.00
Old Fund Outstanding, but Good and Interest-bearing		12,357.00
Old Fund in hands of Treasurer, Interest-bearing -		8,000.00
Total Interest-Bearing Endowment - - -		51,231.00
Grand Total of all Funds - - - - -		60,701.55

ABINGDON COLLEGE CONSOLIDATED WITH EUREKA COLLEGE.

In the summer of 1884, committees of the respective colleges, one committee from each, negotiated terms of consolidation, and the combination went into operation in the following September with a Faculty composed as follows:

J. M. ALLEN, A. M., President,
Professor of Mental and Moral Philosophy and Sacred History.

B. J. RADFORD, A. M.,
Professor of the Bible and Sacred Literature.

CARL JOHANN, A. M.,
Professor of Modern Languages.

A. S. FISHER, A. M.,
Professor of Mathematics.

ANDREW J. YOUNGBLOOD, A. M.,
Professor of Ancient Languages.

H. L. BRUNER, A. M.,
Professor of Natural Sciences.

W. S. ERRETT, A. M.,
Professor of Mathematics.

N. L. RICHMOND,
Professor of Penmanship, Bookkeeping, Business Forms and Stenography.

J. W. METCALF,
Prize Graduate of Royal Conservatory, Leipsic, Germany, Director of School of Music.

MISS LETTIE BRUNER,
Vocalist and Assistant Teacher of Piano and Organ.

PROFESSOR HAROLD PLOWE,
Instructor of Violin.

MISS SADIE GARRETT,
Instructor of Drawing and Painting.

H. L. BRUNER,
Curator of Museum.

H. N. HERRICK.
Librarian.

THE ALUMNI ET ALUMNÆ.

At the Annual Meeting of the Board of Trustees in 1885 the following preamble and resolutions were adopted :

WHEREAS, an arrangement has been made by which all our educational interests of a higher order shall be merged into one institution of learning, therefore

Resolved, by the Board of Trustees of Eureka College :

1. That the consolidation of Abingdon College with Eureka College, at Eureka, is an event deserving formal recognition by us.

2. That we fully appreciate the unselfish and catholic spirit in which the concessions were made that led to this result by those most directly concerned and interested in perpetuating the existence of Abingdon College.

3. That we accept the task imposed by this merging of the existence of Abingdon College into the existence of Eureka College, and, also, which was the controlling motive in bringing it about, viz.: To provide for the general control and support of our educational interests in the state.

4. That the Alumni et Alumnæ of Abingdon College are hereby accepted and recognized as the children of Eureka College, and entitled to all the rights, privileges and honors of students of Eureka College who have received like degrees, and that the Secretary of the Board is hereby instructed to secure the names of such graduates, to be enrolled among those of Eureka College.

5. The name of the consolidated schools shall be Eureka College, and shall be perpetuated under the charter of Eureka College.

6

CHAPTER VI.

UNION OF ABINGDON COLLEGE WITH EUREKA COLLEGE.

All the friends of Christian education had felt for many years that the prospects for establishing a strong college, such as the brotherhood in Illinois needs, were not flattering, while our forces and means and patronage were divided between two colleges. It was felt that one of them must ultimately give up the struggle, and the uncertainty as to which one would survive induced many to withhold their help, no one desiring to invest his means in an institution of learning that might close its doors at any time.

As a result of this, both colleges, though doing much good with their limited means, were greatly hampered for lack of sufficient support. Tuition fees alone never can support a college, and unless material assistance is obtained in the form of

(82)

donations, legacies and endowments, the institution must either go in debt without prospect of ever liquidating its obligations, or it must so reduce its corps of teachers and pay the remaining ones such small salaries as to interfere materially with the quality of the work. This had long been apparent to the Trustees of the two colleges. Financial support for each came almost exclusively from the localities in which the buildings stood The brotherhood in the State took very little interest in the work of education. Financial agents sent out by the college authorities received very little encouragement, and the future looked very unpromising.

During the few years just preceding the union of the colleges, Abingdon had been even less successful than Eureka in winning the confidence and support of the brotherhood, so in the summer of 1884 the Trustees of Eureka College entered into correspondence with Pres. F. M. Bruner, who was then at the head of Abingdon College, with a view of uniting all our educational interests in Eureka. Several meetings were held, and as a result of these meetings Abingdon College ceased to exist as a school under the control of the Church of Christ.

Pres. F. M. Bruner and Profs. H. L. Bruner and W. S. Errett and Miss Lettie Bruner, who had been members of the Faculty of Abingdon College, became teachers in Eureka, and it was felt on all sides that the cause of Christian education in Illinois had been greatly strengthened by this union.

THE MISSION TABERNACLE.

Attendance at the Christian Missionary Convention, which meets annually in Eureka during the early part of August, had so steadily increased from year to year that the Christian Church, in which the meetings were held, became too small to hold the audiences. Being always ready to do their part, and even more than their part, the friends of the college in Eureka decided in 1884 to build an audience-room on the college campus, sufficiently large and commodious to accommodate all who might come. This audience-room was also to be used for Commencement exercises and for other large public meetings.

The Mission Tabernacle, which was erected for this purpose, is a room 80 feet wide by 100 feet long; it stands on gently sloping ground and forms a natural amphitheater, the speakers' platform standing at the lower end. Back of the platform there are two rooms, 14 by 16 feet, used as committee rooms. The audience-room contains 1,200 chairs, and is admirably adapted to the purpose for which it was erected. The structure cost about $4,000.

THE TABERNACLE.

FACULTY FOR 1885-6.

J. M. ALLEN, A. M., President,
Professor of Mental and Moral Philosophy and Sacred History.

W. F. BLACK, Vice President,
Lecturer on Biblical Subjects.

F. M. BRUNER, A. M.,
Professor of Bible and Sacred Literature.

CARL JOHANN, A. M.,
Professor of Modern Languages.

A. S. FISHER, A. M.,
Professor of Mathematics.

ANDREW J. YOUNGBLOOD, A. M.,
Professor of Ancient Languages.

H. L. BRUNER, A. M.,
Professor of Natural Sciences.

N. L. RICHMOND,
Professor of Penmanship, Bookkeeping, Business Forms and Stenography.

MISS EMMA GOODSPEED,
Professor of Elocution and English Literature.

W. WAUGH LANDER,
Director of School of Music.

MISS LETTIE BRUNER,
Vocalist and Assistant Teacher of Piano and Organ.

L. E. HERSEY,
Instructor of Violin.

MISS SADIE GARRETT,
Instructor in Drawing and Painting.

H. L. BRUNER,
Curator of Museum.

H. N. HERRICK,
Librarian.

PROF. A. S. FISHER.

During the summer of 1885 Prof. A. S. Fisher severed his connection with Eureka College and moved to Kansas City, Mo., where he is living at the present time. He was the first teacher of Walnut Grove Academy, now known as Eureka College, and was connected with the school from 1848 to 1886. Not often does a teacher remain in the same school for thirty-eight years, and this long service is in itself sufficient evidence of his ability and of his zeal in the cause of education. He saw the institution with which he was identified develop from a little country school, taught by one teacher in one little room, to a prosperous college with six buildings, fifteen teachers and nearly three hundred students. His influence among the students was always good, he was highly respected and greatly beloved by all his pupils, and hundreds, yea, thousands of young persons were led into paths of usefulness by his advice and example.

SESSION 1886-7.

During this entire session the President, Dr. J. M. Allen, was in the field soliciting means for the college, and Carl Johann acted as President *pro tem.*, otherwise the Faculty was substantially the same as during the previous session. At the end of this session Dr. Allen resigned the presidency to become the financial agent of the college, and Carl Johann was elected to take his place in that responsible position. He accepted the honor thus conferred on him, and the session 1887-8 opened with the following Faculty:

CARL JOHANN, A. M. LL. D., President,
Professor of Modern Languages.

W. F. BLACK, A. M., Vice President,
Lecturer on Biblical Subjects.

F. M. BRUNER, A. M.,
Professor of the Bible and Sacred Literature.

A. J. YOUNGBLOOD, A. M.,
Professor of Ancient Languages.

H. N. HERRICK, A. B.,
Professor of Mathematics.

SETH E. MEEK, M. S.,
Professor of Natural Sciences.

JAMES CHALMERS, A. B.,
Professor of English Language and Literature.

G. W. HOOTMAN,
Professor of Penmanship, Bookkeeping and Business Forms.

MISS ESTELLE FRANKLIN,
Director of the School of Music, Piano.

L. E. HERSEY,
Instructor of Violin.

MRS. S. E. MEEK,
Teacher of Vocal Culture.

MISS MINA VANDERVORT,
Instructor in Drawing and Painting.

LIDA'S WOOD.

Slowly but steadily the attendance of students had been increasing during the last few years, owing mainly to the better work done by the college and to judicious advertising. One of the greatest needs at this time was better and more abundant boarding facilities, especially for young ladies that came to Eureka. The college had two boarding halls at this time, a two-and-a-half story frame house occupied by young ladies and a two-story brick hall for gentlemen, but both were crowded. The halls were not very modern in appearance. A large, new, modern boarding hall was imperatively needed, and the Trustees were formulating plans to secure the means to erect one when Bro. and Sister W. J. Ford tendered them the gift of their beautiful residence located on a four-acre tract of ground adjoining the college, said property to be used as a boarding hall for young ladies. Only two conditions were attached to the gift. These were:

1. That the property should be known as "Lida's Wood," in memory of their deceased daughter Lida, a beautiful and noble girl 13 years of age who had died a short time before, and

LADY'S HALL.

to whom the natural grove of noble forest trees
on the premises had been an especial and con-
tinual delight.

2. That the Trustees should during the following summer build an addition to the residence,
sufficiently large to provide accommodation for at
least fifty boarders.

At a meeting of the Board of Trustees held
April 19, 1888, the generous offer was accepted and
the following resolution adopted:

Resolved, That the Trustees of Eureka College, in session
assembled, tender to Bro. W. J. Ford and his wife their sincere
thanks for the liberal donation of their residence property near
the college, said property to be used as a boarding hall for the
purpose of assisting in educating worthy young ladies who may
attend said college.

A soliciting and building committee was immediately appointed, and preparations were made
to build a hall that should be a model in every
respect.

The residence already on the ground was built
of brick, two-and-a half stories high, substantial,
commodious and lavishly decorated. The interior
finish was of polished hardwood, and the mantels
were of white marble. The ground surrounding
the building is covered with magnificent shade
trees, and is as lovely a playground for the
boarders as can be found anywhere.

The soliciting committee met with success, and

before the college session opened in September
the addition was completed at an expense of
$10,000.

Though Lida's Wood contained forty rooms, it
was filled with boarders from the very beginning, and went far toward making the college
more popular.

During the encampments of the Missionary Convention, which are held annually in Eureka,
Lida's Wood is thrown open to the delegates, and
hundreds are boarded there. Lida's Wood was
always popular with the students, and would
have been so for many years to come had not the
fire-fiend reduced it to ashes January 11, 1894.
At 4 o'clock P. M. fire was detected in the roof; it
spread rapidly, notwithstanding the heroic efforts
made to extinguish the flames, and before 7 o'clock
P. M. the beautiful building was a heap of smolder-
ing ruins. Thanks to the help rendered by the
students and citizens who arrived upon the scene
soon after the fire began, all the property of
the boarders, as well as much of the furniture, was
saved and no one was injured.

While the fire was still raging all the young
ladies who boarded at Lida's Wood were provided
with comfortable homes by the residents of
Eureka. Insurance on the building, amounting
to $9,000, was paid by the underwriters without
bickering or quibbling.

The Trustees of the college have already decided to rebuild Lida's Wood, and it is hoped
that the $9,000 insurance money, together with
voluntary contributions from the friends of the
college throughout the State, will enable them
to replace the building before the beginning of
the session of 1894-5. The college has enjoyed the
benefits of Lida's Wood for six years, and the hall
has been of such marked advantage to the success
of the work that a failure to rebuild immediately
would greatly hinder our progress. Many parents send their daughters to Eureka College because they can here secure home comforts for
them in a boarding hall under the immediate
supervision of the Faculty, and there is no doubt
that the attendance would in the future be materially reduced if the hall was not rebuilt.

CHAPTER VII.

Burgess Memorial Hall—Session of 1892-3—Session of 1893-4—
The Present Condition and Needs of Eureka College.

BURGESS MEMORIAL HALL.

On the 8th of January, 1890, the following resolution was adopted by the Board of Trustees:

WHEREAS, the attendance in Eureka College has more than
doubled in the last few years, and

WHEREAS, the buildings now used by the College are entirely
inadequate to accommodate the students attending, and

WHEREAS, we anticipate a still larger attendance next session,
therefore

Resolved, That three new buildings are now needed, to wit:
One recitation building and two boarding halls, and that we
earnestly request the friends of the college to assist us in obtaining means to erect them.

This resolution indicates the condition of the
college at that time. The boarding halls were
full and the college buildings so crowded that
there were not rooms enough for the number of
teachers employed. In several instances, two
teachers had to occupy the same room on alternate
hours to hear their classes. The work was thus

(92)

retarded considerably and made very unsatisfactory to all parties concerned.

This resolution was quite appropriate, but resolutions do not provide funds. To carry out the purposes therein indicated at least $50,000 were necessary, and the Trustees, through many years of experience, had learned how difficult it is to induce persons of means to give a part of the wealth accumulated by them for educational and religious purposes. Financial agents had been in the field for years, and notwithstanding their best efforts they were scarcely able to collect means enough to cover the deficit that must of necessity appear annually in any college whose income from tuition is not supplemented by large revenues from invested endowment funds. The Trustees also remembered that Eureka College was largely founded on faith; that faith had sustained them and the Faculty during the darkest hour of the history of the college, and it was faith in the friends of education that prompted them to adopt the resolution and publish it to the world.

The President of the Faculty and the Financial Agent were then instructed to correspond with the friends of the college, with a view to inducing them to make liberal donations toward the three buildings desired. The recitation building was an absolute necessity, and all efforts were directed into that channel.

Many persons were written to and visited, but no one was found who would or could begin a subscription list with a considerable sum. Progress was very slow, and it seemed as though nothing would be accomplished, when, after an extended correspondence, and after having made two visits to her home in Indianapolis, Ind., President Johann was able to report to the Board of Trustees at a called meeting, December 15th, 1890, that Sister O. A. Burgess had decided to give the college $10,000 for the purpose of erecting a new building, provided $10,000 more be subscribed for the same purpose by the friends of the college in Illinois before the first day of June, 1891.

After the report had been made the Board adopted the following resolution:

Resolved, That the Board of Trustees of Eureka College hereby take great pleasure in acknowledging the proposed donation from Sister O. A. Burgess, for the purpose of erecting a college building. We hereby, in a body assembled, unanimously tender Sister Burgess our most sincere thanks for her substantial appreciation of the good work our worthy institution is accomplishing, and pray that God may bless both the giver and her gift to His glory.

A copy of this resolution was ordered sent to Sister Burgess by the Secretary, and in due course of time the following characteristic letter was received in return:

INDIANAPOLIS, IND., Dec. 21st, 1890.

MR. R. D. SMITH, Secretary Eureka College.

Dear Brother: Yours of the 16th received, informing me of

BURGESS MEMORIAL HALL.

the action of the Trustees of Eureka College, touching the donation which I propose making to be used by them in the erection of a new and modern college building.

I wish to thank them for their courteous consideration and to assure them that their action is appreciated. It is my desire to do the greatest possible good with the means that our Heavenly Father has seen fit to intrust to my keeping, and it is with that end in view that I have decided to aid the Trustees of Eureka College in providing more ample facilities for the education of young men and women.

The demand for educated men and women to do the Lord's work was never more urgent than now.

Hoping that Eureka College may very soon be thoroughly equipped and ready to do well her part toward meeting the demand, I remain, Respectfully,

(Signed)   MRS. O. A. BURGESS.

This letter is here given in full because it so beautifully sets forth the disinterested generosity of the donor, and because it is hoped that it may be an example to others who have been blessed with abundant means.

A gift made with such evident cheerfulness and for such a noble purpose, is a source of constant blessing both to the giver and to the receiver.

May the influence of the religion of our Lord Jesus Christ induce many others to imitate the worthy example of Sister Burgess.

In 1890 Eureka College was 35 years old, and the above named gift was the largest single donation ever made to that institution.

The Board of Trustees now felt that a new building was practically assured, and they excused

President Johann from class work during the winter term, that he might go out to solicit the $10,000 necessary to make Sister Burgess' donation available.

Before the 1st day of June arrived, the President and Brother J. G. Waggoner, who at that time was pastor of the Church of Christ in Eureka and who volunteered to assist in raising funds, had succeeded in securing pledges for $13,000, and on the above named day the President went to Indianapolis to report to Sister Burgess and to show to her that the Trustees had done the work assigned to them. The report was satisfactory, and her donation was turned over to the Trustees.

The solicitors who visited the friends of the college were well received everywhere and liberal donations were made by nearly all who were approached.

An architect was engaged and plans made for a three story modern building which, when completed, cost $21,000.

It was named Burgess Memorial Hall for two reasons :

1. Because Sister Burgess made the largest contribution to the building fund.

2. Because her deceased husband, in whose memory she made the donation, had been a Professor and Acting President for a time in the college.

As soon as all the preliminaries had been arranged, contracts were let and building operations were commenced. The cornerstone was laid with imposing ceremonies October 14, 1891, and work was continued throughout the winter, whenever the weather would permit.

Though not yet provided with the necessary furniture, the building was de licated to the cause of Education and Christianity during the State Meeting in August, 1891, when friends were present from all parts of Illinois and adjoining States.

The subscriptions made had been sufficient to pay for the building, and it was dedicated free of debt, but no heating apparatus and no furniture had yet been provided. Pledges were asked for at the State Meeting, and in a few moments $3,-000 were subscribed. A steam heating plant was at once ordered, and elegant, substantial modern furniture was purchased for all the rooms, so that Burgess Hall was thoroughly equipped and ready when the students returned in September, 1892.

Burgess Hall is by far the best college building we now have, and, together with the other buildings, gives us ample accommodations for 500 students. It is built of pressed red brick with gray sandstone trimmings, and contains the following rooms :

Ground Floor.—President's office, three rooms

7

for the department of Natural Sciences, and one each for Modern Languages and Latin.

Second Floor.—Two rooms for the Bible department, and one each for the departments of Greek, English and Mathematics. The Library is also on this floor.

Third Floor.—One room for the Art Department and two for the Commercial Department. The room for Actual Business Practice on the third floor is eighty feet square and is undoubtedly the largest and best equipped business room in the State.

The furniture throughout the building is of solid oak, elegantly varnished and exactly adapted to our wants.

SESSION 1892-93.

The erection of Lida's Wood in 1888 and the completion of Burgess Hall in 1892 gave the college such an impetus that even the warmest friends of Eureka were surprised. During devotional exercises the chapel was every morning crowded with as bright and well behaved a body of students as could be found anywhere. Without the new buildings we would have been utterly unable to provide for their wants. The increase in the number of students compelled the Board of Trustees to enlarge the Faculty, and the session was begun with the following corps of instructors :

HISTORY OF EUREKA COLLEGE.

CARL JOHANN, A. M., LL.D., President,
Professor of Modern Languages.

B. C. DEWEESE, A. M.,
Professor of the John Darst Chair of Sacred Literature.

H. N. HERRICK, A. M.,
Professor of Greek and Sanskrit.

J. M. ATWATER, A. M.,
Professor of Latin and History.

G. A. MILLER, A. M., PH. D.,
Professor of Mathematics.

R. E. CONKLIN, A. M.,
Professor of Natural Sciences.

R. E. HIERONYMUS, A. M.,
Professor of English Literature.

H. A. MINASSIAN, A. M., M. D.,
Professor of Sacred History.

W. T. JACKSON, A. M.,
Assistant Professor of Natural Sciences.

G. W. HOOTMAN,
Principal of Commercial Department.

O. J. PAGE,
Assistant in Commercial Work.

MISS MELLIE ALVEY,
Director of School of Music, Piano.

MISS JANIE VANDERVORT.
Teacher of Vocal Culture and Harmony.

MRS. JESSIE MINASSIAN, M. E. L.,
Teacher of Drawing and Painting.

MISS ANNIE J. JONES, M. A.,
Teacher of Elocution.

MISS BELLE EGGERT,   .
Teacher of Type Writing and Shorthand.

R. O. SMALLEY,
Teacher of Type Writing and Shorthand.

F. W. BURNHAM,
Teacher of Telegraphy and Railroad Bookkeeping.

F. M. BUZICK,
Teacher of Penmanship.

386 students attended college during this session, the largest attendance the college ever had. The work done was eminently satisfactory, and prospects brighter than ever.

SESSION 1893–94.

Progress and development being ever our watchword, this session could not be an exception to the rule.

Knowing that young people who spend much of their time in study must take regular and systematic physical exercise, the Trustees purchased, in 1890, a five-acre park near the campus and gave it to the students as an athletic park. This action greatly stimulated interest in athletic exercises, but, unfortunately, a park can be used for physical exercise only in the fall and spring, when the weather is mild. In the winter, when students were most in need of such exercise, it could not be had. A gymnasium was needed and the Trustees made arrangements for it. The four rooms on the second and third floors, on the east side of the old recitation building, were set apart for this purpose. Partition walls and the floor between the second and third stories were removed, throwing the four rooms into one. This room was neatly finished and provided with a full set of the best apparatus to be had. To-day Eureka College has a first-class gymnasium, giving students abundant opportunities to keep their physical faculties well developed while improving their mental and moral natures.

The years 1893 and 1894 will ever be memorable on account of the great and disastrous financial panic, affecting all the enterprises of our country. All enterprises are suffering because of the lack of confidence and money. Colleges are not exempted. Many persons still consider an education as a luxury, and refrain from sending their children to school when hard times come.

Though many colleges suffered severely and some lost as much as 50 per cent in attendance, when compared with the preceding session, Eureka College held her own remarkably well. Though the attendance is somewhat smaller than last year, the decrease is only about 8 per cent, giving us no good ground for complaint. A remarkable circumstance in connection with this appalling financial depression is that, notwithstanding this distress, Eureka College has received larger donations during the last six months than during any period of equal length since the institution was organized. Two of the friends of the college, who have often made donations in the past, gave us this year $5,000 each, and two other friends, who had remembered the college in their wills, passed away and left us $2,500 and $10,000 respectively. Other smaller donations were received which swelled our available assets by about $25,000. We have, therefore, abundant reasons to be grateful to our Heavenly Father for the great prosperity that has attended us. At the present time the Faculty consists of the following members :

CARL JOHANN, A. M., LL. D., President,
Professor of Modern Languages.

B. C. DEWEESE, A. M.,
Professor of the John Darst Chair of Sacred Literature.

B. J. RADFORD, A. M., LL. D.,
Professor of Latin and History.

H. N. HERRICK, A. M.,
Professor of Greek and Sanskrit.

S. D. VAWTER, A. M.,
Professor of Mathematics.

R. E. CONKLIN, A. M.,
Professor of Natural Sciences.

R. E. HIERONYMUS, A. M.,
Professor of English Literature.

G. W. HOOTMAN,
Principal of Commercial Department.

MISS MELLIE ALVEY,
Director of School of Music, Piano.

A. T. SMITH,
Teacher of Vocal Music.

MISS MATTIE NARAMORE,
Teacher of Drawing and Painting.

MISS ANNIE J. JONES,
Teacher of Elocution.

THE PRESENT CONDITION AND NEEDS OF EUREKA COLLEGE.

Ever since 1848 the work of educating the hearts and heads of the young people who have come to Eureka for an education has been continued without interruption. From a very insignificant beginning, the enterprise has gradually developed until to-day the Board of Trustees hold in trust for the brotherhood of Illinois the following real estate:

A beautiful campus covered with stately forest trees on which are located the following buildings. The Old Recitation Building, the Chapel, Burgess Memorial Hall and the Mission Tabernacle. Adjoining the campus to the west is a three acre lot on which stand the two boarding halls for gentlemen. Adjoining the campus to the northeast is a four acre tract on which Lida's Wood, the Ladies' Boarding Hall, stood till it was destroyed by fire January 11th, 1894. This hall will be immediately rebuilt. Southeast of the campus lies the five-acre Athletic Park.

This property, worth at least $75,000, is encumbered by a mortgage of $9,000. The productive Endowment Fund is very small, amounting to not more than $30,000, and is entirely inadequate to provide the means necessary to carry on the work as it might be done and to make necessary improvements. Nine-tenths of all the means expended in developing Eureka College from its humble beginning, have been contributed by the citizens of Eureka and vicinity, yet nearly every community in the State of Illinois is reaping the benefits of the work done in Eureka, by having among its most influential citizens men and women educated in Eureka.

Hundreds of Eureka students have gone to other states, and we are proud to say that, wherever they are, their influence is for the good, the pure and the noble.

Eureka students are filling pulpits in nearly every State in the Union, and eternity alone can tell how much good has been done, is being done and will be done in the future by men and women educated in Eureka.

The primary aim of this college is to send Christian scholars out into the world, for we believe that the best results can be obtained only by Christianizing learning.

What the college needs now is an Endowment Fund sufficiently large to give the Trustees an assured permanent income, and we earnestly plead with those who have been blessed with an abundance of this world's goods to help our work with liberal donations. We can not conceive of any way in which money could be used to better advantage to the glory of God and the welfare of humanity. Many could help us while they are living and have the satisfaction of witnessing the good results produced by their liberality. Many more should remember Eureka College when making final disposition of the means intrusted to their care by Providence. Within the last year several friends have remembered the college while making their wills, and two legacies amounting to $12,500 have come to us during the last six months. May we not hope that the good work will go on, and that the coming years will bring many more such gifts? In making your will, the following form might be used :

"I give, grant and bequeath to the Board of Trustees of the Eureka College, located in Eureka, Illinois, the sum of —— dollars, said sum to become part of the permanent endowment of said college."

Harvard College has an endowment of eight million dollars, Columbia College has eleven millions, and the young Chicago University already has four millions. Think how much good Eureka might do if she had a large endowment fund, and help, to the utmost of your ability, to make it larger.

Eureka College is steadily growing in efficiency. The catalogue to be issued this summer will show that the course of studies has been enlarged so as to require of the student one year more of work before graduation, and requirements for admission will henceforth include the following :

Knowledge of Mathematics through Geometry ; two years of Latin, one year of Greek or German, an elementary knowledge of Botany, Zoology and Physiology and a thorough knowledge of English Grammar and Rhetoric. The curriculum of Eureka College is now as complete and comprehensive as that of any college in the West.

BIOGRAPHICAL.

1 John T. Jones.   2 E. Dickinson.   3 A. G. Ewing.

CHAPTER I.

JOHN T. JONES.

In 1795, in Bucks county, Penn., there was gladly welcomed into the family of Joshua Jones and
his wife Eleanor Thomas, a son, who received the
name of his maternal grandfather, John Thomas.
They were of Welsh descent, and young John
T. grew up under the stern discipline and constant
toil usual at the time.

The community was, religiously, Quaker and
Baptist. The old stone Baptist church called
Pennepek, that five years ago celebrated its second
centennial, still stands, and here the subject of
this sketch received his first religious impressions.

Soon after attaining his majority, he went to
Cincinnati, where he married Miss Ann B. Law-
rence, who was called home in a few years, leaving one son.

In 1827 he married Miss Emily Woodward, and
(109)

in 1831 moved to Jacksonville, Ill. His business capacity, habits of industry and acknowledged integrity of character, gave him many positions of honor and trust. At an early day in " The Reformation," having united with the Church of Christ, he decided to prepare himself for the ministry and devoted his spare time to Bible study.

He loved the society of the children of God and was most loyal to his brethren. His house was the preacher's home, and in dispensing his generous hospitality was ably assisted by his wife, a lady of rare refinement, amiability and intellectual culture.

He was liberal almost to a fault, and the church with which he was connected ever found him one of its most reliable supporters. Mr. Jones was reticent, grave and dignified in demeanor and had an habitual reserve of manner that repelled familiarity ; but his heart glowed with a fervor of affection that his exterior did not indicate.

In 1847 he moved with his family to Walnut Grove, Woodford county, Illinois. He entered with zest into all the plans for the moral and intellectual development of the place. He was chosen a trustee of the infant college and for twenty-five years never failed to be present at the annual meetings of the Board.

In so limited a sketch it is impossible even to *touch* upon the events of a life covering 82 years ;

BEN MAJOR.

but what one *is* is of far greater importance than what he *does*, and here we can only mention the prominent traits forming a character of rare firmness and conscientious activity.

Mr. Jones was progressive and never grew too old to be the friend and adviser of the young preachers. They have called him their "father."

His last years were spent in the family of his son, J. Janvier Jones, in Eureka, kindly and tenderly cared for by his son's wife, Mrs. Lucy Major Jones, until his change came, May 14th, 1877, at the age of 82 years.

Like the setting of the sun in a clear sky, his life closed peacefully and beautifully, with the firm assurance that for him a new and brighter day would dawn. S. E. G.

BEN MAJOR.

Ben Major was born in Franklin county, Kentucky, Oct. 31st, 1796. He was the son of John and Judith (Trabue) Major. His paternal and maternal ancestors were French Huguenots, who came to the colony of Virginia in 1699, after the revocation of the Edict of Nantes in 1685. Previous to this they had been refugees in England, and were sent to Virginia by the charity of King William, and became naturalized by a particular law for that purpose.

In all, there were about eight hundred men, women and children who had fled from France on account of their religious opinions.

They first settled in Powhatan county, but from that point they scattered throughout the colony, some settling on a rich tract of land about twenty miles above the falls of James River, the Majors and Trabues going to Franklin county.

The memory of their first home was preserved by the name Powhatan being given as a Christian name to their children.

About 1790 many families came to Kentucky from Virginia, among them Mr. Major's father and mother and other relatives. Coming there before Kentucky was admitted to the Union, they settled in that part of the State that was afterward Franklin county, supposed to be named from the county they had left in Virginia.

That they were people of culture and refinement will be seen from books, silver and furniture over one hundred years old still in possession of the family. Here the subject of this sketch was born and passed his childhood. His father was a farmer, as were nearly all the settlers in Franklin county at that time. They made homes similar to those still seen in the blue grass regions, and they were like no other farms in the United States.

The farms were large, the farm houses being placed in the center, surrounded by wide pastures, more like parks in England. They engaged in stock-raising, and in the cultivation of corn and tobacco, and in a few years were in easy circumstances. . They spun their own cotton, flax and wool, and wove cloth, sending the surplus to New Orleans, and exchanging it for foreign goods.

In such surroundings Ben Major's youthful days were spent. His education was derived from private teachers, as schools were few in number. Two or three families would employ a teacher, or they would employ one in each family; rarely some were sent away to college.

His education seems to have been above that of the average young man of the day, as well-worn volumes of Shakespeare, Paradise Lost and Lalla Rookh will attest, and he was ever a reader and student throughout his life.

When about eighteen years of age, an older brother, John, went to New Orleans to engage in business, and the following year Ben went to assist him. They continued in business for almost five years.

While they were there their mother died, in 1817, and the next year John died with yellow fever, leaving Ben alone in New Orleans. He closed up the business the following year and returned to Kentucky.

His father, in the meantime, had sold his farm in Franklin county and moved to the southern

8

part of the State, into Christian county, which was being settled at that time. After his return from New Orleans, he spent some time in the neighborhood of his old home, visiting relatives and renewing old acquaintances. Here he met Miss Lucy Davenport, whom he married Jan. 15, 1820. About this time his only sister, Eliza Major, married William Davenport, a brother of his wife.

After his marriage he went to Christian county, and opened a new farm, and soon made for his family a comfortable home. His father had brought his slaves from Virginia, and when he moved to Christian county, took them with him. Here, with the help of his slaves, Ben Major soon had his farm under cultivation, and was one of the foremost business men of the county.

About 1827 or 8, his health failed ; indeed his health had not been good since leaving New Orleans. After trying many doctors with little or no success, he was led to try the Thompsonian system, and after much study and successful treatment of himself he began the practice of medicine, and continued it for over three years before leaving Kentucky, and afterward in Illinois, where doctors were few, and from eight to twenty miles distant. As he was a good nurse as well as a physician, he was often called upon for his services, and there are people in Eureka to-day who owe their lives to his skill and gentle nursing.

He was almost a physician without price, as his services were nearly always gratuitous. If any of the neighbors were sick, he would leave his work and stay with them until the danger was past.

From his childhood he had serious doubts on the slavery question, and with such doubts made the subject one continuous study. As he reached mature years, these doubts were swept away, and he became convinced that the whole system was radically wrong; and being a man who acted upon his own convictions of what his particular duty was to his God and fellowmen, he marked out a course and matured plans for his own guidance; a course which was at variance with all his early teachings, and antagonistic to all his family and society relations.

But fully realizing his duty to the dependent creatures under his control, and the obligations he owed to his children fast gathering around him, he never once hesitated (although at that time it meant almost financial ruin), but determined not only to liberate and colonize his slaves, but at the same time to liberate himself and his immediate family from even a taint of the curse of slavery. He realized that his slaves were not fully prepared for so great a change, and spent many months, even years, in educating them to the proper point; spent long evenings in reading to them all available matter that would in any way shed light on their darkened minds. At first they absolutely refused to entertain a thought of freedom on any grounds. With a kind and considerate master and mistress, and surrounded by all the comforts of which their ignorant minds could conceive, they had no desire for a change. But by a careful and well-devised system of teaching, he finally brought them to consider the matter in the proper light, and consent to be colonized and become free men and women.

Late in the spring of 1831, leaving all his farming operations in the care of his trusted slaves, he started with buoyant spirits, a light heart, and, we may add, a clear conscience, to find a home in some free State ; and and after a long journey alone and on horseback, he reached what is now Woodford county, Illinois, and found a small settlement on the banks of Walnut Greek.

This being the spring after the deep snow, he found in June evidences of it in the drifts along the few fences. He was well pleased with all the conditions and with the noble band of men and women whom he found here. His practical mind was much impressed with the boundless prairies and the grand forests, and with his penetrating vision he saw in this land great possibilities for the future, where he and his sons and daughters might, by their own exertions and toil make free homes for themselves and those that might follow.

Being now fully satisfied that he had found that
for which he sought, his mission in Illinois for the
present ended, he returned to Kentucky, not being
able or prepared to purchase or enter land. He
returned to Illinois in 1833, and entered and purchased about eight hundred acres of land, locating on the east side of the Grove, choosing for his
future home a tract one half mile southeast of
where Eureka College now stands. He then returned to Kentucky to fully carry out all his
plans, for which he had been working so long.
He could make no arrangements for the transport-
ation of his colored people in 1834, so they were
hired out to other planters for one year, the slaves
to receive their own wages.

In the fall of 1835, all things being in readiness,
he sent his agent to New York with the slaves,
who were taken in charge by the American Colonization Society and sent to the colony of Liberia,
Mr. Major being a life member of the Society
and an earnest reader for many years of the *Afri-
can Repository*, its official organ. He incurred all
the expense of sending the negroes, and furnished
them with clothing, supplies and implements.
After reaching their new home, a regular correspondence was kept up, and many welcome letters
were written and received, they invariably ad-
dressing him as "Dear Father." Many of these

treasured letters are still kept by members of the family as sacred mementos.

Nothing had been heard definitely from these people since 1858, when one of the negroes, whose father and mother had been slaves of Mr. Harlan and Mr. Major, was sent to this country on official business for the colony, and while in the United States visited Eureka and spoke in the old church, and gave an account of their manner of living, describing their school system and church advantages.

He thought the prospect for the future of Liberia was good. But of late years news has come that the native tribes have caused much trouble to the colony.

In 1827 or 8, Ben Major, who had long been a member of the Baptist Church, with many others in that part of Kentucky with like views, united and organized the Christian Church at Noah Springs, which was a noted landmark in the early days of the A. Campbell reformation.

In October of 1834 he loaded his goods in wagons drawn by oxen, and started for the Illinois home. The family at this time numbered seven persons, Ben Major and wife, Lucy, and five children, John, Judith A., William, Ben and Lucy. (After coming here they were blessed with three other children, Jo, Ann Eliza and Chastine.) Mrs. Major with the three youngest children rode in a buggy, the other two children, fourteen and ten years of age respectively, riding on horseback. Two of the slaves assisted with the stock as far as Carlinville, Ill., returning to Kentucky from there. And thus began what would seem to us a long, tedious journey. But in after years the trip between Illinois and Kentucky was often made, before railroads were in existence.

The time taken in moving out, some two weeks, was enjoyed by all, the weather being delightful. Reaching Walnut Grove the last day in October, they, after viewing their future home, went to William Davenport's, who had moved out the spring before, and had settled at the head of the Grove. It was a joyful meeting in a new land, with an untried future facing them.

After resting here a few days, he moved on his own farm into a house built of logs and containing two rooms, in which they lived two years, the time being passed in opening up a new farm. Prairie had to be broken and fences made. While there was no clearing to be done, as in Kentucky, yet rails had to be made, and there being at that time excellent timber, the ax formed an important factor. Neighbors were far apart, but neighbors they were in fact and deed. They found such men as John Oatman, Joseph Henry, Noel Meek, Caleb Davidson, David Deweese, Daniel Travis, William

Davenport and Mordecai Bullock, with some others.

In 1835 and 6, many more came, prominent among them, B. J. Radford, Elijah Dickinson, E. B. and A. M. Myers and Thomas Bullock, all seeking and finding pleasant homes in this free land.

The planting of fruit trees of all varieties was one of their first cares, sending to Tennessee and even as far as Harper's Ferry, Va., for them, which in a few years yielded them abundant crops. Small fruits grew wild in great abundance. Game of all kinds was plentiful, and to be had merely for the taking.

After living in the log house for two years, Mr. Major began the erection of a frame house, which required several years for its completion. The frame in all its parts had to be hewn in the timber, and all the lumber hauled from a saw-mill on the Illinois River, more than twenty miles distant, but, after completion, making a very comfortable and, in those days, rather an imposing farm house.

Here he planted fruit, shade and ornamental trees, many of which remain. On his arrival here he found a few members of the Christian Church, and a church organization, but weak in numbers, under the care of Elder John Oatman. In 1835 it was reorganized, and Ben Major chosen as one of the elders, an office which he retained until his death. At first the meetings were held in the log

houses of the settlers. In warm weather the meetings were regularly held in the barns of Uncle
Caleb Davidson and David Deweese, and in the
shady forest. Afterward meetings were held in
the school-house until the old church was built,
on the site of the present cemetery. This old
church has been gone many years, but around it,
for many of the older people of Eureka, cling
many sweet memories.

As the children of these early settlers grew up,
they one and all realized the need of a higher education, the teachers they then employed not
being able to instruct their pupils farther than the
"three R's." After much thought and consultation, they determined to make personal sacrifices
and if possible employ better teachers.

Money was scarce, and how it was accomplished,
and how they builded better than they knew, is
recorded in this history. Of the many personal
sacrifices made, only those who made them know.
After many unsuccessful attempts, they finally
procured the services of A. S. Fisher, and the
foundation-stone of Eureka College was laid.

Though death claimed Ben Major in the prime
of his useful manhood, he yet lived to see the beginning of his fondest hopes realized. In the
spring of 1852, his brother-in-law, William Davenport, while in St. Louis, came in contact with
some cases of cholera, and after returning home

was taken sick, but recovered, no one supposing at that time that cholera was in our midst.

His wife, Mr. Major's sister, was the next victim. They sent hastily for her brother. The family were at breakfast when the messenger arrived, and without a thought for himself, leaving the meal untasted, he hastened to his sister's side, there to remain until death released her from her suffering.

All then knew that the dread epidemic had gained a firm foothold. Returning home accompanied by his nephew, Joseph Davenport, both were taken ill. From the first Mr. Major seemed to realize that his case was a hopeless one, and showed great presence of mind and unselfish devotion to others in directing their treatment. So, heroically and without complaint, he breathed his last. Joseph Davenport survived him only a few hours. Another nephew, John Davenport, also died, making four deaths in so short a time.

These were indeed sad times for the bereaved families. Many were the kind offices rendered. The loving sympathy of the entire community was tendered the saddened families, all feeling keenly the loss of a dear and tried friend. Departing this life with so many of his Christian plans only fairly begun, yet he died in the firm, unshaken faith that his many co-workers would complete the work which they had so auspiciously begun.

Elijah Dickinson, son of Richard and Ann (Quarles) Dickinson, was born Jan. 26, 1795, in Spottsylvania county, Virginia. He was of Scotch-English descent.

In 1814, during the war of 1812, he joined a volunteer cavalry company and served till the close of the war.

He came to Christian county, Kentucky, about the year 1817. Here he was married October 6, 1819, to Miss Mary Ann Burrus, and in June 1821, they united with the Baptist Church. A few years later the preaching of the primitive gospel was begun in that community by some of our pioneer Disciple preachers. He heard it frankly, and in 1831, with nineteen others, left the Baptist Church and united in organizing a Christian Church, of which he was made an elder.

In the fall of 1835 he removed with his wife and six children—J. Quarles, Cynthia M., Celia B., M. Elizabeth, Elmira J., and Elijah W.—to Walnut Grove, Illinois. Here two sons were added to his family, Charles R. and Roger B. A church of Disciples had been organized here several years before. In 1837 he was made one of the elders, and was kept in that office the remainder of his life.

In his early life schools were few and inferior

about his boyhood home, and his opportunities for
that kind of education were very limited indeed. But he was a thoughtful man, a diligent
reader, a close observer, and a good judge of
human nature, and so gathered much general information. He was a staunch friend and promoter
of thorough education and labored earnestly for ·
the upbuilding of Walnut Grove Academy and
Eureka College.

Was elected one of the Board of Trustees of the
Academy at its organization in 1850. After the
death of President Ben Major, in 1852, he was
elected President of the Board, and so continued
till his death.

During his early manhood he was a carpenter,
but after his marriage he chose farming as his oc-
cupation, and continued in it first in Kentucky,
then in Illinois. He peacefully fell asleep, July
28, 1862, at his old homestead one and a half miles
southwest of the college, and his body reposes in
Eureka Cemetery.

ALBERT G. EWING.

A. G. Ewing was born in Nashville, Tenn., Feb.
28th, 1804. His parents were natives of Scotland.
It was a tradition in his father's family that their
ancestors were of the same family as that most
famous of Scottish heroes, Sir William Wallace.

His parents were among the earliest settlers of
Nashville. His father gave his six sons the best
opportunities in the way of education that that day
afforded, and they all became prominent men in a
worldly way except Albert, the subject of this
sketch ; his life was even more energetic and earnest than theirs, but his chief ambition was to serve
his God and save his fellowmen. He graduated
in Cumberland College when only sixteen years
old. Was a good Greek scholar, and throughout
his life his Greek Bible was nearly as often in his
hand as his well-worn English Bible. Gen. Jackson's name is appended to his diploma as one of
the college trustees. The noted General was
known and admired by the youthful student. Soon
after Albert graduated, he was honored by a part-
nership with the then celebrated Dr. Rush in a
drug-store ; he gained a good knowledge of medicine at this time Alexander Campbell preached
in Nashville when Albert was nineteen, and his
parents and himself were among the first converts
Campbell made there. The reformer and his
young convert loved each other. Albert gave up
fine prospects of earthly honor and riches and followed the then persecuted Campbell to Bethany,
became a student under him, traveled with him on
some of his extensive preaching tours, and finally
married Campbell's eldest daughter. She died

young, like all of Campbell's first family of gifted and beautiful daughters.

In 1837 Mr. Ewing married Miss Mary J. Marsilliot of Wheeling, Va., and removed to a farm on the Ohio River near the village of Clarington. She outlived him fifteen years. Farming and the building and managing of a large steam flouring and saw-mill enabled him to give employment to a number of men. He chose this river locality for his home, because religious and educational work was sadly needed there. During the twenty years of his life there all that he had and was, was freely given to educate and Christianize the people. He met with opposition and persecution for a time, but also had good success, and came to be much beloved. He preached, made converts and organized churches in a number of places, built the church house for his home church with very little aid, and was its pastor for sixteen years. He made the same mistake others of our pioneer preachers made, he required too little of others and caused them to depend too much on him. Finally his health failed and he was crippled financially. He brought his family to Eureka, Ill., in 1858. Although broken in health and mental power by a long illness occurring shortly before his coming West, his life in his new home was not useless; he soon became a working elder in the church. His active eldership in Ohio and Illinois covered

JOHN DARST.

a period of forty years. He was a trustee of Bethany College for a number of years before he came to Illinois. He was President of the Board of Trustees of Eureka College for eleven years before his death, and was deeply interested in its welfare.

President Everest once said of him, that of all men he had come in contact with, he had the least admixture of selfishness. The good of *The Cause* was always first with him. Another who knew him well said, when notified of his death, "If ever the words which Christ applied to Nathanael applied to any other man they did to A. G. Ewing. He was an Israelite indeed in whom there was no guile." He fell asleep on August 28th, 1873, at his home in Eureka, Illinois.

JOHN DARST.

John Darst was born November 6, 1816, in Greene county, Ohio. Both of his grandfathers came from Germany. His boyhood and youth were characteristic of that early pioneer life. He learned to read and write, went as far into practical arithmetic as his teacher's limited knowledge would take him, and barely tasted grammar.

Ruhamah Moler became his wife, November 22, 1838. She shared the hardships of those early times, assisted heartily in carrying out the plans

to better the condition of their family, and has co-
operated fully in all his efforts for the church and
college. The support of a devoted wife, man's
greatest earthly stay, he has never lacked. She is
now the quiet, home-keeping, home-loving companion of his old age. Their golden wedding, November 22, 1888, brought to their home forty-three
children and grand-children. Three others could
not be present. In the company were nine sons
(one, John W., having died at 18) and their only
daughter. Their children honor them while living
and will revere their memory after they shall have
passed on to the other shore.

For thirteen years Mr. Darst continued his farm
life in Ohio. He attempted to raise the standard
of education at his birthplace in the interest of his
children. For them he wished to secure a better
education than he had received. The old ideas
were too firmly established, however, to be uproot-
ed. About this time he learned that the newer
west offered special inducements to the farmer.
Influenced by the hope of obtaining better educational and material advantages, he removed his
family to Eureka, Illinois, September, 1851. For
more than thirty years he continued to farm exten-
sively and successfully at this place. He was also
interested in milling for some years. In 1882 he
became president of the Farmers' Bank, which had

just been organized. In business his career has been long, prosperous and honorable.

He has always taken an active part in the advancement of the community in which he resided. In 1856 he laid out the town of Eureka. His fellow citizens have shown their appreciation of his public spirit by calling him frequently to serve their interests in local offices. While a young man he recognized the evils of the drink habit. Ever since he has been its foe, and is now a party prohibitionist. During our National struggle he was an abolitionist and had five sons in the Union army. His political action is governed by the sole consideration of right. He allies himself with those who stand for moral issues and breaks all party ties which interfere with this most worthy exercise of Christian citizenship.

In early life Mr. Darst became a Baptist, but soon united with the Disciples of Christ, among whom he has held official positions to his credit and to their advantage for nearly half a century. He first served the church as deacon, but for many years he has been an elder, and faithful to the spiritual welfare of the congregation..

On arriving at Walnut Grove, now Eureka, he found that kindred spirits had already established an academy. He identified himself at once with the enterprise. Eureka College was chartered in 1855, and at the first business meeting he was

9

elected a trustee. He acted in that capacity until 1873, when he was elected president of the Board of Trustees on the death of Mr. Ewing. This office he has since filled continuously. He has had a leading part in the erection of the college buildings, which the prosperity of the college made needful. To superintend their construction he has taken the time from his private business. For many years he always looked after the gratuitous work necessary in caring for the college property. His interest, his energy and good business judgment have naturally given him a prominent place in the management of college affairs. It is a pleasure to add that other members of the Board of Trustees show a willingness to relieve him of labors which are too onerous for the growing infirmities of age.

Mr. Darst has made it the rule of his life to put a large share of his earnings into the college funds. He prefers to see his money do good while he lives. All who know the facts must freely acknowledge that without his co-operation and financial support the college work would have been most seriously crippled. Brief mention of some of his characteristic acts may provoke others to more liberally support a worthy cause. It is also proper, too, that the facts be recorded before they are forgotten, that he may receive honor while he lives. Lovers of Christian education can also better appreciate how much their cause is indebted to this faithful friend. When the college was young, it was difficult to secure money for buildings, without which the work could not go on. Plans were made for the recitation building and pledges obtained to meet the expense. Financial distress became so great that many subscribers could not pay their pledges. Mr. Darst and William Davenport gave their note for the college debt, and mortgaged their property to secure its payment. Depression in money matters continued and the note fell due. A new note had to be given. For good reasons Mr. Davenport asked to be released from taking up the burden anew. Mr. Darst then bought more land that he might properly secure a new note, and mortgaged all he had, even the home of his family, to assume alone the payment of the entire college debt. As an illustration of his faith in God and his love of the cause, his conduct on this occasion will serve. He went to the harvest field and told his sons what he had done, and added: "If we can save this crop and have another good one next year, we will be able, I think, to save our home." One dollar was harder to get then than five are now. His first donation to educational interests in Eureka was $250, in 1852. His largest at any one time has been $6,000. His larger contributions aggregate not less than $25,000. Besides these he always responds to minor calls.

Recently he has given liberally to the select library for the Biblical department, and has promised twice the amount to the general library of the college. In a recent letter he speaks of his work in the following words: "I wish now I had kept an account of what I have done, but not caring whether other men knew or not, I knew the Lord knew how much and the motive with which it was given. This I could not have done without the co-operation of my wife and children. And if I could, I would not take one dollar of it back." No additional words could emphasize the faithful consecration of this man and his family to the interests of Eureka college. Disciples of Illinois, Mr. Darst's sons were kept from college privileges to pay off a college debt, and thus provide for your children the advantages which Eureka College affords. Will not this persuade you of your abundance to give liberally to endow a work which is so full of promise, if well equipped?

Finally, it remains to speak of Mr. Darst's interest in young men preparing for the ministry. Their work and worth lie nearest his heart. Often he gave them board, furnished them horses to carry them to their appointments, loaned them money, attended regularly their devotional meetings until age prevented his going, and talked to them plainly about their life and work. He wished them to have a proper conception of the ministry of the

Gospel. There are many who have reason to remember his wise counsel, and some for personal
reasons, too, recall with gratitude the Scripture,
"Faithful are the wounds of a friend." Of his
helpfulness the following is a good example: B.
B. Tyler, of New York, early in the sixties devoted
part of his time to business, to obtain a support for
his family. His Sunday services were full of
promise. Seeing this Mr. Darst "persuaded him
to relinquish his business engagements and devote
his energies to the saving of souls, stipulating to
supply all necessary funds to support him in the
work." Of this offer Mr. Tyler says: "I want the
world to know that John Darst did this for me and
for the Church of Christ. If I have been worth
anything to the world, let this grand, good man,
still living, have the honor that belongs to him."

Such, in mere outline, is the life of this plain,
earnest, self-sacrificing, unassuming Christian
man. The world is always better because of such
lives.

CHAPTER II.

A. S. Fisher—Sue Jones Grant—John Lindsey—Sarah Fisher Conover—Caroline Neville Pearre—Elmira J. Dickinson—O. A. Burgess—R. A. Conover—C. L. Loos—George Callender—J. M. Allen—B. W. Johnson—Richard H. Johnson—J. H. Rowell—Mary Clark Hawk.

A. S. FISHER.

Asa S. Fisher was born in Clinton county, Ohio, December 10, 1824. In 1829 his parents moved to Illinois, locating in Tazewell county. There he lived with his parents until the winter of 1842, assisting his father on the farm and attending the crude schools of the locality during the winters. In September, 1843, he entered Tremont Academy, where he remained till the following March. In 1844 he entered the Preparatory Department of Knox College, Illinois. In August, 1845, he removed to Marshall county, and was there engaged as a school teacher until July, 1847. In the fall of 1847 he entered Bethany College, returning to Illinois in July, 1848.

(134)

A. S. FISHER.

In September, 1848, he commenced the school in Walnut Grove that developed into Eureka College. He was a constant and zealous promoter of the in-stitution for thirty-eight years of his eventful life.

In 1866 he reluctantly withdrew from the college, conscious of having aided, to the extent of his ability, in the establishment of an efficient literary auxiliary to the Christian Church, leaving its future to the management of younger men.

During his connection with the institution thousands of young men had been received under its fostering care, and had there received a literary training and development, making them valuable citizens in their respective localities. They had gone forth and were to be found in the valleys, on the plateaus, the hill-tops and mountain-sides of our vast western domain. They had penetrated the western mountains, had looked out upon the great ocean and visited the islands of the sea. They were cultivators of the soil, watchmen on the towers of Zion, active agents in legislative halls and fearless defenders of their country's honor; college professors and presidents, popular political orators, eminent at the bar, *drawing* lecturers and profound jurists.

Educators, like poets, are born, not made. Mr. Fisher was a born educator, and early in life set about fitting himself for that, his chosen life-work,

as best he could with the advantages within his
reach. It was in the pioneer days when times are
always hard and money always scarce and schools
nearly always poor.

But as the country developed advantages improved. The young man went to college, stead-
fast in pursuit of his purpose, not knowing, but
often wondering, where his field of labor during
life was to be.

Meanwhile, among the enterprising citizens of
Walnut Grove, the spirit of education was becoming more and more rife, and they were wondering
how, in their poverty, they could ever educate their
children. Under the leadership of Elder Ben
Major they discussed over and over again the
building up of a seminary or academy for the
higher education of their sons and daughters,
than the irregular, inefficient subscription schools
of the time afforded; but where the man and
whence the money for this work, were the ever-re-
curring and ever unanswered questions that con-
fronted them.

But during the session that Mr. Fisher attended
Bethany College, a nephew of Mr. Major's was
also there, Mr. J. M. Major of Bloomington, Ill. To
him Elder Major wrote asking if there was not
among the students there some one who was fitted
for, and willing to undertake such a work as was
wanted here; and the gladsome answer came back

highly commending "a Mr. A. S. Fisher from near Tremont" for the position. The result was, in August he came on for a conference with some of the leading men in the community, and early in September, 1848, the school opened in the little frame schoolhouse, and lo, *Eureka College was begun;* though not one of those devoted souls dreamed how well they were building, nor whereunto their work would grow.

The coming of the "new teacher," fresh from college, was a notable event in our quiet, country neighborhood. We were not used to college men then, had scarcely ever seen one. This young man was tall, fair, beardless, bashful, and looked much younger than he really was. But the fire of a noble purpose burned bright in his soul and gleamed forth from his eye. Character was stamped on his mien. He had a work to do and he meant to do it, was the language of his actions. And so he went into his little school of children and half-grown boys and girls, resolute to do his part in making of it a school of higher grade.

He boarded in the home of Elder Major. A warm friendship grew up between them, as, congenial in spirit, they counseled and planned and worked for the realization of their common hopes. The school enterprise proved eminently successful, and before the session of ten months closed it was so well reported of in the surrounding counties

that a goodly number of young men and young
women were arranging to enter it at the beginning
of the second session, in September, 1849. All
this led to its organization, during vacation, as
Walnut Grove Seminary.

During that summer, Mr. Fisher took an' important social step. The bachelor became a
benedict. Several years before, while teaching in
Marshall county, he had met Miss Susan S. Palmer, daughter of Elder Henry D. Palmer, a prominent preacher of the Gospel, and July 25th they
were married, thereby a real help-mate being
gained. With their limited means a house was
built near the school, and they kept boarders at
$1.25 a week, fuel and lights included. This was
at a time when there was no store of any kind,
nor butcher-shop nor post-office nearer than
Washington, eight miles away.

The school, as seminary, academy and college
continued to grow, though with varied experiences,
adverse and prosperous, and many changes of
teachers were made ; but Prof. Fisher stood un-
flinchingly by it through times of sorest trial as
firmly as through most prosperous seasons. It
never had a truer, more devoted friend than he.
He never had much money to give, but he gave
freely in proportion to his means ; and gave without reserve the mental and physical strength of
his early and mature manhood, toiling in and for

it through periods of financial stress ; through the straits of the civil war, when it almost had to suspend; through perils within and perils without. In course of time he became overwhelmed in financial reverses and these seriously involved his relations with officials in the college management, and led to his separation from the college, and his going to Kansas City, where he now resides.

MRS. SUE E. GRANT.

Susan E. Jones was born near Jacksonville, Ill., April 4, 1832. She was the oldest daughter of Elder John T. Jones and Emily Woodward, his wife. She was educated at Jacksonville Female Academy, the oldest ladies' school in the State, and began teaching in 1847.

Prof. Fisher says in a recent letter to Mrs. Grant, "You conducted the first school in the series that developed into Eureka College, and well do I remember who assisted me during my second year in Walnut Grove."

Four years later she accepted a position in Christian College, Columbia, Mo., then in the efficient hands of Pres. John Augustus Williams of Kentucky.

In 1852 she was married to Prof. Robert A. Grant, of Boone county, Mo., and removed to Can-

ton, Mo., where she was present at the laying of
the corner-stone of Christian University in 1853.

For several years she was principal of the De
Soto Young Ladies' Institute at this place, and her
husband continued teaching in Christian University until 1875, when they removed to Woodland,
Cal.

On account of financial reverses, Mrs. Grant re-
entered the school-room after reaching California,
and taught for some nine years. During this time
she served for some time as the President of the
California Home Missionary Society, and afterward as President of the Christian Woman's
Board of Missions of California, when the Home
Mission became merged in the National organization.

In every emergency of life, Mrs. Grant has
proved a woman of unusual force of character, remarkable intelligence, and exceptional energy,
cheerfulness and courage.

"The heart of her husband doth safely trust in
her," and her children may well "rise up and call
her blessed." The latter are all educated Christian young men and women, acting well their part
in life's arena.

Thus loved and honored by the community in
which she lives, her family, church and friends,
may she spend a serene old age, until she is
called up higher to enjoy the broader opportuni-

ties, the higher ideals, the nobler affections, the grander motives of the future, Just Beyond.

ELDER JOHN LINDSEY.

Elder John Lindsey was born in Christian county, Kentucky, June 15, 1821. Was of Scotch descent. His father, Elder James A. Lindsey, was for many years a Baptist preacher, but in the year 1827 he with his church took his stand with the Reformation with no name but that given in the New Testament and no creed but Christ. He moved with his family to Tazewell county, Illinois, in 1834.

He obeyed the Gospel at fifteen years of age, and began preaching at eighteen, receiving many into the church. He was a strong temperance man, and came near being excluded from the church in 1841 for delivering a temperance lecture, signing the pledge, and inducing others to do so. About 1843 he visited Kentucky with Dr. G. P. Young, and while there was chosen by the Disciples of that State to receive the education given by Bethany College to the State. He entered college in the fall of 1844 and graduated in 1848. Spent his vacations preaching in Virginia, Pennsylvania and Ohio, averaging over one hundred additions each year. Returning to Illinois in the fall of '48, he was made district evangelist with Elder John T. Jones.

Was married to Maria K. Mason, sister of Prof. Mason, of Bethany College, in 1850; located in Walnut Grove, and with John T. Jones and Wm. Davenport began soliciting means to build Walnut Grove Academy, which was soon erected, and began teaching there September of the same year, with Prof. A. S. Fisher. In 1852, his wife's health failing, he resigned as teacher to travel with her, and at the same time to raise means to build what is now known as "Gentlemen's Hall, No. 2." He afterwards located at Washington, Ill., with the little church of 30 members, which grew to 145 during his stay there. Early in 1855 he and Elder Wm. Davenport spent two weeks in Springfield at their own expense to obtain the charter for Eureka College, the loss of time from his church in Washington being deducted from his salary of $600. He was one of the committee of three to name the town. He reported "Eureka," and Elder J. T. Jones "Althea."

When Alexander Campbell canvassed the State for endowment for Bethany College Mr. Lindsey traveled with him. Mr. Campbell being indisposed much of the time, Mr. Lindsey filled his appointments.

He held a successful debate at Metamora with Mr. Davis (Universalist), and one at Lincoln with Mr. Luckock (Methodist).

Later he moved to Peoria, and while there he

married Miss Frank Redding of that city. Also organized the church there with seventeen members, and ministered to it; taught school for a support; secured a lot and built a small house of worship, and increased the membership to sixty-five. Left it in care of I. N. Carman at a salary of $600, he and O. A. Burgess each paying $150 of that.

He was then elected a professor of Abingdon College, but on conferring with the Board of Trustees his work was changed to that of financial agent, and in one year he raised six thousand of the nine thousand dollars indebtedness, and nine thousand dollars endowment.

On Oct. 12, 1858, he was married to Miss Martha M. Davidson, of Walnut Grove, and then located in Atlanta. Soon the State Board sent him to liquidate the debt on the house of worship in Quincy, which he did in one month's time. He was elected President of the college at Monmouth, Ore., in 1858, but declined, and accepted a call to the church at Palmyra, Mo. While there was elected President of the college at Kirksville, Mo., but declined, preferring to preach. Somewhat later he returned to Eureka, and at the close of the war took charge of the church at Duquoin, and while there was elected about the same time President of Carbondale College, Ill., and President of Princeton College, Ky. He accepted the latter, and recommending Clark Braden for the former, began the arduous labor of building up a school in his native State just after the ravages of the Civil War, and used this opportunity given to show his high appreciation of the favor Kentucky had conferred on him. The school opened with seventeen and closed with ninety-seven. He taught through the week and traveled on horseback from Friday till Monday, preaching and soliciting money and students. By the end of the second year his health was so impaired that he resigned, leaving the school in good condition. He then took charge of the church at St. Joseph, Mo., where his labors were crowned with great success in additions to the church and in work at mission points. But the work was too arduous, and before the end of the third year his disease, which proved to be a growth around the heart, became so serious that, on the advice of his physicians to abandon his pastoral work, he again returned to Eureka in the winter of 1873. But his rest was short. He could not resist the many calls to hold meetings, and was very successful. Had more than 150 additions in one at Mackinaw.

He traveled one year as State Evangelist. The remainder of his life was spent preaching for different churches. His last sermon was at Twin Grove, McLean Co., July 3, 1887, on The Resurrection. He was then barely able to stand. His

1 Susan Jones Grant. 3 Sarah Fisher Conover.
2 Elmira J. Dickinson. 4 Mary Clark Hawk.
5 Caroline Neville Pearre

disease had gradually progressed, and on the morning of Oct. 15, 1887, the weary spirit passed to its heavenly rest. "Blessed are the dead that die in the Lord."

SARAH FISHER CONOVER.

Sarah Fisher was born near Tremont, in Tazewell county, Illinois, December 17, 1833. Entered Walnut Grove Academy in its third year, September, 1850, and attended its sessions three years. Taught one year in the preparatory department. Was married October 3, 1854, to Dr. R. A. Conover.

Is still living at her home in Peculiar, Cass county, Missouri, where she settled on removing to that State in 1868, loved by all who know her.

CAROLINE NEVILLE PEARRE.

"Miss Callie," as she was called in *auld langsyne*, began the voyage of life near Clarksville, Tenn., April 15, 1831, and in infancy was brought by her parents to Mackinaw, Ill. After Walnut Grove Academy was started she spent several terms in it as student, also as teacher. Then after teaching about sixteen years, chiefly in Columbia, Mo., and Harrodsburg, Ky., she was married in 1869 to Dr. S. E. Pearre, and became a most efficient associate in his ministerial work.

Hers was a strongly missionary spirit, and in
10

1874, while living in Iowa City, Ia., she developed the idea of enlisting the sisterhood of the Church of Christ in systematic effort for the spread of the Gospel. With the encouragement and assistance that she received from the editors of the *Christian Standard* and the *Christian-Evangelist*, and a few others, she planned a convention to be held in Cincinnati, Ohio, in October of that year.

About seventy-five women responded to her call, and under her leadership organized the Christian Woman's Board of Missions, which has proved a mighty power for good in many ways.

She always loved young people. Long she was accustomed to lead them, especially in their literary and social training. She loves them yet, but though no longer associated with them in the school-room, from her quiet home in Irvington, Ind., she still holds sweet and helpful communion with them through the *Young People's Standard*.

Hers is the graceful pen of a ready writer. Long may she wield it.

ELMIRA J. DICKINSON.

Elmira Jane Dickinson, daughter of Elijah and Mary A. Dickinson, began life in Christian county, Ky., January 9, 1831. Is of Welsh-English descent. Came with her parents to Walnut Grove in 1835. Was baptized July 6, 1845. Was educated in Waluut Grove Academy, taking the full academic course, but before diplomas were conferred. Taught, at different times, several years in the academy, also several years in the college, retiring finally from the work in June, 1870. In 1869 the Board of Trustees conferred on her the degree M. A.

She aided in the organization of the Christian Woman's Board of Missions at Cincinnati in October, 1874. Was, at the beginning of this work, made State President of the Board in Illinois. Three times she resigned this office and others were elected, but she was as often recalled to it as those others resigned it to enter other fields of labor, and she still has charge of that work.

She was one of the deputation sent by the C. W. B. M. in January, 1887, to visit its mission on the Island of Jamaica. The trip occupied about three months.

In June, 1887, she was elected one of the trustees of Eureka College, the first woman called to that position, which she continues to fill.

She has long been an earnest worker in the temperance cause, and was three years W. C. T. U. President in the Ninth Congressional district, in which she resides, and gave that up only because she could not carry on that arduous work in addition to her missionary duties, to which she felt specially called.

A friend and promoter of education always and everywhere, she has been especially interested in and thoroughly loyal to Eureka College, and has long wished that a record of its origin, work and experiences might be arranged in permanent form. Therefore she rejoices that this is now being done by the Alumni Association, and is glad to aid in the work.

God has blessed her with a busy, happy life. The evening of it she is spending in her quiet home in Eureka, doing whatsoever her hand finds to do.

O. A. BURGESS.

Otis Asa Burgess was born in Thompson, Windham county, Connecticut, August 26, 1829. His ancestors, both paternal and maternal, were of the Pilgrim stock.

When about eight years of age his parents moved to Norwich, Chenango county, New York. He attended "Munich Academy," near his home, completed the course (except the classics) in the spring of 1847, and in the fall of the same year "went west" to Woodford county, Illinois, and taught school till 1851, in that and in Marshall county.

It. was during this time that he first heard of the Disciples, and at Washburn that he first heard a full, clear statement of their doctrines. This was a forcible presentation of. the gospel and its conditions, by Elder Henry D. Palmer, based on Acts

O. A. BURGESS.

2: 38. His own words concerning it were, "It was new, wonderful. It opened a new world." He was immersed July 1, 1850; went to Bethany College in the fall of 1851; graduated July 4, 1854, and was married October 17 of the same year to Miss N. J. Ledgerwood, of Washburn, a granddaughter of Elder Palmer.

During the winter of 1854-5 he was solicitor for Walnut Grove Academy, and was instrumental in obtaining the charter for Eureka College that same winter.

In the spring of 1855 he took charge of the church in Washington, Illinois, but resigned in the fall and became a professor in Eureka College, continuing one year. From May, 1861, to May, 1862, he was in his country's service, but his health failing, he returned home.

Late in the fall of 1862 he took charge of the Central Christian Church in Indianapolis. After a pastorate of nearly eight years, he accepted the presidency of Northwestern Christian (now Butler) University, in which capacity he served two years, resigning to take charge of the church on the corner of Indiana avenue and 25th street, Chicago. After a pastorate of three years he returned to the presidency of the university, where he remained eight years.

In the spring of 1881 he decided to go back to the same little church in Chicago. This was his last work. He passed away March 14, 1882, and was laid to rest in the quiet little cemetery at Forest, Illinois.

He was a man of great force of character, full of energy and persistence, of great physical power and mental vigor, *and was always at work*.

He was strong in controversy, and held a number of important and successful discussions in defence of Christ and his teachings. Was firm even to sternness in refuting his opponent, and seemed cold as an iceberg, but it was only seeming. His heart was as warm and tender as a little child's, and large enough to take in all the world. And so it came to pass that both his friends and his enemies were strongly so. While he was eminently successful in debate, he was just as successful as an evangelist in winning souls to Christ by his own strong personal convictions, his tenderly persuasive power, and his knowledge and use of the Word of God.

Moreover, he was successful in the management of his finances. Was deeply interested in politics, benevolence, education, Christianity at home and abroad, and freely used his means for whatever would uplift and ennoble humanity.

O. A. Burgess was a good man. In his death the church lost a pillar, and the whole world a friend.

R. A. CONOVER, M. D.

Richard Ashton Conover was born in Morgan county, Illinois, December 28, 1831. Received his literary education at Eureka, Illinois. In 1856 began the study of medicine under Dr. R. B. M. Wilson, of Washington, Illinois. Graduated from St. Louis Medical College in 1858. Was married to Miss Sarah Fisher of Tazewell county, Illinois, October 3, 1854. Taught one year in the preparatory department of Walnut Grove Academy. Practiced medicine in Eureka, Illinois, from 1858 till the breaking out of the war of the Rebellion. He entered the service in August, 1862, as Assistant Surgeon in the 108th Regiment, Illinois Volunteer Infantry. In 1863 was promoted to Surgeon and served in that capacity until the close of the war. Removed with his family to Peculiar, Cass county, Missouri, in 1868, where he practiced his profession sixteen years, when, his health failing, he lingered two years, then passed away with heart disease, February 15, 1886. At the time of his death was president of the Medical Association of Kansas City District.

PRESIDENT LOOS.

Charles Louis Loos was born December 22, 1823, at Woerth-sur-Sauer, Department of the Lower Rhine, France. His father was Jacques G. Loos, a native of France; his mother a native of Bavaria, consequently, German.

After his fourth year he attended the academy of his native place until his departure for the United States, in 1834. He was reared in the family of a pious grandmother, and by her was carefully train-ed in the Lutheran faith. In 1837 he was confirmed in the Lutheran Church. Soon afterward he be-came acquainted with the teaching of the Disciples, and in 1838 united with them under the preaching of J. Wesley Lampheare, being immersed by John Whitacre. This caused great bitterness and oppo-sition among his Lutheran relatives, but he had taken the step under an earnest conviction of duty, and did not stop to confer with flesh and blood.

He began to teach school at sixteen years of age, and at seventeen began to preach the gospel. In September, 1842, he entered Bethany College, where he graduated in 1846, and then remained three years as teacher in the primary department. July 6, 1848, was married at Bethany to Rosetta E. Kerr, daughter of Rev. John Kerr, a Presbyterian minister, of Newry, Ireland. She was his devoted companion and helpmeet for forty-five years, and very recently has fallen asleep.

In 1849 he was ordained to the work of the min-istry. Served the church at Wellsburg, Virginia, one year, then the church at Somerset, Pennsylva-nia, five years. During two years of this time he edited a monthly paper called *The Disciple*, and two years was principal of an academy. In January, 1856, he took charge of the church on Eighth and Walnut streets, Cincinnati, Ohio, and became assistant editor of the *Christian Age*. In January, 1857, having been elected President of Eureka College, in Illinois, he removed to that place and work, remaining until September, 1858, when he was recalled to Bethany College, to the chair of Ancient Languages and Literature in that institution.

In May, 1880, he resigned his professorship in Bethany College, and soon after accepted the Presidency of Kentucky University and the chair of Greek, which position he still occupies.

He was a regular contributor to the *Christian Standard* from its beginning in 1866, until the death of its editor and founder, Isaac Errett. He was a contributor to *Moore's Christian Quarterly* and has been a writer also for the *Christian Quarterly Review*. Of late years he has been writing for the *Christian-Evangelist*.

He has now been preaching fifty-two years, and engaged in higher educational work more than forty years. His best loved work has been the ancient languages as connected with the Holy Scriptures in preparing young men for preaching the Gospel.

Since the death of Isaac Errett he has been the President of the Foreign Christian Missionary Society.

GEORGE CALLENDER.

George Callender was born in Edinburgh, Scotland, July 14, 1807. There he attended school, beginning the study of Latin when only eight years of age, and becoming in it so proficient that Greek was learned with a Greek-Latin lexicon. He was also fitting himself for the ministry of the Presbyterian Church, in which faith he had been brought up, until about his fifteenth year, when, threatened with serious lung trouble, was obliged to give up his studies and enter his father's tannery, where he served his apprenticeship to the trade. His health while there was in a great measure restored, but though obliged to give up serving God from the pulpit, he was not idle. He joined heartily in church and Sunday-school work, in work of the Society for the Destitute, visiting the sick and needy, rendering necessary substantial aid, and ever ready with words of comfort and encouragement, which few knew better how to give.

On leaving the tannery he engaged in the commission business in Glasgow, removing later to Liverpool, England, where he married Miss Isabella Dunlop, and where they lived nine years. For the sake of the children, especially the boys—two sons and a daughter having been born to them—he determined to leave the vice and confinement of the city for the pure, free air of an American farm. In

May, 1852, he came to the United States, seeking a suitable location for their new home. He was greatly attracted to this locality by its natural beauty and fertility, and, after purchasing property, returned to England to settle up his business. The following year he removed his family to the property purchased the previous year, near what is now Eureka, Illinois, and soon identified himself with the best interests of the community. One daughter was born to them there; and, alas for the father's hopes and sacrifices, in 1856 one son died, and in 1858 the other.

In 1855, through the preaching of Rev. William Brown, Mr. Callender and his wife were buried with Christ in baptism, having learned of the Disciples while in Liverpool by reading the discussion between Alex Campbell and Robert Owen on the Evidences of Christianity. Soon after becoming acquainted with the young people of the neighborhood he gathered them together at his home on Sunday afternoon for Bible study. The little Sunday-school soon outgrew his rooms, and was removed to the academy, which, too, was soon not large enough to accommodate those who came, and. it was moved again, to the church, where he was still its faithful superintendent and teacher of the Bible class. Such was the beginning of our Sunday-school in Eureka, not that this was the first time or the second that one had been organized in

the community, but it was given to this good man
to successfully begin and carry it through its early
discouragements, till it became second only to the
church service.

He who knew the advantages of an education
could not but feel a deep interest in the struggles
of our school to gain and maintain a place among
our people. Mr. Callender was President of the
college for two or three years, during which time he
awarded the first diploma given by the institution,
and under him also graduated the largest class of
its first twenty-six years. Being a thorough student of the Bible and having a mind well stored
with useful information, the lectures he frequently
delivered before the students were exceedingly interesting and instructive. He was very fond of the
society of young people, over whom he had a remarkable influence for good; he made himself their
friend, joined in their amusements, sympathized
in their sorrows, and gave substantial aid to
ambitious, deserving students, struggling to obtain an education. He gave freely of time and
means to further the interests of the college.
He was one of the Charter Trustees and its efficient secretary of the Board for a number of
years, and only retired from the trusteeship
when age and failing health warned him to lay
aside some of the burdens of earlier years. In
his dealings with others and in his daily life he

was above reproach. It was a comfort when
age was creeping on, to feel that all his life through
he had striven to be just and honest toward all
men. Having made his peace with God he did
not doubt, and often, when he felt the powers of
mind and body failing, would repeat, "He that hear-
eth my 'word, and *believeth* on him that sent me
hath everlasting life, and shall not come into con-
demnation, but *is* passed from death unto life"
(John 5: 24), receiving untold comfort from Christ's
words. As the shadows of forgetfulness closed
about him, he still remembered passages of God's
word and could express himself in prayer when
speech concerning the common affairs of life failed
him. After a lingering illness, most patiently en-
dured, his spirit took its flight July 17, 1891, and
his body was laid to rest in the cemetery at Eureka.

Such is the brief history of a noble life, a life not
unsuccessful as the world counts success, but eminently successful in its best sense, in its influence
for good upon all with whom he came in contact.

GEORGINA JOHANN.

J. M. ALLEN.

James M. Allen was born in Fleming county,
Kentucky, July 1st, 1827. Father's name, Simeon
B. Allen; mother's maiden name, Mary Stamps

Shackleford, both of Fayette county, Kentucky.
Their parents moved from Virginia to Kentucky.
He was educated at home, in country and village
schools, until sixteen years of age. Then attend-
ed Transylvania University, Lexington, Kentucky,
under Methodist supervision, H. B. Bascom, presi-
dent, and afterward Bacon College, Harrodsburg,
Kentucky, James Shannon, president. Studied
medicine with Dr. David Clinton Higbee, Lexing-
ton, Kentucky. Attended course of lectures in
Medical department of Transylvania University.
Following year continued study of medicine with
Dr. Shackleford of Maysville, Kentucky, and Dr.
Flamming, of Elizaville, Kentucky.

Year following this took course of lectures in
Ohio Medical School, Cincinnati, and received diploma from this school.

Practiced two years in Mayslick, Kentucky, and
moved to Illinois in fall of the year 1853.

Entered the ministry and was ordained at Eureka
in 1856. Began teaching in Eureka College 1857.
July 31, 1860, married Sarah E. Watkins, Eureka,
Illinois. Connected with Eureka College as professor, president, financial agent, etc., from 1857
to summer of 1891, when he moved to Sprague,
Washington, where he preached for the church a
year and then took charge of the church at Spokane, Washington.

1 C. L. Loos.
2 Geo. Callender.
3 B. W. Johnson.
4 H. W. Everest.

B. W. JOHNSON.

B. W. Johnson was born in 1833 in the log cabin
of a pioneer settler, in Tazewell county, Illinois.
On his father's side his ancestry was English, but
was settled in South Carolina before the Revolu-
tion. His mother was of Scotch descent. Until he
was seventeen his education was that of a prairie
farm in the summer and of a log school-house in
the winter. At that age he entered Walnut Grove
Academy, then conducted by A. S. Fisher and
John Lindsey. For a portion of three years he attended its sessions, the last two reciting in Greek
and Latin to John H. Neville. After teaching a
district school for two terms, he went, in the fall
of 1854, to Bethany College. He graduated there
in 1856, and after teaching in Bloomington one
year, accepted a place in Eureka College.

In 1858 he married Miss Sarah Allen of Bloomington, Illinois, sister of Dr. J. M. Allen. They
have three children, all daughters and all married.

Five years later he accepted the position of Corresponding Secretary of the General Missionary
Society, and one year after that of Professor in
Bethany College. In 1868 he accepted the Presidency of Oskaloosa College. For the last twenty
years he has been engaged as editor of the *Christian-Evangelist*, and at intervals of editorial work

has found time to write a dozen volumes, all commentaries on portions of the Bible, except a volume of travels in the Holy Land.

RICHARD H. JOHNSON.

Richard Henry Johnson was born at Washington, Illinois, March 2, 1835. His parents, John and Martha (McCorkle) Johnson, were, the first of English, the second of Scotch ancestry.

When about eighteen years old he entered Eureka College, and was graduated from Bethany College, Virginia, in 1859. The next year he was made a professor in Eureka College. Was married to Miss Susie S. Smith, of Bridgewater, Vermont, in 1862. Three years later he removed to Williamsville, New York, to take the position of principal of the Classical Institute at that place. Thence he removed to Lock Haven, Pennsylvania, to engage in the ministry, returning a few years later to Illinois, thence in 1878 to Oskaloosa, Iowa, where he assumed the pastoral work of the Christian church.

In 1881 he accepted a professorship in Oskaloosa College and was advanced to its presidency the next year.

He gave up his official duties in the college in 1888, and is subsequently actively engaged in the work of the ministry, being pleasantly located at New Sharon, Iowa.

1 John Lindsay.   2 R. H. Johnson.
3 R. A. Crevier.   4 J. H. R__n.

J. H. ROWELL.

Jonathan Harvey Rowell was born at Haverhill, New Hampshire, February 10, 1833. His father was a well-to-do farmer and his ancestors were among the earliest settlers of New England. The first sixteen years of his life were spent on his father's farm, working in summer and going to district school in winter.

In 1849 his parents moved to McLean county, Illinois, where his father died the following year.

From sixteen to twenty-two he taught school in winters and worked at whatever he could find to do in summers. At the age of twenty-two he united with the Church of Christ at Stout's Grove, and soon after entered Eureka College, where he graduated in 1861.

During the time he was going through college he taught one year at Washington, and also more than a year at Eureka in the preparatory school, then under the control of the college authorities. In 1860 he was appointed Professor of Mathematics in the college.

In May, 1861, he enlisted in Company G, 17th Illinois Infantry, a company largely made up of college students. Was first lieutenant of the company one year and captain two years, succeeding Elder O. A. Burgess, who was the first captain.

He graduated from the Law department of Chi-
11

cago University, valedictorian of his class, in 1865, and the same year commenced the practice of law in Bloomington, Illinois, where he has since resided.

He was married in 1866 to Maria S. Woods of Alton, Illinois, a native of Illinois but of New England parentage. They have five children. His oldest son is a graduate of Michigan University, and now a student in Germany. His oldest daughter also graduated from Michigan University, and is now teaching in California. His second and third sons are in school in Bloomington.

He was State's Attorney of the eighth judicial circuit of Illinois, from 1868 to 1872; Master in Chancery of McLean county two years; member of the Board of Education of Bloomington six years; Garfield elector in 1880, and a member of the 48th, 49th, 50th and 51st Congress. Was chairman of the Committee on Elections in the 51st Congress; was active in securing the passage of the Inter-State Commerce, the monetary and the tariff legislation now upon our statute books, and he also, with the best help he could get, prepared the Federal Election bill, which passed the House, and which has since been miscalled the " Lodge Bill " and the " Force Bill."

Has taken an active part as a Republican in all political campaigns in this State since 1864, and is still good for several more campaigns.

MARY CLARK HAWK.

Mary Gertrude Clark was born near Eureka,
February 12, 1841, daughter of Robert M. and Cynthia M. Clark. Her father was one of the original
trustees of Eureka College. Among her first teachers was Professor A. S. Fisher, under whose efficient instruction she continued until her graduation in 1861. During her senior year she taught
in the Preparatory department of the college, and
continued teaching in Eureka's public schools until 1865, when she married Major R. M. A. Hawk,
92nd Reg. Ill. Vols., to whose home in Mt. Carroll
she removed and there has since lived.

Major Hawk was County Clerk of Carroll county
for twelve years, resigning to accept a seat in the
Forty-sixth National Congress as a Republican
representative from the Fifth district of Illinois.
On the eve of a renomination for a third term in
Congress he was suddenly stricken down at his
post of duty, in the strength of a vigorous and
noble manhood. Left thus alone, Mrs. Hawk bravely devoted herself to the rearing and education of
her children—a daughter and two sons. Her son,
Harry, class '85, was the first child of a member
of the Alumni to graduate from Eureka College—
the first grandchild of his mother's Alma Mater.
The names of Prof. A. S. Fisher and Dr. J. M. Al-

len, two of his mother's instructors, appear on his diploma.

Mrs. Hawk has always been an ardent supporter of Eureka College and its interests, and feels a personal pride in the welfare of the institution.

CHAPTER III.

TEACHERS FROM 1860 TO 1880.

H. W. Everest—H. O. Newcomb—B. J. Radford—A. M. Weston.
—O. P. Hay—D. M. Blair—James Kirk—Carl Johann—E. W.
Dickinson—A. J. Youngblood.

H. W. EVEREST.

Harvey W. Everest was born at North Hudson,
Essex county, New York, May 10, 1831. Leaving
the public schools of his native village, he continued his education at Geauga Seminary and at
Western Reserve Eclectic Institute (now Hiram
College), Ohio; Bethany College, West Virginia,
and at Oberlin College, Ohio, from which he graduated.

He had served as tutor while attending the Eclectic Institute, and immediately after his graduation became its principal, and held this position
until he resigned it to accept the presidency of Eureka College in 1864. Leaving Eureka in 1872, he
served the Christian Church at Springfield two
years as its pastor. In 1874 he was chosen one of
the professors in Kentucky University and remained there two years. Then was pastor of the church

at Normal,.Illinois, one year, when he was called, in 1877, to be a second time president of Eureka College.

This position he held till the spring of 1881, when he accepted the presidency of Butler University at Irvington,Indiana, remaining there till 1886, when he went to Wichita, Kansas, to take in hand, as Chancellor, the work of organizing Garfield University. For three years this institution seemed eminently successful, but then, on account of financial difficulties, was forced to suspend. In June, 1890, President Everest became pastor of the church at Hutchinson, Kansas.

For years he has contributed very largely to our current literature, both papers and magazines. In 1884 he published "The Divine Demonstration—A Text-Book of Christian Evidence" which was at once adopted by our own Bible Schools, and also has recently been adopted by Center College, Danville, Kentucky, one of the leading Presbyterian colleges in the United States.

H. O. NEWCOMB.

Henry Obediah Newcomb was born January 5, 1838, at Wadsworth, Medina county, Ohio. His parents were of English descent and his paternal grandfather was one of the first Disciple preachers of the Western Reserve.

His early education was obtained at the Eclectic Institute, Hiram, Ohio. He afterwards entered the Junior class, Michigan University, from which university he graduated at twenty-three, having completed the required curriculum and also the usual course in French and German literature. Soon after.he was called to a professorship in Eureka College, where he taught Greek, modern languages and history during the last seven years of his life. After a thorough course of law reading he was admitted to the bar at Warren, Ohio, and later he organized and carried on the Law department at Eureka College.

His health failing, he returned to Hiram, where he died, at his father's home, September 16, 1870, at the age of thirty-two.

As a scholar he was accurate and profound; as a teacher, popular and successful, having at all times the full appreciation and respect of both faculty and students.

B. J. RADFORD.

Benjamin Johnson Radford was born December 25, 1838, at Walnut Grove, Illinois, within a mile of the present village of Eureka. His parents were Virginians of English stock, with a slight admixture of Scotch on the father's side. His life, until he attained his majority,was upon the farm, work-

ing in summers and attending school during the
winters. In January, 1859, he began his first school
teaching, at Mt. Zion, near Eureka, continuing until June. The next winter he attended Eureka
College, and the next taught again, near Washington, Illinois. In the spring of 1861 he again
entered college, expecting to complete his junior
year. Then the war came on and he went a-
soldiering with the majority of his fellow students.

He was mustered out of service with his regiment in June, 1864, having served more than three
years. Having secured a clerkship in Springfield,
at a good salary, he was married in October of this
year to Rhoda J. Magarity, of Mt. Zion, whose acquaintance he had made while teaching there, and
to whom he was engaged before he enlisted. In
the spring of 1865 he was induced by O. A. Burgess, his old college teacher and captain, and who
was then corresponding secretary of the General
Christian Missionary Society, to enter the ministry.
He resigned his clerkship, and after spending a
part of the summer traveling for the Society under
the direction of Mr. Burgess, that fall again entered
Eureka College, graduating in June, 1866. The
year 1867 was spent in farming, and in the spring
of 1868 he was installed as pastor of the church
at Niantic, Illinois. The next spring he returned
to Eureka, purchased the *Woodford* (now *Eureka*)
Journal, and while conducting that preached in the

neighboring congregations on Sundays. The next year he was appointed Professor of Latin in his Alma Mater, and entered upon his work with the fall term of 1870. He continued in this work until 1881, occupying the presidency of the college part of the time. In July, 1881, he accepted the pastorate of the church in Des Moines, Iowa, and the next year was elected President of Drake University. Double labor of pastorate and the presidency caused a physical break-down which compelled a resignation, and in July, 1883, he returned to Eureka. After a short rest he was as good as new, and that fall found him teaching again in the college and preaching for the Eureka church, in both of which labors he had spent so many years.

In September, 1885, at the earnest solicitation of Isaac Errett, Mr. Radford accepted the pastorate of the Richmond Street Christian Church in Cincinnati, of which Mr. Errett was an elder. During the next summer he was chosen as Mr. Errett's associate in editing the *Christian Standard*, and still occupies the position of associate editor on that paper. In connection with Miss Jessie Brown, he edited several volumes of *The Disciple*, a periodical that met with great favor among the Disciples. In 1890 he became pastor of the Central Christian church of Denver, but returned to Eureka in 1892 and resumed his work in Eureka College, where this sketch leaves him.

As preacher, lecturer, editor and poet, Mr. Radford has become known throughout the brotherhood, and whatever reputation he has, has been justly earned by hard and continuous work. He was honored with the appointment of representative of the Disciples of Illinois in our World's Fair Congress in connection with the Parliament of Religions, and gave eminent satisfaction as such representative.

A. M. WESTON.

Asa Minor Weston was born September 24, 1836, at Cleveland, Ohio, and reared on a small farm six miles east of that city. His ancestors were among the first settlers of Massachusetts. His preparatory education was at Shaw Academy, Colamer, Ohio. Then he spent several years in Oberlin College, completing the Sophomore year, when, attracted by the fame of Horace Mann, he, with seven of his class-mates, went to Antioch College, where he graduated in 1857. From a child he was very fond of books, and apt in studies of all kinds.

He taught during his college course, in part paying his own way. After graduation he taught in a select Normal School in Clinton county, Ohio. In 1860-1 was local editor of the *Cincinnati Press*, a daily paper of wide circulation in the city and vicinity. Gave up the paper to enter the army in August, 1862. Was first private in Co. K, 50th Reg. Ohio Vol.Inf. Promoted at various times, he became Sergeant-major of the regiment and second Lientenant Co. E. Served till the close of the war without absence or wounds. Was in the Atlanta campaign, also in the engagements at Perryville, Franklin, Nashville and other places.

After the war was Superintendent of Schools and Principal of Jennings Academy, Vernon, Indiana, two years. Then Professor of Mathematics in Hiram College, Ohio, the first two years of its existence as a college. Declined to remain longer when the responsibility and management were placed in the hands of one man. Married Miss Julia E. Pardee, one of the teachers in the college. This union was blessed with one child, a daughter, now Mrs. Rowlison, of Troy, Pennsylvania. Then after one year in charge of Major College, a school for young ladies, in Bloomington, Illinois, he came to Eureka in 1870, remaining six years, three years as professor and three as president, succeeding President Everest. During his presidency there was a good increase each year in the number of students.

In 1876 removed to Indiana, and has greatly enjoyed fitting up a home and preaching according to occasion. Three years, from 1888 to 1891, had a delightful service as pastor of the church at

Troy, Penn. Since then has been living on his farm near Mount Summit, Indiana.

He considers that his forte was undoubtedly teaching, and was always exceedingly popular in school work, but never so anywhere else. All his life he has been subject to severe headache, and, as a teacher, worked too hard, and for this cause felt constrained to abandon this calling, declining some lucrative offers to take charge of schools.

In politics he has been independent.

Was reared in the influence of the Presbyterian Church, in which his father was a deacon. When a young man he fell into skepticism, caused by the unreasonableness of certain dogmas which he had been taught. After his graduation he heard preaching by ministers of the Church of Christ, which in time so disabused his mind of false impressions, and gave him keys to an understanding of the Bible, that he determined to obey the Gospel at the very time that he decided to enlist in the service of his country. He was baptized by David S. Burnett in Cincinnati, and the next morning found him on his way to camp Denison. Never since has he lacked faith in or enthusiasm for the cause of the ever blessed Son of God.

His life has been a busy one, but he has found time to write a book entitled, "Evolution of a Shadow." The point of view is the Sabbath as a type (or "Shadow"); hence the name. It is an

interesting work and has been very generally com·
mended by those who have read it.

O. P. HAY.

Oliver Perry Hay was born in Jefferson county,
Indiana, May 22, 1846. His parents, Robert and
Margaret Hay, were of Scotch descent. A. B.,
Eureka College, 1870. Married to Mary E. Hows·
man, June 30, 1870. Professor in Eureka College,
1870-3 ; in Oskaloosa College, Iowa, 1874-6. Student at Yale University, 1876-7. Professor in Abingdon College, 1877-9. Professor in Butler University, Indianapolis, 1879-92. Ph. D., Indiana
University, 1887. Assistant on geological surveys
of Indiana and Arkansas, 1887 to date. Fellow
of American Association Advanced Sciences, 1889.
President of Indiana Academy Sciences, 1891. Author of various papers published in " Proceedings
of the United States National Museum," " Bulletin
United States Fish Commission," "American Nat-
uralist," etc., on fishes, batrachians, reptiles, etc.;
also of a report to State Geologist on the " Batrachians and Reptiles of Indiana ; " also of a report
to State Geologist of Arkansas on the "Batrachians
and Reptiles of Arkansas." At present Honorary
Fellow in department of Palæontology in University of Chicago.

D. M. BLAIR.

D. M. Blair was born near Elizaville, Fleming county, Kentucky, Thursday, January 17, 1839. His father was of Irish and his mother of French descent. He entered Ohio University as a student in 1857 and was graduated from the same in June, 1863. In the fall of that year accepted the professorship of ancient languages in Flemingsburg College, Flemingsburg, Kentucky, where he was associated with Hon. John A. Brooks.

In June, 1864, was elected professor of ancient languages in Battle Ground Collegiate Institute, at Tippecanoe Battle Ground, Indiana, and in 1866 was made president of the same. In 1867 removed to Ladoga, Indiana, and taught in Ladoga Academy.

In 1873 came to Eureka College and remained till 1878. In the fall of 1882 was elected superintendent of schools in Mason county, Illinois, and served four years, living in Havana. Since December, 1886, he has lived in the quiet village of Topeka, Illinois, and taught most of the years in the public schools of Mason county.

God blessed him in large measure with the gift of song, and in its exercise he has served faithfully his day and generation.

JAMES KIRK.

James Kirk is of Scotch-Irish parentage, and is forty-five years of age. His father was characterized by industry, frugality and sobriety; his mother by self-reliance and integrity; both by piety. These qualities were his heritage.

Because of the long illness and early death of his father, his youth was oppressed by poverty and hard work, which, combined with close study, overtaxed even a vigorous body.

He worked as a farm-hand, carpenter, school teacher, to obtain the means of procuring collegiate instruction. He entered Eureka College in 1867, and was graduated in 1871. In the meantime he was a student of law, but chose the work of education as a life employment.

After a successful experience as principal of schools, he was called, in 1876, to teach natural and physical science in Eureka College. He gave the institution eight years of faithful service, resigning in 1883 to give more time to the county superintendency of schools, a work which he had undertaken in 1881. This office he resigned in 1889 to become superintendent of schools in Pekin. He served the schools of this city until called to be assistant State Superintendent of Public Instruction in 1891. To the value of his service in this office, the State Superintendent has given highly appreciative expression in his last State report.

In addition to his school duties Mr. Kirk has taught for several years, from the pulpit, the way of the Lord ; and the fruit of this labor is a reward of inestimable value.

Mr. Kirk was happily married in 1874, and has had five affectionate children.   God has blessed him.

CARL JOHANN.

The subject of this sketch was born in Chaux-de-Fonds, Switzerland, March 2, 1849.   The place of his birth is in the Jura Mountains, only a few miles from the boundary line between Switzerland and France, and here, among the beautiful scenes of the marvelously grand Swiss landscape, he spent the first fifteen years of his life.   His parents, Albert and Mathilda Johann, who were only in moderate circumstances, required nothing of their children except that they should attend school faithfully and labor diligently to secure an education. This the children seemed to do cheerfully.   Carl entered the public schools of his native city at the age of six, and when he was fifteen years old he graduated from the high school.   Up to this time he had attended school eleven months each year without interruption, for, in that country, the only vacations students ever got were two weeks at

Christmas and two weeks in August. In this city nearly all the people speak both French and German, consequently the children learn both languages simultaneously without knowing it. There it is no uncommon thing for children at play to ask a question in French and to receive an answer in German without having the least idea that two languages have been used.

Having graduated from the high-school, his parents sent him at once to the famous college of Lausanne,where he made an excellent record,selecting mathematics and language as his major studies. Having developed a marked fondness for mathematics and mathematical drawing, he here decided to prepare himself more specially to become a civil engineer. At the age of 18, having completed the course in Lausanne, he became a student in the University of Aarau and afterwards in Zurich, all in Switzerland. At the age of twenty, with the consent of his parents, he went to Paris, France, where he studied for a time, and when he was not yet twenty-one years of age he decided to emigrate to the United States, where better opportunities are offered to young men of energy and education than anywhere else in the world.

Though he had devoted much time to the study of ancient languages and to German, French, Italian and Spanish, he had never studied English, and he landed in New York, as many have done
12

in the past and as many will do in the future,
without knowing one word of the language spok-
en by the people among whom he had decided to
live. He did not have a single friend or relative
on this side of the Atlantic and was therefore thrown
entirely upon his own resources.

Knowing that his slender pocket-book would not
sustain him long in idleness, he left New York two
days after landing, going—he did not know where
—looking for something to do to make an honest
living. In a few days he arrived in Collinsville,
Connecticut, where he was hired as a farm hand by
a refined, religious and highly cultured Yankee
who had made a fortune through his genius as an
inventor.

It is very probable that the new immigrant did
not make a model farm-hand, for he had never
done a day's work on a farm in his life, but he was
willing to learn both how to farm among the stony
hills of New England and how to speak the English language. The retired capitalist and farmer
for whom Carl Johann began to work, soon discovered that his hand had had excellent educational advantages, in fact that he had as good an education
as he had himself, and they soon became warm
and intimate friends. To show how easy it is to
learn a new language when one already knows
several others, it is sufficient to state here that
three months after landing in America, he had learn-

1 B. J. Radford.   3 J. M. Allen.
2 A. M. Weston.   4 Carl Johann.

ed English sufficiently well to be engaged as private tutor, for his four children, by the very man for whom he had been working on the farm. His field of activity was transferred from the farm to the comfortable sitting-room, and here, with salary doubled, he began his career as a teacher. Of course, all the teaching had to be done in English, as the pupils knew no other language, and the teacher who three months before did not know one word of English was now, among many other branches, actually teaching English grammar.

He remained in this family thirteen months, and the work done during that time was eminently satisfactory to all parties concerned. Dr. Johann left that place in the summer of 1870 to go West and grow up with the country. Not until 1894 did he again meet with the gentleman whose children he taught in Connecticut. Then he came to Eureka to make his former farm hand a visit, and stated that the year of instruction given at that time to his children directed their thoughts into right paths and started them on the road to usefulness and success.

From Connecticut the young teacher went to Chicago by way of Niagara and the great lakes. After suffering many disappointments in that city, and after having been out of employment nearly three months, he secured employment as a surveyor with a railroad company intending to build a road from Houston to Austin, Texas. He left Chicago without further delay in company with twelve other surveyors and reached Houston, Texas, by way of New Orleans and Galveston, in the fall of 1870. From Houston they traveled in ox-carts a distance of nearly one hundred miles to their destination, a point twenty-five miles east of Austin, from which point the road was to be surveyed to the capital.

The work was done in six months, to the satisfaction of the company, and this surveying party had the honor of preparing the way for the first railroad that entered the capital of Texas.

The sojourn of the surveying party was not altogether uneventful, for they were working in a practically uninhabited wilderness and were twice attacked by Indians, two of the surveyors being killed in one of the encounters, but Carl Johann came through unharmed.

Returning to Illinois, the subject of this sketch went to Menard county, near Tallula, where he warked on a farm for a few months, and then was offered a position as teacher in a country school at $35 a month.

His work was so successful that in less than two years he was receiving the highest salary paid to any teacher in the county, and had just been offered the principalship of the High School in Petersburg, the capital of Menard county, when, in the summer of 1876, he was offered the professorship of Modern Languages in Eureka College. As college work suited him better than public school work, he accepted the position and immediately moved to Eureka, where he began teaching in September of the same year.

For the last eighteen years he has been constantly identified with Eureka College as a teacher. In 1886 he was elected Acting President, and in 1887, when Dr. Allen resigned the Presidency, Carl Johann was elected President by the unanimous vote of the Board of Trustees, and he is still filling that office at this writing.

In October, 1889, Carl Johann was married to Miss Georgina Callender, daughter of George Callender, a former President of Eureka College, and they have been blessed with four children, Helen, Agnes, George and Albert, all of whom are living.

Dr. Johann's parents being Lutherans, he was sprinkled when seven days old (he still has a certificate from the pastor of the church certifying to this) and was "confirmed" at the age of fourteen. While teaching in Tallula, Menard county, Illinois, in 1872, he had the privilege of attending a protracted meeting held by Brother D. R. Lucas, now of Indianapolis, Indiana, was convinced of "the better way," made the "good confession" and was baptized in the manner commanded by the Scriptures. Tallula had a strong congregation at that time and their pastor was one of the most elo-

quent, logical and convincing pulpit orators in the
Brotherhood. He was none other than W. D.
Owen, who has since been member of Congress
from Indiana, having served three terms, and who
was appointed Commissioner of Immigration by
President Harrison. For more than one year the
new convert listened weekly to the "pure Gospel"
as it was presented by that eminent man of God,
and was thoroughly taught in the doctrine of the
Restoration.

President Johann has been quite an extensive
traveler. During the last five years he has been
in Europe twice, visiting England, Scotland and
Ireland, besides all the important cities on the
Continent, from Paris to Rome and Constantinople.
He has also been in the West Indies three times,
visiting Cuba, Jamaica, Hayti, San Domingo, Porto-
Rico and many of the smaller Antilles. In the
United States he has been in nearly every State
from Canada to the Gulf and from the Rocky mountains to Maine. Knowing how to travel, he has
gathered up many valuable facts and incidents,
which he gave to the students in a series of about
twenty interesting lectures.   .

His disposition is well adapted to the management of a large number of young people, and he
has never had any serious difficulties with the students. Under his system of government, students
are largely controlled by calling on their own ap-

1 H. O. Newcomb.   3 A. J. Youngblood.
2 E. W. Dickinson.   4 Jas. Kirk.

preciation of the right and on their own sense of. honor.

ELIJAH W. DICKINSON.

E. W. Dickinson was born in Christian county, Kentucky, July 18, 1835. His parents, Elijah and Mary A. Dickinson, and family moved to Illinois the following October and settled on a farm, now . owned by R. B. Dickinson, about two miles south of where Eureka is now situated. Here the subject of this sketch spent his youth and early manhood, working on the farm during the farming season and attending school in the winter time. He commenced his career as a teacher, by teaching a district school in White Oak Grove during the winter of 1855 and '56. The next September he entered Eureka College as a student and continued there until he graduated in 1860. For several years following this, most of the time was spent either in farming or in teaching, the greater part of the latter being done in or near Eureka, having taught years in the public schools of the village and two years in Eureka College as Professor of Mathematics. In the War of the Rebellion he served as First Lieutenant of Co. C, 139th Reg. Ill. Vol. Infantry. On the 5th day of September, 1861, he married Miss Anna M. Dennis, with whom he lived happily until she died, March 8, 1889.

Mr. Dickinson is now a citizen of Eureka, Illinois,

and takes a lively interest in all affairs pertaining to religion, education and politics.

A. J. YOUNGBLOOD.

Andrew Jackson Youngblood was born near Veedersburgh, Fountain county, Indiana, January 27, 1843. Graduated at Depauw University, Greencastle, Indiana, in 1869. Professor of Latin and History in Howard College, Kokomo, Indiana, in 1872. Took the chair of Ancient Languages in Columbia Christian College, Columbia, Kentucky, in 1876. In 1879 was called to the same position in South Kentucky College, Hopkinsville, Kentucky. Was elected President of West Kentucky College in 1880 and served one year. From 1831 to 1891 held the chair of Ancient Languages and of Latin and History in Eureka College. Now a resident of Kokomo, Indiana.

CHAPTER IV.

N. L. Richmond—J. V. Coombs—F. M. Bruner—Henry Lane Bruner—W. S. Errett—S. E. Meek—H. N. Herrick—G. W. Hootman—James Chalmers—Sina Stickel Thomas—H. A. Minassian—Roland Ellsworth Conklin—B. C. Deweese—J. M. Atwater—R. E. Hieronymus.

N. L. RICHMOND.

N. L. Richmond was born near Rising Sun, Indiana, Ohio county, August 29, 1856. His father of English and mother of Dutch descent. Both parents descended from first settlers. He had the advantage of a common school education; worked at the carpenter's trade until 21 years of age. He then began a course of study in the Indiana State Normal School at Terre Haute, with a view to teaching. Taught in the public schools of Indiana for six terms of six months each, spending the intervals in college. Was a student in the Normal College at Danville, Indiana, when the president had a call from Eureka College for a teacher of commerce and kindred branches. Owing to his proficiency in this work, at the request of the Faculty, he accepted the position.

He was employed in the above College four years, after which he engaged to teach in the Commercial department of Grand Prairie Seminary, Onarga, Illinois. Was in this school five years.

He was married to Miss Theona Ward of Kentland, Indiana, June 18th, 1889.

June 1st, 1892, he took a half interest in the Ottawa Business University, Ottawa, Illinois, where he now resides.

J. V. COOMBS.

J. V. Coombs was born on the farm in Boone county, Indiana. In 1867 he entered the academy, Ladoga, Indiana. He began teaching in 1868. In 1870 he became a student at Northwestern Christian University, where he remained two years. In 1873 he entered Eureka College. After teaching several years in the public schools, in 1879 he was elected to the presidency of the Indiana Normal College, Ladoga, which position he held two years. In 1882 he graduated in the Classical department of Chicago University. In the fall of 1883 he was elected to the chair of Literature and History in Eureka College. In 1885 he entered the lecture field and achieved much renown as a platform lecturer, filling engagements in forty States and Territories. In 1889 he became a general evangelist for the Christian church, in which calling he continues up to this date. He preached one hundred and eighty nights without the loss of one night. After a few days rest he started again and spoke one hundred and ninety nights in succession. Thousands have been added to the church under his preaching. In the last four months he has added four hundred and fifty. In 1888 he was married to Miss Allie Marlatt, Covington, Indiana. God has blessed them with one little girl. They now reside in Irvington, Indiana.

F. M. BRUNER.

Francis Marion Bruner was born in Breckenridge county, Kentucky, December 28, 1833, of parents who were of pure German descent. He entered Knox College at Galesburg, Illinois, in 1851 and took a thorough classical course, graduating in 1857. Next year was spent in teaching and preaching at Henderson, Illinois. He married Esther Lane in the spring of 1858 and, accompanied by her, soon went to Europe to pursue his studies. He spent two years at the Royal University at Halle, Prussia, where he came in contact with Professor Tholuck, some months in Berlin, followed by a tour from Cologne to Manheim, thence to Lake Constance, and through Switzerland to Paris, where he spent five months in L'Ecole de Paris, returning to the United States after an absence of three years. During the first three years after his return he evangelized in Knox, Warren and Henderson counties of Illinois. In the summer of 1863 he was commissioned a captain in Co. A, 7th Reg. U. S. Colored Infantry, and served in Southern States one year, when he was discharged for "disability caused by his arduous and faithful services."

In 1865 he was ordained to the ministry at Monmouth, Illinois, where he was minister five years, serving one year in the Legislature of the State during that time.

In 1870 he was elected President of Oskaloosa College, in which capacity he served until 1876, when he was called to the presidency of Abingdon College, Illinois, where he remained until the union of Abingdon and Eureka Colleges, in 1885. Then he moved to Eureka and had charge of the Bible department from 1885 to 1886, when on account of failing health he was compelled to resign and seek rest and a more healthful climate. These he found on a mesa in northwestern Texas, and while still continuing his ranch life, he preaches at El Paso, Texas, every Lord's day.

HENRY LANE BRUNER.

Born in Knox county, Illinois, 1861; graduated from Abingdon College, classical course, in 1880;

1 F. M. Bruner.   3 W. S. Errett,
2 H. L. Bruner.   4 H. A. Minassian.

spent the year 1880-81 in the Sheffield Scientific School of Yale University, and the following year began teaching natural sciences in Abingdon College; during the summers of 1881 to 1884 was employed, also, as assistant on the United States Fish Commission; in 1884, when Eureka and Abingdon Colleges were consolidated, was elected to the chair of Natural Science at Eureka; in 1886 resigned on account of failing health and spent the following years recuperating in Colorado and Texas; in 1890 married Miss Carolyn L. Aumock, of Colorado Springs; elected to chair of Biology and Geology in Drake University in 1891, and the following year removed to his present home at Irvington, Indiana, to occupy a similar position in Butler University.

W. S. ERRETT.

W. S. Errett was born in Pittsburg, Pennsylvania, August 6, 1841. He is of English-Irish-Scotch descent. At the age of fourteen years his father removed with his family to Knox county, Ohio, where young Errett had seven years' experience in farm life.

In the fall of 1862 he entered the army, serving as a private in the 65th Reg. Ohio Vol. Infantry. Soon after returning from this service he entered Bethany College, and was graduated from there with the degree A. B. in June, 1871. In September of the same year he began his chosen work of teaching, in charge of the public schools at Madison, Ohio. His father dying the next spring, he returned to Knox county. Was married to Selena H. Bakewell at Normal, Illinois, February 27, 1873. The same year was chosen elder of the church at Mt. Vernon, Ohio, and soon after began preaching at their instance.

Removed to Missouri in 1878; to Greenville, Illinois, in 1880; to the chair of Mathematics in Abingdon College in 1881; thence to the same work in Eureka in the fall of 1884. Since then has taught in Ash Grove, Missouri, and preached in Kansas and Illinois, and is now pastor of the church at Carbondale, Illinois.

S. E. MEEK.

Seth E. Meek was born near Hicksville, Defiance county, Ohio, at 1 o'clock A. M., April 1, 1859. He is of Welsh Anglo-Saxon ancestry. Was brought up on a farm. After leaving the High School spent four terms in Valparaiso, Indiana, Normal. Then spent three years in Indiana State University, at Bloomington, from which he was graduated in 1884.

He held the Cornell Fellowship in Cornell University, Ithica, N. Y., in 1885-6. Taught in Eureka

College from January 1887 to January 1888, and in Coe College from January, 1888, till February, 1892, when he was called to his present position of Adjunct Professor and Curator of Museum in the department of Biology and Geology in Arkansas Industrial University at Fayetteville.

He has been temporary assistant to the United States Fish Commission ever since his graduation, and has conducted for it Scientific exploring parties in Iowa, Nebraska, Missouri, Arkansas and Indian Territory during summer vacations. Was also member of a party under Dr. D. S. Jordan in the Virginias and the Carolinas, and has published a number of scientific papers.

His degrees are from Indiana University—B. S. in 1884; M. S. in 1886; Ph. D. in 1891.

He became a Christian March 5, 1877, and was married to Miss Ella Tourner, of Bloomington, Indiana, December 25, 1886.

H. N. HERRICK.

Horace Nelson Herrick was born in Lewis county, Kentucky, August 24, 1862. His father, George W. Herrick, was born in Vermont, and was of good old Puritan extraction; his mother, Josephine Hendrickson, was of Irish descent.

In 1864 the family moved to Manchester, Ohio, and in 1865, on account of the father's failing health, to Wapella, Illinois.

When eighteen years of age, Professor Herrick taught a country school. He entered Eureka College in 1881 and graduated in '86. The two years following he was Professor of Mathematics in his Alma Mater. In 1888 he became a student at Harvard College, graduating there in 1890. Professor Herrick is a self-made man, the means used in procuring his education having been obtained by his own labor.

He was married July 29, 1890, to Miss Mary Musick, of Eureka Illinois. They have two sons.

In September, 1890, Professor Herrick took charge of the Greek department of Eureka College, which position he holds at present.

G. W. HOOTMAN.

G. W. Hootman is the fifth son of Christopher and Sarah Ann (Winbigler) Hootman. Born July 29, 1861, in a log cabin near Hicksville, Ohio, his advent into the world at that time, in the northwestern part of the State, started him in the experiences of the early pioneer life of that region. He grew to young manhood among the deprivations incident to farm life in a new country.

His ancestors are, for the most part, of German-English descent, with a marked tinge of Scotch blood, and have transmitted, as a rich inheritance to their children, the hardy physical constitution

1 G. W. Hootman,   3 R. E. Hieronymus.
2 H. N. Herrick.   4 R. E. Conklin.

of the former, coupled with the more active and vigorous mentality of the latter.

When old enough he began to attend the country school and, of course, to help in the work of the farm. This he continued to do until he had reached his twentieth year. His time in school had been so well employed, that, with the addition of a few weeks of special preparation at the Newville Academy, Newville, Indiana, he was granted a permit to teach, and taught his first school, near his home, during the winter of 1880-1.

After this he immediately began his work as a student in the Northern Indiana Normal School and Business Institute, Valparaiso, Indiana, and continued to attend school and teach until five years later, when he was employed as principal and instructor of the Commercial department in the Defiance Normal College, Defiance, Ohio. The management of this institution not proving satisfactory, he resigned his position, and after two months of work in the office of the Defiance Machine Works, entered upon the organization of a Summer Normal at St. Joe, Indiana. Before his term had closed he was engaged as manager and Principal of the Business Department of Eureka College, a place he has now creditably filled for seven years.

His preparation for the special work in which he is now engaged, has been thorough, and is further

13

supplemented by a careful study of numerous cognate branches.

At the age of twenty-five years he was married to Miss Clara E. Richardson of Farmer, Ohio, who has proven a true help-mate to him in their eight years of wedded life. To them have been born three loving children, Beulah Alice, Helen Mabel, and Hugh Donald.

With these extra gifts of God's sunshine to cheer him, and the consciousness that the success of the past may only foreshadow the possibility of still higher achievements and greater usefulness in the future, he can hopefully anticipate the brighter days of the years that are before him.

JAMES CHALMERS.

James Chalmers was born in Ontario, Canada, November 22, 1859. He is of Scotch-Irish parentage. In his seventh year his parents moved to Grand Rapids, Michigan, and he received his elementary education in the excellent public schools of that State. He was afterwards educated at the University of Michigan and Eureka College, the latter institution conferring upon him successively the degrees of Bachelor of Arts and Doctor of Philosophy. In 1892 Western Michigan College conferred upon him the degree of Doctor of Laws.

He was Professor of English and Philosophy at Eureka College in 1887-89 and was then elected to

1 D. M. Blair,   3 Jas. Chalmers,
2 J. V. Coombs,   4 S. E. Meek,

the chair of English Literature at Ohio State University, a position which he still holds.

In 1888 he was married to Miss Lizzie Anderson of Grand Rapids, Michigan, then a student in the University of Michigan. Two children have been born to them—James A. and William Wallace. They have a beautiful and happy home in Columbus, Ohio, with one of the largest and choicest libraries of English literature in the State.

SINA STICKEL THOMAS.

Sina Stickel Thomas was born in Putnam county, Illinois, March 11, 1865. Her parents, Hiram and Sarah Stickel, were both of English descent. The family moved to Princeton, Illinois, in 1880. Here she attended the public schools, and graduated at the township High School in 1886. She entered the School of Oratory, Northwestern University, in the fall of 1886; received her diploma from this department in the spring of 1888, and was engaged as teacher of Elocution in Eureka College the following fall.

She was married to L. R. Thomas, September 10, 1890, and resigned her work as teacher in the college in the fall of 1891, having served the institution three years.

She now resides at Milford, Illinois, where her husband is pastor of the Christian Church.

H. A. MINASSIAN.

Harootune Avedis Minassian was born June 13, 1867, at Sevas, Turkey, from pure Armenian parentage. In 1879 he completed the high school course of the missionary school in Sevas, the same year filling a vacancy in the staff of teachers in that school.

From 1880 to 1886 he studied at Central Turkey College, nearly completing the Scientific course, and graduated from the Medical department.

Spent the summer of 1885 traveling in Mesopotamia; was assistant to Surgeon F. D. Shepherd at Aleppo in 1886 until the fall, then came to America. Entered Bellevue Hospital Medical College as a graduate student and obtained its degree in March, 1887; served as physician to two of the dispensaries of the New York Medical Missionary Society until September of that year, when he came to Eureka College. Entered the Biblical department. Received the degree of B. S. in 1889, B. S. and B. S. L. in 1890. The same year accepted the position of Professor of Sacred History in Eureka College, in which capacity he has since served.

He was joined in wedlock with Jessie Bruner December 25, 1890.

R. E. CONKLIN.

Roland Ellsworth Conklin was born at Chambersburg, Illinois, December 16, 1860, of New England ancestry.

He attended the public schools until his father's death in 1877.

Two years later he entered Abingdon College, completing the academic course in 1883. A year later he entered Eureka College and graduated in the class of '86. After two years' teaching in the public schools he was elected to the chair of Natural Science in Eureka College. During the summer of '89 he accompanied a Harvard Geological party on a tour through the Eastern and Middle States. Having been granted leave of absence from the college, for the further study of Natural History, he entered Harvard University in 1891, receiving his degree the following year. The present year is being spent in graduate work in Zoology in the same institution.

B C. DEWEESE.

Benjamin Cassel Deweese was born August 10, 1851, near Jacksonville, Illinois, of Kentucky parentage. The toil necessary for the support of the family deprived him, during early life, of most educational privileges. Self-instruction partially made good this loss.

He obeyed the gospel in February, 1867, and was baptized by Elder Enos Campbell. In September, 1870, he entered Kentucky University at

Lexington, Kentucky. After five years of student life he graduated in June, 1876, from the College of the Bible, at that time one of the colleges of the university.

His life has been devoted to the ministry and to teaching. At the first his preaching was divided between general work and serving churches in smaller fields. In 1879 he located at Cadiz, Kentucky, where he preached for four years. The next church to which all his time was given was at Henderson, Kentucky. From this field he was called to succeed B. J. Radford in serving the Richmond Street Church, Cincinnati, Ohio. Thence to Columbia, Missouri, from which church he removed to Eureka, October, 1889, to become Principal of the Biblical department in the college. · In 1876 he began a course of study preparatory to the work he is now doing. This was rigidly pursued for the fourteen years which passed before the call to Eureka College.

In 1881, without previous consultation, he was elected principal of the Cadiz High School. This spontaneous call was accepted, and before the school year closed he was elected to the chair of Ancient Languages in South Kentucky College, Hopkinsville, Kentucky. Soon after taking this new position he was elected President. His connection with the college continued until the build- ings were burned, when he accepted the care of the

1 Sina Stickel Thomas.
2 N. L. Richmond.
3 B. C. Deweese.
4 J. M. Atwater.

church at Henderson, Kentucky. Besides this regular work a number of young men received private lessons in Greek and Latin in preparing themselves for college. Several schools have secured his services for part of his time, where he preached, to teach classes in Greek and Latin.

As a preacher Professor Deweese has always specially labored for the spiritual growth of his congregations. He loves teaching, and every call for such work has come without solicitation from him or his friends.

April 13, 1875, he married Miss R. E. Downing of Lexington, Kentucky. They have had but one child, whom they buried several years ago. His wife has devoted her life towards making his work a success, and to her belongs much of the credit for whatever of good they have wrought.

In 1890 he was called to take charge of the Bible department of Eureka College, which position he still holds. He loves his class work and is eminently successful in it.

J. M. ATWATER.

John Milton Atwater was born June 3, 1837, at Mantua, Portage county, Ohio. His four grandparents were all New England people.

His early life was spent on the farm, where milking cows, handling horses, chopping wood, hauling logs, building fences, breaking steers, running sugar camp in spring, haying and harvesting in summer, gathering apples and husking corn in fall, and going to school in winter, made every year a busy one, and developed brain and brawn for the work of life.

The religious influence under which he grew up was earnest and devout. His father, Darwin Atwater, was a charter member and officer of the first church of Disciples organized in northern Ohio, at Mantua. His mother, Harriet Clapp, was a charter member of the church at Mentor, formed a little later.

` At the age of fourteen he entered what is now Hiram College. At twenty-one he was made a member of the faculty, Mr. Garfield being at that time President of the school, and continued there three years. He began preaching in 1859 at Hiram. In 1861 he entered Oberlin College, graduated in 1863, and then took a two years' postgraduate course there.

In 1866 he was called back to Hiram to be the head of the school there, and continued in that position till 1870. From that time till 1887 he gave his time almost entirely to preaching, holding pastorates in Syracuse, N. Y., Worcester, Mass., Springfield, Ill., and Cleveland, Ohio.

In 1887 he was chosen a professor in Garfield University, Wichita, Kansas, and later was made

Dean of the College of the Bible in that institution. After the suspension of that school, he was elected, in 1891, Professor of Latin and History in Eureka College, Illinois. From there he was called in 1892 to be President of Oskaloosa College, Iowa, where he is now engaged.

R. E. HIERONYMUS.

The ancestors of Robert Enoch Hieronymus came originally from Germany to Virginia. Emigrated later to the "Blue Grass" region, Kentucky; then came to Illinois in 1828.

His parents, Benjamin R. and Susan Mary (Mountjoy) Hieronymus, lived in Logan county, Illinois, where he was born, December 8, 1862.

After the district school, he attended and graduated from Illinois State Normal University, and later from Eureka College. He then spent one year in the University of Michigan at Ann Arbor.

His mother died when he was eleven years old, and from that time until he attained his majority he lived with an uncle, Enoch Hieronymus.

Since the fall of 1889 he has been teaching in Eureka College, in the department of English Language and Literature.

He was married June 26, 1890, to Minnie Frantz, at Wellington, Kansas. Two children bless their home—Faith Helene, and Frank Mountjoy.

CHAPTER V.

Susie Smith Johnson—Belle Johnson Allen—Emma Smith DeVoe —Eugene Plowe—Eva M. Wright—Ella F. Taylor—Emma E. Page—W. W. Lauder—Mina Vandervoort Miller—J. W. Metcalf—Charles W. Campbell—Sarah Garrett Humphrey—Clara Hatch Stevens—May Irene Burrows—Jessie Bruner Minassian.

SUSIE SMITH JOHNSON.

Susie (Smith) Johnson was born January 14, 1839. Her youth was spent at Bridgewater, Vermont. She completed her education at Ludlow Academy. Came West in 1858 and engaged as teacher of Music in Eureka College, giving instruction for several years before and after marriage.

Was married to Professor R. H. Johnson, in Vermont, August 11, 1862, and was associated with him in his work the remaining years of her life.

She died, beloved by all, at Oskaloosa, Iowa, September 20, 1890.

BELLE JOHNSON ALLEN.

Belle (Johnson) Allen was born February 20,

1843, at Washington, Illinois. Was graduated from Eureka College in 1865.

She assisted her brother in the Academy at Williamsville, N. Y., shortly after graduation. Returning to Eureka in the fall of 1866 she entered upon the work of teacher of Music in the college.

On the 29th of June, 1867, she was married to John W. Allen, removing with him to Johnstown, Pennsylvania, where he was in charge of the Christian Church. In April, 1868, Mr. Allen being called to the charge of the church in Omaha, Nebraska, they removed thither, where Mrs. Allen died in December of the same year.

EMMA SMITH DE VOE.

Emma Smith was born in Warren county, Illinois, in 1848. In 1859 she removed with her parents to Washington, Tazewell county, Illinois, where she was married to J. H. DeVoe in 1880. She received a very liberal education.

Her public life began when she took charge of the Music department in Eureka College in the year 1870, where she taught through the session of 1870-71.

Whatever success she has attained she attributes largely to influences started and aspirations born at Eureka. Especially does she feel herself indebted to Father and Mother Darst, and she never tires of singing their praises.

In 1881 she removed with her husband to Huron, D. T., where they remained until 1891, when they came to Harvey, Illinois.

Mrs. DeVoe took active part in the temperance wars that finally made two prohibition States out of Dakota Territory. In 1889 she became State Lecturer for the Equal Suffrage Association. She is now National Lecturer in her chosen field. She devotes all her time to this work and is in demand everywhere.

EUGENE PLOWE.

Eugene Plowe was born May 17, 1851, in Wadsworth, Medina county, Ohio. He is of German descent on his Father's side, and Canadian-American on his mother's.

Attended Hiram College, and later taught vocal music there.

Studied Voice under the celebrated Carlo Bassine, and Piano under A. R. Parsons in New York.

Took charge of the department of Music in Eureka College in September, 1871, and resigned in the summer of 1877 to locate in Peoria, where he has been engaged in teaching Music ever since. He is now President of the Peoria Conservatory of Music, which is just closing its third year.

EVA M. WRIGHT.

Eva M. Wright, daughter of S. and C. A. Wright, was born in Indiana, near Rockville, in 1859. Her father is of Welsh, and her mother of Scotch descent. She removed to Eureka, Illinois, while yet a child, entering the college as a student at the age of 13, remaining for the greater part of four years, after which she took a two years' course at Wesleyan University, Bloomington, Illinois. She studied music under Professor E. H. Plowe, Professor J. W. Metcalf, and Professor J. R. Gray, all of whom were connected with the Musical department of Eureka College.

Miss Wright taught music in the college during the year 1878. She removed to Pittsburgh, Kansas, in 1890, where she is still engaged in teaching music.

ELLA F. TAYLOR.

Ella F. Taylor was born at Geneseo, Illinois, March 2, 1854. In 1868 removed to Brooklyn, N. Y., and while there made a specialty of the study of music, under such instructors as Miss Hanly, Professor Albert Rowse, and Professor John Zundel.

In 1875 returned to the West. After several years spent in teaching music in Illinois and Kansas, went to Boston, Mass., where she spent three years in studying and teaching music.

In 1889 completed the Normal course of Music in public schools, and in 1890 graduated from the Teacher's Vocal course at the New England Conservatory of Music.

Is now located in Tempe, Arizona.

EMMA E. PAGE.

Emma E. Page was born at Metamora, Illinois, in 1852. The English, Scotch and German are interwoven in her remote ancestry. The Pages were among the sturdy planters of the Plymouth Colony.

Her father, A. N. Page, was a minister of the Church of Christ, and her mother was a great worker for the Master. They removed to Tazewell county in 1856, and in 1874 went to Champaign, that their children might have the advantages of the State University.

Miss Emma graduated there in 1878, taking the honors of a class of forty. She took a post-graduate course and a second degree. From 1879 to 1881 she was the music teacher in Eureka College. Later she taught music in Ottawa, Kansas, and in Kansas City, Missouri.

In 1888 she went with her parents to Mannville, Wyoming, which is still her home. In 1892 she

1 Emma Page.
2 J. W. Metcalf.
3 W. Waugh Lauder.
4 Emma Smith DeVoe.
5 Mina Vandervort.

was made chairman of the Prohibition State Central Committee, and she is now in the lecture field for the W. C. T. U.

W. W. LAUDER.

W. Waugh Lauder was born in 1856 in Canada. He is of Scotch, Huguenot and German descent— Armstrong ("Belted Will") and Brechleugh, Scotch; the famed historian Grotius, German ; the Huguenot noble De Toof, French. His father was a well known parliamentarian and barrister.

Mr. Lauder has been pianist of the Toronto, Canada, "Philharmonic Society ; " leader of the Anglican Choir of Leipzig, Saxony ; member of the famous " Riedel Verein " of Leipzig ; of the St. Cæcilia Society of Rome, Italy ; and has trained choruses in Bloomington, Cincinnati and London.

He has been director of music of Helmuth College, Canada; of Eureka College, Illinois ; of Cincinnati Wesleyan College, and Ohio Conservatory of Music, Cincinnati ; and Professor of the New England Conservatory of Boston.

He is now a leading critic, teacher and virtuoso of Chicago ; special critical correspondent to the *Musical Courier* from Chicago for the Columbian Exposition, and organist and choir-master of the Central Church of Christ, Chicago.

MINA VANDERVOORT MILLER.

Mrs. Mina Vandervoort Miller was born at Cedar
Point, on a farm near Peru, La Salle county, Ill.,
June 26, 1863. Her father, Dr. I. A. Vandervoort,
was born in Ohio, of Holland Dutch and German
descent. Her mother, Isabella Noble, was born
in Ohio, of Scotch and French descent, whose gen-
ealogy is traced back to the French Huguenots
who left their country and went to Scotland, and
came from there to Maryland.

Dr. Vandervoort and family moved to Tonica,
Illinois, in 1864, where they lived until 1890, when
they moved to Normal.

After finishing the course in the High School in
Tonica, Mrs. Miller went to Eureka and studied
music under Professor Metcalf, and painting under
Miss Sadie Garrett, during the years 1882-3-4-5
The last year she assisted Miss Garrett in the
painting department, and the following year
studied under Mr. Waldo, a well-known artist in
Chicago. In 1887-8 she took Miss Garrett's place
in the Art department of Eureka College.

In May, 1891, she was married to Mr. G. A.
Miller, an alumnus of Eureka College, who was
then preaching in Monroe, Wisconsin. In December, 1891, he was called to succeed Mr. A. P. Cobb,
pastor of the Christian Church in Normal, Illinois,
where they are now living.

J. W. METCALF.

John W. Metcalf is a native of Illinois, having been born at Waverly, Morgan county, December 10, 1856, of American parents.

At an early age he developed a talent for music and was placed in charge of the best instructors obtainable. His literary education was secured at Knox College, Galesburg, Illinois, and at Chicago University, Chicago. He took charge of the Music department in Eureka College in September, 1874, and remained through two school years. In the fall of 1877 he went abroad to further pursue the study of music. Was accepted as a regular student at the Royal Academy of Music, at Leipsic, Germany, where he remained four years, finishing with honor, and was awarded a prize and a special diploma.

On his return to America he again took up the work at Eureka, where he spent several years, then taught a few years in the Boston Conservatory of Music.

The last two years he has been teaching in Leland Stanford, Jr., University, his home being in Oakland, California. He has composed quite a number of works for the piano forte that have been published, and has been quite prominent as a public performer.

14

CHARLES W. CAMPBELL.

Charles W. Campbell was born in Cincinnati, Ohio, January 22, 1849. He was a son of George Campbell, one of the pioneers of the Reformation in Indiana.

Leaving the common schools he spent two years in Fairview Academy under Professor W. M. Thrasher.

He served a few months in the army in 1864; was a student in Northwestern Christian University in 1865-6-7; became a student in Eureka College in 1869, and graduated with the class of '72. Was at once employed as Professor of Drawing and Painting. Studied law and was admitted to practice at Bloomington in 1874.

Was married March 30, 1875, to Miss Jean E. Neville, a graduate of Eureka College. They soon removed to Tazewell county, and thence to Topeka, Kansas, which is now their home.

At Topeka he has served as Assistant in the State Adjutant General's office, and in the office of the Auditor of State, and is now in the United States Pension office at Topeka.

His best work has been rendered to the church. In season and out of season he has served it well. As treasurer, he. has systematized the business management until the church in Topeka is a model in the administration of its business affairs. As

1 C. W. Campbell.
2 Sadie Garrett Humphrey.
3 Emma Hatch Stevens.
4 Jessie Bruner Minassian.

Elder of the church he is chairman of the Official Board, and has always maintained harmony and unity in its work.

He is a member of the Kansas State Board of Missions, and its treasurer, and is greatly useful in its business management and methods.

B. L. S.

SARAH GARRETT HUMPHREY.

Sarah Jeanne Garrett was born July 26, 1860, at Peoria, Illinois. She was the second daughter of Auren and Wilhelmina Garrett, being of Scotch descent on her mother's side, while her father was a native of New York State.

From childhood she chose an artist's life, commencing her life work at the age of eighteen. At the age of twenty she took charge of the Art department in Eureka College, remaining four consecutive years. After an absence of one year she returned, continuing until her marriage to Andrew B. Humphrey, when she went West. Still following her chosen profession, she became Directress of the Art department at Hall Institute, Iowa. In 1889 she returned to Illinois, and is now in Chicago.

CLARA HATCH STEVENS.

Mrs. Clara Hatch Stevens was born in Harrodsburg, Kentucky, April 22, 1855, of English descent

on her father's side, and French on her mother's.
Was graduated from Jacksonville (Illinois) Fe-
male Academy in 1873. Afterwards took a post-
graduate course at Hamilton College, Lexington,
Kentucky. Studied Art during the entire time at
these institutions under the best teachers; and
afterwards at the Art Students' League, New
York city, under Mr. J. Carroll Beckwith, and pri-
vate lessons of Mr. Frank Fowler and Mr. R. M.
Shurtleff in the same city ; also had lessons of Mr.
Dennett Grover and Mr. Louis C. Earle of Chicago.
Has exhibited paintings in the Academy of Fine
Arts, Brooklyn, New York, St. Louis and Chicago.
Had charge of the Art Department three years at
Drury College, Springfield, Missouri, and after-
wards at Eureka, Illinois.

In 1893 she received an appointment from Mrs.
Potter Palmer, President of the Board of Lady
Managers, Chicago, of the World's Columbian Ex-
position, to assist in the mural painting of the
Woman's Building.

MAY IRENE BURROWS.

May Irene Burrows was born in Atlanta, Illinois,
December 16, 1861, to Dr. and Mrs. C. H. Burrows.
She was educated in Atlanta High School and Illinois State Normal University, and was a teacher
seven years in the public schools of Minier, Atlanta

and Tonica, Illinois, during which time she was pursuing the study of Art.

She spent the session of '86 and '87 in Eureka College as Art instructor, since which time she has studied art in New York under the ablest artists of this country.

Her life has been a steady advance toward success in her chosen profession.

At present she is finishing her third year as Art instructor in St. Mary's Hall, Faribault, Minnesota.

Her mother was of Swiss and her father of English descent.

JESSIE B. MINASSIAN.

Jessie Bruner Minassian was born February 6, 1867, at Monmouth, Illinois. Ancestry, German and Scotch. She lived with her parents at Monmouth, Oskaloosa, Abingdon and Eureka, successively. Attended the public schools and Abingdon College, graduating from the latter in 1884, and taught school the following year. In 1886 she studied music at Eureka College, and since 1887 has devoted her entire time and attention to her chosen profession—Art. Studied painting in oil with Professor L. A. Loomis, graduate of Royal Academy of Berlin; portraiture with Mr. J. A. Bunch of Chicago, and Professor C. C. Minor of the Chicago Art Institute, and watercolors with Artist

White. Taught art at Cambridge, Illinois, through the fall and winter of 1889.

She gave her hand in marriage to Dr. H. A. Minassian, December 25, 1890.

Took charge of the Art department of Eureka College, January, 1892, and has since removed to Des Moines, Iowa.

She spent the summer of 1892 sketching in Wisconsin, making a large collection.

REMINISCENCES.

REMINISCENCES OF EUREKA.

Woodland, Cal., March 2, 1893.

Miss Elmira Dickinson :

My Dear Friend—You ask me to give you a chapter of ".Reminiscences of Eureka" and my memory goes back to the summer of 1847, when my father, John T. Jones, first made his home in Walnut Grove. The name "Eureka" had not then been thought of. The stately walnut trees were standing in their original majesty. The wild blackberry vines were loaded with their luscious fruit, and hazelnuts hung temptingly overhead and upon each side of the narrow footpath. The mocking-bird and the whip-poor-will sang undisturbed in their native forest, and the quail, pheasant, wild turkey, gray squirrel and red deer lured the hunter to spend many a day in the leafy grove with only his gun for a companion.

All the features of a pioneer settlement were here, and the neighborhood was especially favored in having leading men of intelligence and high moral and religious principles. No physician's services could be had without sending many miles, but Ben Major, everybody's "Uncle Ben," was

always ready to leave his own work to answer the
call of distress. Whether the angel of life or the
angel of death had called, his kind voice and ready
skill were there to rejoice with the happy or to
comfort the broken-hearted.

I have heard my father say that "the difference
between Uncle Ben and other men was this; that
while the latter would say, 'If I had not such a
piece of work to do I would visit Brother A., who
is sick;' Uncle Ben would say. 'If Brother A. were
not sick, I would plow that field to-day.'" This
good man was a native of Kentucky, and becoming convinced of the evils of slavery, wished to remove his family from its influences, but could not
conscientiously *sell* his slaves in order to get rid of
them.

About this time Colonization Societies were being
formed to send negroes to Liberia, and Uncle Ben
became convinced that this was the best solution
of his difficulty. He therefore sent his slaves to
Liberia, having first taught them to read and
write, and regularly sent them needed supplies until their coffee and sugar plantations were matured
and would enable them to provide for themselves.
Others united with him in this benevolent scheme
and a Colonization Society was formed in Walnut
Grove. At one of its annual meetings, Uncle Ben
read aloud a letter from one of his former slaves,
who addressed him as "My dear father," and said

that he had sent him a sack of coffee from his own plantation. The tears were in 'Uncle Ben's' eyes as he read this letter, and his voice trembling with emotion said, "Brethren, that coffee will drink sweet without any sugar."

There was but one church building in Walnut Grove in '47, and all meetings of general interest were held there. That house stood where the Eureka cemetery now stands. It was customary to announce all matters of importance after the Lord's day services. If any were sick it was then made known, and arrangements made for their being properly cared for during the ensuing week. Young men would volunteer to go upon a certain day to feed the stock, chop the wood, sit up at night, if necessary, until every day was provided for. The busy matrons would find time to ride to the house of affliction, carrying a basket of ready-cooked food, such sweet home-made bread and glasses of jelly for the sick, and for the well more substantial supplies. This was done, not as a deed of charity, humiliating to the recipient, but as one sister might offer needed help to another.

At one time, a young man, upon whom fell the support of his father and sisters, was sick. The young men of the neighborhood assembled, plowed his land and put in his crop, so that when he was again on foot he had not lost the season and thus fallen financially behind. This kind of practical Christianity was the rule, and not the exception in this community.

In the summer of '47 or '48 my uncle, Joshua Jones, and his wife,"Aunt Sally," made us a visit, bringing with them two school friends of mine from Jacksonville, Illinois. Uncle Joshua was slow and deliberate in all his ways. He was an intelligent man; a deep thinker, of good education for the times. Afterwards he moved to the Grove, and for a long time served as an elder in the Christian Church. Aunt Sally was an energetic, impulsive woman, with a quick appreciation of the humorous. One day we were visiting a friend, when our hostess asked me how Brother Gorin was. Aunt Sally spoke up quickly and said, "What is the matter with that Brother Gorin? Everybody asks about Brother Gorin." Our kind-hearted hostess answered, with a face full of sympathy, "Indeed, I don't know, Sister Jones, just what's the matter with him, but I believe the poor man has a *spine* or something in his back." My friend, Mary, sat demurely in her chair, but it was more than Betty and I could stand, and Aunt Sally, seeing our unsuccessful efforts to control our laughter, came to our relief and suggested that we go out and see "Aunt Liddy's" (?) loom, which we certainly found to be the most *amusing* loom that had ever been constructed.

The actors in this scene are all gone, all but myself. Their life work well and faithfully done, "they have entered into their rest."

Large families were the order of the day, and it is told, truly, no doubt, that a mother whose children had all grown out of babyhood had set out for "meeting" in the wagon with her husband. For some reason she was nervous and could not ride comfortably in her chair. At last she said, "Stop, old man, stop! I know what's the matter. Get out and get me a chunk to carry in my lap. I'm so used to carrying a baby I can't ride without holding something."

In '49 a protracted meeting was held by D. P. Henderson and A. Procter, then just returned from Bethany College. A large number, about one hundred, were added to the church. William Davenport and my father administered the ordinance of baptism, standing at the same time in the clear, pebble-lined stream, and receiving the candidates as they were lead to them.

One of our neighbors had long been the only member of his family in the Christian Church, his wife professing a different faith. At this time he had the pleasure of seeing his wife and five of their children and a son-in-law go, following their Saviour, down into the waters of baptism. Every heart was touched and many an eye was filled with tears. It was an interesting time when this army of new converts was received into the fellowship of the church. As was always then the custom, they were called to the front and received from the lips of the evangelist or pastor, instructions as to their duties. Every effort was made to deepen the impression already received and to plant their feet more firmly in the untried path before them. The importance of Bible study and prayer was especially enjoined. Then followed the right hand of fellowship with much rejoicing and many tears. Objections are often made to an emotional religion; but we claim that our religion is from God, and "God is love," and love is surely an emotion as well as a principle.

My home in Eureka was one of peculiarly loving associations. It was here that were passed the last hours given me to spend with a dear mother. The most intimate confidences of our lives were here enjoyed, as I was just budding into womanhood, and here I learned most fully to appreciate the loveliness of her character. Her elasticity of spirit rendering her habitually cheerful, her rare unselfishness and thoughtfulness of others, the mutual sympathy with which we appreciated the same authors, the unvarying neatness of her attire, her deep conscientiousness and her love for me, made hers a character to be loved and revered. When I left her for the last time she was standing by the yard gate as I bade her goodbye and rode away, and never can the picture of her earnest, wistful face fade from my mind. She knew it was the last time, but I did not, but I know she awaits me on the other shore, and that that loved face now wears a happier expression than it ever wore on earth. "Thanks be to God for his unspeakable gift.".

The settlers of Walnut Grove fully appreciated a liberal education, and at an early day in the forties decided to improve the privileges of their children in this regard. Soon after my father became a citizen here he erected for me a log schoolhouse in his own yard, where the labors of my life were inaugurated. Here I presided over seventeen girls, twelve of whom were somewhat my seniors in age. "Many remain to this present, but some are fallen asleep."

My methods of teaching at that time need not be criticised now, but could doubtless be improved. The teacher, at the age of fifteen, was herself learning many a lesson to be utilized in future fields. My school was broken up by an epidemic of measles, and never reassembled. The sorrows of that winter will long be remembered. Many homes were made desolate, and those who were not afflicted were kept busy caring for the sick. Death claimed one of my pupils, Miss Amanda Wilkinson, of Metamora.

The name "Eureka" was chosen for the new post-office, and I well remember when my father and

"Uncle Davenport" announced the fact at our house. I think they had selected the name.

A school-house was built not far from the church in '48, and A. S. Fisher installed as teacher. He had been educated at Bethany College and was unsurpassed for thoroughness and conscientious devotion to his work. Later he became a profes- sor in Eureka College and served in this capacity for many years. In the early records of this insti- tution his name must ever stand prominent—a synonym of faithfulness. His wife was Miss Susan Palmer, a daughter of the pioneer preacher, Henry D. Palmer, and an aunt of Mrs. O. A. Burgess, the National President of the Christian Woman's Board of Missions.

Every step accomplished only encouraged these earnest men to plan for greater things, and at length to determine to plant a college in the grow- ing town of Eureka. You know, my friend, that I had then returned to Jacksonville, Illinois, to com- plete my course of study, and you and others who remained on the ground can more faithfully chron- icle the subsequent events connected with the his- tory of the college. If, however, a community ever merited the success it has achieved, that place is Eureka. And, although the heads are laid low that originated the idea of a great educational in- stitution here, and the hearts have ceased to throb that worked and sacrificed for its accomplishment, still, "their works do follow them" in the noble college, whose influence is so broad, and which stands a lasting monument to their memory.

It was my privilege in '92 to revisit this spot, so linked with the past, and once more to be the honored guest of those friends of former years. There are still the descendants of the Majors, the Dickinsons, the Radfords, the Davenports, the Mitchells, the Bullocks, the Joneses, the Darsts and others, whose sterling traits show them to be worthy representatives of their worthy sires.

O Eureka! Eureka! How shall my pen do justice to thy generous hospitality! How my heart responds to the love-feasts with which thy tables were spread! How the past, with all its tender memories of mother, father and home, crowds upon me—scenes no more to return in this life! Many happy days have been mine, but adown the vista of time no skies are more bright than thine, no memories more dear to my heart! Yours sincerely,

MRS. SUE. E. GRANT.

15

OLD ACADEMY DAYS IN WALNUT GROVE.

Over forty years ago—in the year 1850—I entered as a student of Walnut Grove Academy, which a college charter, a few years later, transformed into Eureka College. The school, opened not long before in a single room, had just been transferred to the new brick, with a chapel and two recitation rooms, a building which, in those days of beginnings, was regarded as a magnificent structure. The teachers in charge were Professor Asa Fisher, who has the honor of planting the germ which grew into Eureka College, and Elder John Lindsey, who has long since rested from his labors. A little later the place of the latter was taken by Professor John H. Neville, who continued long after the two or three years had ended that I passed in the academy. Among my fellow students in that period I recall Miss Elmira J. Dickinson, so well known in our missionary work; Miss Nannie Ledgerwood, now Mrs. Burgess, the beloved President of the Christian Woman's Board of Missions, and the founder of Burgess Hall, and Miss Caroline Neville, better known in these later times as Mrs. Pearre, to whom the conception of the Woman's

(226)

Board of Missions is to be credited. It is enough to enshrine Walnut Grove Academy as a sacred memory that it has equipped three women so nobly for their beneficent work.

It would be hard for one who has only seen Eureka in these later times to picture the primeval condition that existed forty years ago. The brush had been trimmed out of a small space around the academy and in the vicinity of the old frame church where the forefathers worshiped. A heavy wood and dense thicket covered the whole area of the present college campus. A path ran diagonally through the tangled undergrowth to "Uncle" John T. Jones's, where I found a home. This dense wood often re-echoed to youthful oratory as the young Patrick Henrys practiced in preparation for the weekly literary society. Occasionally some flight of eloquence awoke a response from a mischievous fellow student who, attracted by the sound, crept up and astounded the orator by his sudden applause. I have a vivid recollection of an experience of that kind myself, which so paralyzed the wings of my Pegasus that he came down with a bounce.

It is still a pleasure to recall those primitive days. Life was so real. All was so hearty and joyous. The student life, though far removed from that of the present, was robust and helpful. Algebra, with the mysterious results worked out by

the unknown quantities, opened to our visions a
wonderland, and the conjugation of *Amo* or *Tup-
to* seemed to bring the ring of the matchless periods of Cicero and Demosthenes. Then the memory of the worship in the low frame church by the
cemetery, and of the ancient worthies who bowed
at the altar there—such men as Myers, and Dickinson, and Major, and Radford, the men who
builded better than they knew—is one that can
never cease to be an inspiration.

One incident of those early times, a part of my
school experiences, seems to me to be worthy of
a place here. In the fall of 1853 Alexander
der Campbell made a visit to Illinois in the interest of the endowment of Bethany College. As
there were no facilities for railroad travel, he was
carried over the country in the carriages of the
brethren. He aimed to make one address per
day, at widely separated points, and came from
Lacon, I think, the day he spoke in Walnut Grove.
A vast audience gathered, from many miles over
the country, long before he arrived. W. W. Happy, of Jacksonville, addressed them for a while,
in order to occupy the time, but the people were
so impatient to hear the great reformer that
the words of Elder Happy fell on dull ears. At
last Mr. Campbell came and entered the pulpit. I
had never seen him before, but none of that audience needed anyone to inform them that the mag-

nificent looking man was the famous President of Bethany College. He was then over sixty-five years old; his hair was iron gray, but his face was fresh and his eye like the eagle's. His superb physical frame showed no signs of decay; he was in the prime of his intellectual strength; his voice rang out like a bugle, and as he spoke that day upon the mystery of Godliness, one of his favorite themes, he thrilled his audience as I had never heard mortal man do before. It is a tribute, not only to the impression which he made, but to the large-hearted liberality of the churches at Walnut Grove and in the vicinity, that $2,500. if my memory is not at fault, was subscribed on that day to the endowment fund of Bethany College. When we consider that the wealth of the region was not one twentieth of what it is now, that the citizens were nearly all small farmers, and that they were burdening themselves to found a literary institution in their own midst, their response was remarkable.

What I have written thus far all pertains to the pre-college period, in which the forces were at work which a little later crystallized into Eureka College. I write of this because it was my period of student life, and the memories of it are rosier than when, some years later, I was burdened with the duties and anxieties of a teacher in the college. I will, however, mention one experience of

the latter period which can be recalled by many
who will read this sketch. In the spring of 1861,
in the month of April, I went down to Peoria to
remain over Sunday. On Saturday evening the
boom of the cannon firing upon Fort Sumter roll-
ed over the land, and came with mighty reverbera-
tions upon our West. On Sunday, thoughts of
battle mingled with the hymns to the Prince of
Peace, and an eagerness for tidings from Sumter
made men forget the glad tidings of the Gospel.
On Monday morning I hurried back to my duties
at the college, over which I was presiding, and as
I came in sight I saw the Stars and Stripes proud-
ly floating from its pinnacle. On the campus I
met the students, engaged in drilling for the tented
field, and the formation of a company had already
begun. That company, Company G, of the Seven-
teenth Illinois Infantry, carried some of the noblest
young men to the front that ever offered their lives
for their country. Of these James Skelton and
Charles Dickinson were shot down at Shiloh,
though the latter lingered, an invalid, for many
years ; J. H. Rowell, after the war, went to the law
and to Congress ; H. D. Clark, J. W. Allen and B.
J. Radford are known, and loved, and praised in
all our churches for their work's sake. T. R. Bryan,
of Kansas City, was another of the band. He is not
a preacher, but is well known as the Treasurer of
the Church Extension Fund.

Memories come so thickly that I am tempted to write a history instead of a brief sketch, and it requires some self-denial to restrain my eager pen.

B. W. JOHNSON.

TRANSITORY REMINISCENCES OF WALNUT GROVE AND EUREKA—1851-1855.

The committee to whom has been assigned the duty of preparing a History of Eureka College, in order to get a few chapters of "early days," had to cast their eyes about for a "back number." Hence my selection as one antedating the familiar things of the present day, with the expectation that nearly forty years of active business life could be passed over without mention in the retrospection of incidents and tales of yore that are expected to be resurrected.

Well, to begin, it was "Walnut Grove" when I first put in my appearance. Then the trees were cut down, and it was "Stumptown." After the trees were removed they were enabled to find it—hence the name "Eureka."

I was not long in finding out that I was at home with kinfolks, as it was, "Uncle Ben" (Major), "Uncle Billy" (Davenport), "Uncle John T." (Jones), "Uncle Joshua" (Jones), "Uncle Davy" (Deweese), "Uncle Elias" (Myers), "Uncle Abisha" (Myers), "Uncle Elijah" (Dickinson), "Uncle Ben" (Radford), "Uncle Caleb" (Davidson), and others, nearly all of

(232)

whom had wives that were "Aunts" of course, to
say nothing of a numerous progeny of descendants
who might have been called cousins.

We boarded around in the neighborhood with
the citizens, as there were no regular boarding
houses. In fact we did not need them, as they "took
us in" for almost nothing—$1.75 per week.

The nearest post-office was at Washington, eight
miles distant. We spent a good portion of the day
Saturday in finding out and visiting those who had
been to town Friday, so that we could get our letters one day in advance, without waiting till Sunday, when the farmers would come to church and
distribute the mail. The Walnut Grove Academy
mail was usually sent by anybody who happened
to go to town.

About the first mail from Eureka (which was
carried on horseback) carried a great many epistles
of which the following will serve as a sample:

"APRIL 1, 1852.

"MR. —————:

"We hope you will not be offended when you find that
you have been April-fooled by the

"STUMPTOWN GIRLS."

One of the striking features of the place—one
not likely to be forgotten—was the frame church
building, now long since abandoned. Whether or
not its body "lies mouldering in the tomb" in the
cemetery which now occupies its former location, I
do not know. It was a low, broad structure with

two doors in the end, and the pulpit between them. It had an inclined floor that would have reached the ceiling had it not fortunately found the rear end of the building just in time to prevent a tall man from bumping his head.

The location of the pulpit served to prevent the running out and in of the youngsters,. some of whom, no doubt, came from neighborhoods where the practice was in vogue, as was the case in most new settlements of the country. At one place I heard of, where the custom had become a regular nuisance, the new preacher was notified by the officers of the church so that he would not be taken off his guard and nonplussed in his sermon. Being thus apprised, he proved himself equal to the occasion. On entering the pulpit he remarked that it was quite cool in the room, and if any of the people had holes in their stockings they were at liberty to go out during the sermon and warm their feet. As none went out, it was said (to the credit of the mothers and wives) that they had attended to the darning on Saturday night, and it was not necessary for the preacher to think about *darning* the stockings, or the wearers either, during the sermon.

"Lida's Wood" had its antetype in the "Bower of Beauty" (only the ghost of itself now—1893—remaining) which was presided over by Professor Fisher and his estimable wife. Many of the young

ladies boarded there, and they were supposed to
be under the strictest surveillance; but many were
the *billet doux* that passed up and down the stove
pipe that went through another room. I sometimes
have wondered if we that have passed through the
"boy and girl" period, ever stop to think of those
by-gone days (when we think we are exercising
the same surveillance), and wonder if we don't
know how it was ourselves. Those *billet doux*
always got there, do now, and always will.

Then there was the "Queen's Palace" that was
kept by those maiden ladies, the Kings. That was
a resort for the male students. Who can now
think of the place without associating with it the
names of John W. Owen and John L. McCune—
generally called John - Leander-Honey-my-dear-
Mitchell-McCune, not for short, but because of a
love affair—as that was their boarding place.

There were no saloons, but there was a famous
drinking place just east of the academy—Walnut
Grove Spring. We all resorted there at recess
and at the noon hour to quench our thirst. Like
the famous spring of Dan, it was the source of a
"Jordan," but its name was not assigned to it on
account of its similarity in that respect, but from
the song that runs, "Jordan is a hard road to
travel, I believe," as was demonstrated by its
steep banks that were wonderfully in the way (during the icy and rainy times) of the boys who

thought they were good enough to "pass over Jordan" to see the young ladies who lived south of that famous gully.

The usual pranks of students ("human natur" is always the same) were played, but the writer being a *good* boy will let some one else tell of most of them. In proof of goodness one incident might be mentioned. It was the custom at the close of the "morning hour" for Professor Fisher to name the person or persons that might need disciplining, to meet the faculty in the "south room," naming the hour that their presence would be, expected. In the morning aluded to, he announced that with others Mr. Pickrell would please meet the faculty. As quick as thought, Mr. George Pickrell jumped to his feet and asked, "Which Mr. Pickrell ? The pupils smiled audibly, even Professor Fisher allowing the rings to spread over the corners of his mouth when he replied, "Mr. George Pickrell." More than one, if they relate reminiscences, will remember *that* room.

Spirit-rappings (ought to be spelled *wrappings*) were creating some excitement about that time. A medium (a woman) was located a few miles from the academy. A party was made up to pay her a visit. The enquirers were requested to place themselves around a box and put their hands on it. After a few communications had been received from the spirit land, it was suggested by some

incredulous person (there are nearly always some
of that kind in such crowds) that perhaps the
spirits communicated through the toes of the medium, and to be certain there was no deception, a
committee was appointed to hold her feet. This
intimidated to some extent the spirits and they refused to respond. As there was likely to be but
little fun, one of the "toe" committee held on with
his hands but did the rapping himself, much to the
relief and amusement of the medium, as it got her
out of a *bad* box and edified the spectators.

Dr. J. M. Allen, who was then a practicing physician, afterwards a minister, and then President
of Eureka College, was a frequent visitor to the
room that Professor Neville and myself occupied.
One night he staid late. The weather was inau-
spicious, a heavy snow was falling, and upon invitation of his hosts he decided to remain over night
in the one-third of the bed that had been so generously tendered him. The guest occupied the post
of honor by sleeping "before," with Professor
Neville in the "middle." The next morning Professor Neville was missing. Neither the Doctor
nor myself having been disturbed, we were at a
loss to know what had become of him. After we
had retired the snow had ceased to fall, so that the
tracks he had made in his escape were plainly
visible. We had roasted him out, and he had
struck for the doctor's bed for a morning nap.

I would be remiss in my duty if I forgot to mention the ladies' and the gentlemen's magazines that were published once a month, printed with a pen. They formed a kind of safety-valve for the school. All were required to write "compositions" but they were not required to read them but three times a month. The fourth week, on Friday afternoon, they assembled at the church, the inhabitants being invited and welcomed to hear the news read from them by the editors, who were succeeded by some aspiring youth and maid every month. The authors who contributed were reported by the editors to the faculty, so as to excuse them from writing a composition and reading it themselves, hence the relief, safety and relaxation from being always solemn, as compositions were rated as serious affairs.

The gentlemen's magazine of March 2, 1855, is before me. Some of the subjects treated were: "Reading" (an editorial), "History," "Views," "Lost, a Heart," "Imagination," "Intemperance," a poem "To the Trustees," "A Ship at Sea" (poetry), "Whiskers or Beards," "The Philosopher's Stone Found," a letter addressed to Miss Fide (who had advertised for a husband) by Timothy Scruggs, "The Last Farewell," "Musing," a few verses styled "I Can't Do It," "Murder," "Bloomers," "Influence of a Woman," "Love," "A Valentine," etc., besides "Ye Locals."

The stirring times came in the spring, when we were invited by Mr. John Darst to visit his sugar camp (now in the heart of the town) at night, to eat maple sugar and wax. One evening is especially remembered, when about half a dozen of his boys —there might have been more—were inclined, fully as much as the big kettles of sugar water, to boil over, their spirits exuberating with fun and frolic. But when their father pointed his finger at them and said, "Settle, boys, settle," they at once subsided, but they didn't stay "settled" very long at a time (though, finally, several of them did *actually* "settle" not very far from the spot where the camp was located). It is needless to add that we had a sweet time.

Space and time forbid, or I might go on and write how we always got lost when we went sleigh-riding in the big sled with four horses, in going, as we always did, to Mr. Kinnear's; or how we got to and from the "Grove" by private convey-ances, as no public ones went that way.

We could not go with the mail, because, even after the office was established, the mail was car-ried in a sack on horse-back. It was a *mail* con-trivance, anyway, while the school was male and female.

Or I might tell about the "Old Folks' Home" that the church established for the benefit of old Brother and Sister Moffett, and about how one of

the elders every Sunday would call for two volunteers to go each night through the week to care
for them ; and about the first store, that was kept
in a room about fifteen feet square, by Mr. Ster-
ritt; and how he brought tin dinner-horns that
were *all* bought one night by some of the boys
who went out and made the welkin ring, till the
merchant was sick of hearing them, but when he
tried to get them to desist, they replied that they
"bought them to blow." And how proud we were
when the firm of Clark & Jones opened a store on
the corner west of the academy, and how big we
felt when we found that we were not in an academy at all, but in a sure-enough college, having
had the good fortune to have it brought to us.
We being *Charter Members* required no matricu
lation fee or initiatory ceremonies, you see, so we
kept right on in the "middle of the road." Or,
I might tell how, when one of the societies held
an election for officers by ballot, one of the boxes
was "stuffed," and when the fact was announced
the member who did it rose very gravely and said,
"If any one is guilty, let him speak."

I will leave these, and many other incidents of
such nature, to be expatiated upon at greater
length by some one who remembers about them,
or others of the same kind.

But before closing let me say that the thirty-
eight intervening years have failed to ex-

tinguish the pleasant memories of teachers and
fellow students. Nor would these reminiscences
be complete without a kind word in memory of
the good men we called uncles,most of whom have,
I believe, "joined the great majority," where they
will receive their reward. My remembrance of them
is of the kindliest sort. They were whole-souled,
liberal, self-sacrificing, social, worthy members of
society. Long live the memory of their good
deeds.   J. H. PICKRELL.

Chicago, Ill.
16

SWEET AND SIMPLE SERVICES.

Eureka College is part of the fruit of the spirit of "attempting great things for God and expecting great things of God," which so characterized the early Church of Christ in Walnut Grove. Among the earliest recollections of the writer some of the sweetest are of the simple services led by Uncle Ben Major and Uncle Elijah Dickinson. As I look back nearly half a century, I see the plain meeting-house. The doors are open, for it is Sunday morning. The windows are open, for it is a summer morning. The sweet-faced, matronly women enter by the north door, and occupy the shady, fragrant north side. "No silks rustle, nor envious eyes encounter." It is literally homespun and harmony. The young men and boys are gathered in the shade of some neighboring tree, satisfying a social hunger begot by six days in the wilderness of the corn-fields. The young women and girls are here and there in groups gathering bloom in hands and cheeks. Then there comes out through the doors and windows the summoning solo, "Safely through another week," and everybody knows that "Uncle Lijah" has begun

(242)

the service of song. The strong, uncultured voices of the men, and the tender trebles of the women help to swell forth, "God has brought us on our way." The young people file in, and at the last verse the chorus is full, and pretty much the whole community for miles around is in the house. Then the little fat hymn-book opens at another place, and "Come let us anew" swells forth, and the congregation is in line to "Our journey pursue." Dear, saintly band of singers! I have heard Thomas' and Gilmore's, and the tuneful "divas" over whom the world runs mad, but I would resign the privilege of ever hearing them more for the sake of listening to you once again. But it may be that among the "lost chords," too sweet for earth, even that may be picked up again over there.

THE FIRST MEETING TO BUILD THE ACADEMY.

The meeting was called in the east room of the Walnut Grove Seminary, afterwards called "The Palace," because a family by the name of King afterwards occupied it for a dwelling. The new academy building was to be of brick, and, what was hitherto unknown as to school-houses hereabouts, two stories high. Plans of the architectural wonder were shown at the second meeting, and after various futile attempts to satisfactorily exhibit them, somebody said, "Put the paper behind the candle." Then everybody saw. Have we so placed the Gospel candle before Eureka College that all the brethren in the State can see it? We have been trying to. Then Uncle Billy Davenport made a speech to arouse enthusiasm. And he knew how. He astonished us by saying, "Yes, and upon this magnificent building we will have a bell that can be heard from Tom West's to Bowling Green." Those were about the limits of the world for some of us. The house came, but not *that* bell. But other belles came, more musical and beautiful, and many of them remain unto this day, but some are fallen asleep. The building of such a house was a great undertaking in that day, but after much discussion, Uncle Ben, the guide and autocrat of the neighborhood, said, pointing to E. B. Myers, "You give $150," and to David Deweese, "You give $150," and to himself, "And you give $150," and then suggested what others might do, and the thing was done. His main contention was that they must build an institution where young men should be educated for ministers of the Gospel. When we stop to think of the scores of strong and successful preachers who have been educated here, and of the three-score young men now in the Bible department, we suspect that these men builded wiser and larger than they knew—perhaps larger than any of us know.

AN EXCITING EPISODE.

During the winter of 1860-61 the political excitement throughout the country was at fever heat,
and, of course, the college did not escape the infec-
tion. Before the end of the winter term seven of
the Southern States had seceded, and the "Confederate States of America" had been organized at
Montgomery, Alabama. There were in the college
some half dozen or more of young men (some of
them from the South) who were avowed, outspoken
and not over-discreet Secessionists. They continu-
ally provoked the anger of the loyal students, both
Republicans and Democrats, by their disloyal
talk. Soon after the beginning of the spring term
the excitement was greatly increased by the attack
upon Fort Sumter, and some of the Secessionist
boys threatened to hoist a rebel flag on the public
park in Eureka. This so stirred the popular wrath
that matters began to look serious for the thought-
less young fellows. At this crisis one of the loyal
students—who a few days afterward enlisted in
the service—undertook to do a little missionary
work among them. He got together four or five of
them in a room of the old boarding-hall, and, after
explaining to them as best he could the state of
the public temper, he kindly advised them to be
more discreet, and by all means avoid giving further offense.

Instead of receiving this well-meant advice in the spirit in which it was proffered, the young men informed their. would-be adviser that when they needed his counsel they would call for him. The latter withdrew, and it was about two o'clock in the afternoon. The more he thought the matter over the hotter he grew, until at last he decided to give the young "fire-eaters," as the boys called them, a lesson. Proceeding to a store, he procured two yards of white muslin, upon which he painted, during the afternoon, a palmetto tree with serpent coiled about it, and a lone star; making what was then supposed to be the confederate emblem. Having attached this to a pole, he awaited the approach of midnight, when he and another student climed one of the most conspicuous trees in the public park and thrusting the pole above the topmost branch, securely fastened it there. Early in the morning they were upon the ground to witness the outcome. Soon men and boys began to collect in front of the business row on the west side of the park, and the news rapidly spread that "those fellows had put up a rebel flag on the square."

It was a bright spring morning with a soft south wind, and before the sun was far on his daily route an excited crowd was gazing upon the "rattlesnake rag" triumphantly flaunting treason in their faces. Finally a young man volunteered to bring it down from its lofty perch. When it was brought into the midst, the crowd looked upon it a moment in dazed wonder, and then made a simultaneous rush for it. In twenty seconds pole and flag were broken and torn into fragments. The pieces were piled upon the ground, a match applied, and the offending rag was reduced to ashes. Then the silence was broken by a prominent citizen who said, in a voice trembling with suppressed emotion, "I will give a hundred dollars to know who put that up." Another, and another, and another spoke up, rapidly swelling the sum to be offered as a reward for the coveted information. Matters were getting serious for the Secessionists, but it leaked out somehow that the thing was a hoax. But the indiscreet fellows learned a lesson. For the first time they concluded to keep their mouths shut, and they soon departed for more congenial places. B. J. RADFORD.

Eureka, Ill.

FROM A STUDENT OF 1855 AND 1858.

On a pleasant April afternoon of the year of grace 1855, with a modest equipment of baggage and books, I first entered Eureka, to become a student at "Walnut Grove Academy." A year or two before some sense of waste of time and energy in the follies of youth had come upon me, and I had taken a round turn upon some of my habits, thus gaining more hours and strength for self-culture. Now in my twentieth year, with the day of my majority nearing, and the graver realities of life at hand, I felt the need of more systematic mental discipline and equipment than the desultory opportunities of local schools, of the printing-office and home offered, valuable as these were in the absence of better; and having heard nothing but good of the Academy of Walnut Grove, may be attracted also by the classic name already chosen for its post-village, I settled upon that school for such short attendance as the remainder of the academic year allowed.

On the morning of the Sabbath day, the day next before my start for Eureka, the large frame flouring mill which, after agriculture, furnished

(248)

the pioneer industry to Lacon, where I then lived, had burned, and my duty as foreman of the local hose company had led me to "the perilous age of battle, where it raged," so that I reached Eureka the next day with a badly scorched and thickly swathed hand. Nothing, however, detracted from the pleasure with which I rode under the noble shades of the beautiful grove which then stretched almost unbroken across the present lines of the railways intersecting at Eureka and across most of the present site of the village.

> "The groves were God's first temples. Ere man learned
> To hew the shaft and lay the architrave,   .
> And spread the roof above them,—ere he framed
> The lofty vault, to gather and roll back
> The sound of anthems,—in the darkling wood,
> Amidst the cool and silence, he knelt down
> And offered to the Mightiest solemn thanks
> And supplication.   .   .   .
>   Be it ours to meditate
> In these calm shades thy milder majesty,
> And to the beautiful order of thy works
> Learn to conform the order of our lives."

Eureka was then a little place. Probably not one-tenth the number of its present population resided permanently in the hamlet. Scarcely a house considered as belonging to it stood on any other road or street than that in front of the Academy buildings. I do not at this moment recall any other store or shop than the small but exceedingly varied mercantile establishment and

post-office kept at the crossing of the roads, by
the hale, good-natured Clark, whose family formed
so large an element in the educational and par-
ticularly social life of the place. There was but
one Academy building proper, besides the boarding-house. The chapel and recitation-rooms were
all under a single roof, occupying a small, but
then sufficient, two-story brick building, called the
Academy. A few rods from it, and nearer the
road, was the frame boarding-house, which, judg-
ing from the picture in the recent catalogue before
me, may be the present "Hall No. 2." Here I
was most kindly and hospitably received by mine
host, John Major, brother of Jo Major, whose
name I am glad to recognize in the list of the
present Board of Trustees. I am sure he has a
warm place in the hearts of all his former boarders. Under a previous landlord it had been a
favorite trick of the boys to accomplish the easy
feat at a meal of eating up everything upon the
table, and then piling the plates. But no one
ever proposed the like in Major's time there; in
fact, it was practicably impossible. An ample
supply of plain but wholesome and toothsome
food always awaited us, whose partaking was always prefaced by pious thanks duly rendered to
the Giver of all good.

The teachers of the time were principally Professor Fisher, whom I had the pleasure to meet at

his present home in Kansas City three years ago,
and Professor Neville, a brilliant young bachelor
who was much the object of tender solicitude on
the part of young lady students and match-mak-
ing mammas, whom I also met with great satisfaction long after in Lexington, Ky., where for many
years he has been a successful teacher. Among
the students whom I remember best, and most of
whom have made reputable if not famous figures
in affairs since, were Ben Radford, later a graduate
of '66, minister, editor and lecturer of large note;
Ben Davenport, who afterwards went to Harvard,
and has since had, I am told, a rather varied, perhaps picturesque career as lawyer and politician;
Noel Meek a few years afterwards Sheriff of Woodford county; the Earls, H. S. and Jo. of whom the
former blessed my sight last year at the State Disciple Convention in this city, on his return from
some years' service in Liverpool, England; Henry
Clay Mannen, a one-armed student of excellent
disposition and culture, who died during his attendance here; Libbie Maxwell (since Shaw, and
now Halsey), grand-daughter of one of the oldest
and most useful ministers in Northern Illinois, the
Rev. Father Palmer, and daughter of one of the
best citizens Marshall county ever had; Anna
Major, and a few others.

My short term passed rapidly and most pleasantly in the lovely grove and among its kindly

and gentle people. Almost every one in the settlement was then of the Disciple faith, and most
of them were Kentuckians. Their warm-hearted
friendliness and hospitality, the seclusion and
quiet of the scholastic retreat, its absolute freedom
from drunkenness or other outbreaking vice, and
the superior advantages offered by the school,
comparatively humble as it was, combined to
make my brief sojourn there one of the brightest
spots of a generally happy and healthful life, now
verging hard upon six decades. One of my favorite walks had been to the verge of the great prairie
but a little distance to the east of the buildings ;
and during the next three years far and away, the
pleasantest excursions I took from my home at the
northward were across the prairies to the dear
school-home in the grove.

> "These are the gardens of the desert—these
>   The unshorn fields, boundless and beautiful,
>   For which the speech of England has no name,
>   The prairies. . . . Lo! they stretch
>   In airy undulations far away,
>   As if the ocean in his gentlest swell
>   Stood still, with all his rounded billows fixed
>   And motionless forever."

I quote this, also the "Forest Hymn" above,
perhaps needlessly, but from (to me) a surpassing
interest of association, since I use in quotation the
identical book that at least once accompanied me
in these delightful rides,—an early edition of

Bryant, lately in my father's library, but since his lamented death last year one of the most-prized treasures of my own. The gifted lady friends who were sometimes my companions in these tours; the remarkably accomplished music teacher for a year at the school, Miss Ellen Frances True, of Ohio, sister of one of the young Buckeye poets of the time, she accompanying me on a Sunday trip to one of Bro. Burgess's church services at a distance in the grove; and others whose memory is delightfully bound up with these occasional visits, are also bright among the recollections of those years.

Progress was observable at every visit. The Academy had become the College in 1855, but took form as such rather gradually. The talented Burgess joined the faculty, also Barton Johnson, of the pioneer Washington family, whose brother, J. B., is my neighbor in Detroit, as the popular pastor of the Central Christian Church; and temporarily others who aided to give the new foundation power and fame.

The sturdy Scotch scholar-farmer, George Callender, was for a time President, but had left the chair he occupied, as had also Burgess for the time being, Neville and Miss True, when I returned in the spring of 1858 to take some further preparation for an Eastern college. The President of the school was now that fine classical and general scholar of German stock, Dr. Charles

Louis Loos, whom I am happy to meet here almost every summer, as he makes his annual visit
to his daughter, Mrs. Campbell, of Detroit. The
faithful Fisher still remained, with Johnson, these
three being the only full professors. S. E. Pearre,
M. D., was assistant professor; Miss M. Josephine
Myers, assistant in the Preparatory Department;
and Mrs. M. Augusta Buckley, teacher of music.
The railroad, then the eastern extension of the
Peoria and Oquawka, by this time connected the
village with Peoria, and hopelessly broke the old-
time solitude and stillness of the place. A busier
village had begun to cover the forest spaces between the college and the tracks; the post-office
had been removed to the new town; the community
had become more mixed, not altogether to its advantage, and generally a new era had set in.
There was still a good school there upon the old
site, however; the first college building had been
erected, though it did not yet contain a full-fledged
college. Again my limited term passed quickly,
profitably and happily. The catalogue of that
year is before me, and bristles with points of
interest. The old families of Eureka and Woodford County, and those of similar names in other
regions, muster strong in the lists of students of
thirty-five years ago. Here are nine Myerses, five
boys and four girls; as many Martins divided
as seven and two; Skeltons, five and two; Clarks

and Joneses, each three and four; Davidsons, four
and two; Wests, three and three, and Wellmans,
three and two; Smiths six, and Darsts five on the
male side only; Hales four; Hayneses, Burtons,
McCulloughs and Conovers, three each, on the
gentler side only (I believe an incidental remark
of mine concerning the Conover home, that had
also some attractive lady boardeis, gave it name
as "The Bower of Beauty"); Majors, four and one;
Bakewells, three and one; Brubakers, two and
one; Dickinsons, Radfords, Bullocks, Grahams
and Paynes, three boys or young men apiece;
Gastmans and Hallams, two each. The two Doug-
las sisters, of Vinton, Iowa, were great social favor-
ites. A number of these students staid by the
college to full graduation—Rowell, since Congress-
man of high repute, in 1861, also the year of
Tommy Bryan, now of Kansas City; of Carpenter,
since a college president at Colusa, Cal.; of Mollie
Clark Hawk, of Mt. Carroll, Ill.; Dave Hallam,
merchant at Los Angeles, Cal.; Rutilia Gillum
Hoyt, of Forest, Ill.; A. H. Smith and Sallie Davidson Crawford, of Eureka; J. Frank Davidson,
Esq., of Hannibal, Mo.; and Rev. H. D. Clark
("Deacon" of old), Mt. Sterling, Ky. Sixty-one
was the great year of the students of '58. The
previous year had brought the pioneer graduate
of the college proper—Lige Dickinson, who I see
remains at the old home. .In 1852 the sole Eureka

graduate was the Rev. Sam Hallam, now of Belton, Texas; the next year came Leroy Skelton, since deceased, and Elder Eli Fisher, whom I gladly met in the summer of 1888,.at his home amid the mountains of Montana ; and in '68 Laura Fisher Gibson, now with or near her people in Kansas City ; S. F. Davidson, a Chicago editor, and Emma Clark Crow, of Pittsfield, Ill.

Others will contribute such abundant and possibly redundant store. of personal reminiscence that I need not take time and space for mine. I simply add that I account the Dedication Address for the H. C. Mannen monument and the Representative Address for the Periclesian Society, during the closing days of my last term at Eureka, as the most satisfactory honors of all my school life. Blessings on the dear old place! I would adopt and adapt for it the personal German benediction, " May you live a thousand years !"

HENRY A. FORD.

Detroit, Mich.

EXPERIENCES OF A MINISTERIAL STUDENT.

Among the many interesting experiences that enter into the life of a college student, it is difficult to fix upon those which ought to have first place in a brief chapter of reminiscences. Perhaps it is as well to begin with a glance at ante college days.

When a little boy, living in Eureka, the writer's notions of the college students were about the same as those of other "youngsters" of the town, namely, that they were a lot of conceited young folks, who felt themselves to be above their juniors, and whom it would vastly benefit to be "taken down a notch." One way in which this desirable end was occasionally realized was by inveigling some of the college students into a spelling match with the children of the "district" school, which would be held in the old red brick Academy on Friday afternoon or night. We always "downed" them in these contests, for, whatever superiority they might possess over us in all the other elements of an education, some of us knew Webster's and McGuffey's spellers by heart, and were simply invincible. How we would gloat over their discomfiture when some tall six-footer from the Junior class would go

17 (257)

down on a huge polysyllable, which would be fairly caught out of his mouth by a barefooted little
"shaver" of ten or twelve, and spelled with a rap-
idity and ease that showed it to be almost a me-
chanical process with him. When, after an absence of several years, I returned to enter college,
I found that this custom had been abandoned, and
that the students had but little intercourse with
the pupils of the public schools. Whether this
was because the former had learned caution from
past experiences, or because the latter had degen-
erated in spirit and ambition, I do not venture to
say.

As a college student I was, of course, thrown into closest relations with those who, like myself,
were preparing for the ministry, and I find the
memories of the associations gathering about this
calling coming back most freshly to my mind.
With one fact, as I look back upon those days, I
am deeply impressed, namely, the uniform respect
with which these theological striplings were treated by the kind people of Eureka and vicinity. In
some colleges the students of theology are looked
down upon by their fellow-students and the citizens of the community. If not openly shown,
there is yet a latent feeling of disrespect toward
them, as though their peculiar calling were less
manly than others. But the very atmosphere of
Eureka always seemed to envelop the young

preacher with kindly influences which gave him most pleasing visions of the vocation upon which he was entering. Most of the ministerial students were poor boys, who had to make their way through college by the most arduous toil and the severest self-denial. As soon as he could muster up courage to stand before a congregation, the candidate for the ministry would begin to "practice" on some of the village or country churches in the vicinity, and if he proved to be at all acceptable as a speaker, he would soon find churches that would pay him a few dollars a visit. The writer recalls vividly the pride with which he returned from preaching his first sermon, carrying in his pocket a five dollar bill, and in his heart the memory of many kind words of encouragement, which to him were better than gold or silver. To some of us who used regularly to administer our very crude ideas to these long-suffering churches, it now seems wonderful with what tenacity the churches around Eureka have held on to life. Some of them even grew under the labors of these raw young preachers, and very few, if any, actually died under the infliction. Among the churches which will always be held in grateful remembrance by the preachers educated at Eureka, for their generous financial assistance, kindly forbearance and thoughtful sympathy, should be prominently mentioned Mount Zion, Secor, Versailles, White Oak

Grove, Pontiac, Flanagan, Saunemin, and others, no doubt, that will occur to the mind of many an old student. The writer remembers one young preacher who, for nearly a year, visited regularly two of these churches, wearing a suit of clothes which he had entirely outgrown, and which were patched in so many places as to reveal a disastrously low state of finances on his part; yet he never heard an unkind or criticising word from any person at his expense. Their sympathy was so real that it could be felt, and was unspeakably helpful to him. Of course, there were some candidates for the ministry who were not very highly esteemed in the community and college, and whose services were not welcomed by the churches; but these were, in the main, young men who had no true conception of the dignity of the gospel ministry, and were aspiring to it merely for a little cheap glory, or to secure, as they supposed, an easy mode of living. They usually found out their mistake very soon, and either left school or, at least, gave up their purpose of preaching. With rare exceptions the earnest young man, whose heart was set on the work of preaching Christ, whether his talents were ordinary or extraordinary, found a welcome place in the esteem of the people and in the pulpits of the churches.

It will readily be understood that the student

who had regular preaching appointments to fill
was under the necessity of working hard, if he succeeded in keeping up his studies and giving satisfaction to the churches for which he spoke on
Lord's days. At the close of a hard week's work,
ending, perhaps, with an oration or debate in one
of the societies, which had required all his extra
time during the preceding days of the week, he
had to start for his appointment on Saturday, preparing his sermons for the next day while on the
train, or after arriving at his destination. If he
drove to his appointment, the buggy became his
study, and he would find himself audibly thinking
out his discourse, as he followed the winding timber road, or pursued the straight and uninteresting
lane that followed the section lines across the
broad prairies. Returning, weary from his journey, often not till Monday afternoon, he must then
make up his Monday lessons, and prepare for his
classes on the following day. It was good discipline, though, and helped to train many of us
for the experience we have had to face in the active ministry of this busy age, when a man must be
able to do two days' work in one, and to keep it
up indefinitely.

These young preachers had their fun, too, even
when it was at their own expense. One of the
writer's classmates, whose name would be familiar
to most of our readers, had such an experience,

over which he yet enjoys a hearty laugh. Preaching in a close and intensely heated school-house,
not a hundred miles from Eureka, he was greatly
annoyed by observing a young lady on the front
seat sound asleep, and attracting attention from a
large portion of the audience by the comical mo-
tions of her head, as it fell forward and backward
and from side to side, at frequent intervals. Determined to win the attention of the congregation
at all hazards, he increased the volume of his voice
and the vigor of his gestures, and concluded an
animated period by bringing his foot down upon
the floor with a resounding stamp, when the "sleeping beauty" sprang from her seat with a cry of
alarm which destroyed all the solemnity of the
service, and forced the preacher to end his discourse without the usual conclusion and exhorta-
tion, since he found himself unable to restrain his
own laughter, or that of the congregation.

Ah, those happy days! How the heart thrills as
it recalls the buoyant spirit that filled our breasts,
and the pleasing visions that flitted before our
imaginations. Life has proved to be more of a
task than we anticipated, and not all of the bright
dreams have been realized; but we have found
much of compensation, nevertheless, in the truer
ideal of life that has come to us, as we have
learned at the feet of the dear Master the lesson of
loving self-sacrifice and service. And we are sure

that at least the alphabet of this lesson was learned from the lips of our beloved Alma Mater.

W. F. RICHARDSON.

Denver, Colo., June 20, 1893.

STORY OF A NEWSPAPER MAN.

In the beginning—but this is not a Scripture lesson, nor am I one of the evangelists of Eureka College, except in an indirect sense. Moreover, it is perhaps better to leave the story of the beginning of Walnut Grove Academy to one of the really old students; for, though my recollection of this educational movement runs back over forty years—to 1852, in fact—my actual connection with it began in 1863, and it was in June of 1893 that I had the pleasure of attending a reunion of the alumni of the college on what happened to be the quarter-centennial anniversary of my graduation, coincident, likewise, with the celebration of the quadro-centennial anniversary of the new world's discovery.

Looked at in that broad verbal way, Eureka College takes on a most venerable seeming; for quarter-centennial and quadro-centennial, literally, are not far apart. To one who has passed the half-century post on life's journey, a hundred years seem all too short for the needs of knowledge-getting and character-building, and one can begin to understand how, in the sight of the ever-living

God, "one day is as a thousand years, and a thousand years as one day."

Therefore it is, that, in the wide view, there is not much difference between one quarter of a century and sixteen of them; for, after all, time is measured by things accomplished, because accomplishment is the stuff of which history is made. Savage nations have existed for thousands of years, but have made no history because they have done nothing in race advancement.

In that view, again, Eureka College stretches far into the world's past; for the third of a century which has elapsed since Elijah Dickinson received, in 1860, the first diploma issued by it, has witnessed the doing of more things by man for man than any full century which preceded it, and for the doing of them the dear Alma Mater has borne her share in the preparation.

On the material side—and material development is always a step toward the spiritual—immense strides have been made. The utilization of electricity to supply human needs, which now holds such a conspicuous position in every-day life, is practically comprised within that span, telegraphy alone ante-dating it. The telephone, the phonograph, the telautograph, the electric lamp, the electric motor, electric ovens, electro-cautery, and other helpful inventions of the sort, were unknown, and mostly undreamed of, when Elijah Dickinson

reached that part in the curriculum scheduled in
the catalogue under the head, "Electricity and
Magnetism"—a brief treatise, made little of, as an
insignificant province in the realm of physics.

In like manner, remarkable advancement has
been made in other material lines. Labor-saving
machinery has, in almost every department of human endeavor, lifted some of the crushing burdens
from toil and shortened the hours of labor, while
cheapening the cost of life's necessaries. Antisep-
tic surgery, improved surgical appliances, and a
wider knowledge of hygiene and materia medica,
have lengthened the span of life. In short, we are
better housed, better clothed, better nourished and
longer-lived than our fathers, because we know
more of the laws of life and death, and take greater precautions to obey them. If we could but
know all of them perfectly and obey them implic-
itly, we might bid defiance to death.

Nor is it only on the material side that we have
advanced in the last thirty years. The world has
learned many lessons in justice and in humanity.
Three great nations—the United States, Russia
and Brazil—have stricken the shackles from the
limbs of their slaves, and have declared that none
but free men shall henceforth dwell within their
borders. Thus did Christianity assert its power
alike in a despotism, a constitutional monarchy
and a republic. The first two were allowed to put

away their sin in peace; but with us, because we had been living a lie before the world, declaring freedom inaleniable while aleniating it, a blood atonement was exacted, and a half million lives— not witting the truth, perhaps, in most cases, but none the less really—were offered as a sacrifice on the altar in God's temple that we might be purged of our sin. It matters not that we of the north did not hold slaves, we paltered with the traffic for a hundred years, knowing it to be wrong, and the Upright Judge pronounced the alternative sentence of national repentance and sacrifice or national death.

Having paid the penalty in full measure, we stand before the Christian world, within whose borders the sun shines on no slave, purified and strong, joined with the rest of the Christian world in saying: "Neither shall any man, Christian or pagan, hold any other man in bondage."

In these same years republicanism has conquered the western hemisphere, and no crowned head now rules at any new-world capital; the flag of peace has been displayed in Rome, the breeding place of war; international arbitration has been accepted and put in practice by the two greatest nations in existence, and the time is hastening apace when the doors of the temple of Janus shall be closed forever.

But the record of material and moral progress

since the foundation of the first Eureka College
building was laid, does not set the full bounds to
the world's advancement. The sweet flower of religion has been unfolding its petals, one by one,
revealing beauties unsuspected in that day when
the horrible was held before the Christian view,
and holy men saw infants in hell not a span long.

Travel and reading have broadened our vision;
contact with the members of other Christian
sects than ours, and with the exponents of other
religions than ours, have taught us that the es-
sentials of the code of ethics are everywhere substantially the same; that the differences in religions are chiefly racial and social; and we are
beginning to get a glimmer of the fact that, in all
ages and to all peoples God has revealed himself in
such form as best suited the time and the condition
of the people to whom the revealment came. To
Abraham, the shepherd, He came as the guide who
would show him a land rich in pasturage, wherein
his flocks would increase mightily, and where his
descendants should make him the head of a great
nation; to Moses, the deliverer of the enslaved, He
came as a warrior unconquerable, ready to lead
the children of Israel out of bondage and to de-
fend them against any who might oppose them.
At His last appearing, to a people looking and
praying for a promised King who should restore
Israel with a mighty hand and set up anew the

throne of David, He came as the Prince of Peace, promising His faithful followers a kingdom not only incomparably more glorious than that of David, but one that neither the powers of earth nor hell could overthrow in time or eternity. To Buddha, the contemplative, He appeared as a teacher of the moralities, promising a forward step in each right action performed toward final absorption in the Godhead. To Mohammed, exemplar to a race of predatory nomads, He promised, in return for abstinence in one direction, indulgence in another, less evil.

Thus to each, according to his needs and capabilities. To a blind race we may suppose he would come as a rushing, mighty wind, to be heard; to a deaf race, as a pillar of fire, to be seen.

To our forefathers, because they were not easily led by the sentiment of love, He came compelling obedience through fear of everlasting punishment.

To us, who look with streaming eyes to Calvary, the fires of hell are without significance. Christ lifted up, draws us to Him, and the smoke of the burning no longer ascends to our sight.

Knowing then that there is but One God, the center toward which all men of good will of all the world are traveling, by whatever road, I trust we have reached a point where we are glad to grasp by the hand and bid God-speed to those whom we

meet on the upward way ; that we have come to a
point where we are willing to admit that a Presbyterian, a Catholic, or a Buddhist may be saved by
God's grace.

This is a long step, and the Parliament of Religions, held in Chicago in 1893, has prepared the
way for another step ; that perhaps the plan of
salvation, the work of the omnipotent, omniscient
God, is not a failure after all, dooming the vast
majority of mankind to eternal punishment; that
perhaps Confucius, and Buddha, and Brahma, and
Mohammed were prophets of God, commissioned
to reveal Him, each to his own people, in such
guise as best suited their characteristics and environment.

In doing this we abate no jot of the faith as it is
revealed to us and are absolved no tittle from the
injunction to preach it to all the world. We merely recognize them as a part of God's children who
have not seen the full light, as it has been revealed to us.

For this work I know no branch of the Christian
church so well equipped in its attitude as ours.
Unhampered by a formulated creed, made to fit
conditions which do not exist in missionary lands,
and which must prove a hindrance to those bound
by them, our evangelists are prepared to preach
the Word in its simplicity and beauty..

In all this world there is nothing so grand as

character; nothing so inspiring as a lofty ideal, and it has been the good fortune of our institution of learning to have instructors who taught that the end of education is not erudition, but the formation of character; that the aim of scholastic training is not to fill the mind with facts, but to enable it to evolve principles of action from them.

It is for that reason that Eureka College, in greater measure than any other school with which I am acquainted, has sent men into the world; men in the broadest and best sense; men controlled by a clear-cut moral standard; men who have been taught to know the right and to dare to do it.   S. F. DAVIDSON.

Chicago, Ill.

BRIGHT MEMORIES.

Miss Dickinson:

You have asked me for reminiscences—college reminiscences. My heart springs lightly to the task and speeds with joyous, winged feet, along the backward stretch of vanished years, to bring up retrieved treasure for the enrichment of "Our College" book.

Task? This is no task. It is only a little outing, on a summer afternoon, to turn away from the burden and heat of life's toil-filled present, and wander, hand in hand with memory, through the elysian fields of youth and gladness, or dream in delicious leisure on memory's couch and lay the haggard cheek of care against the soft plush lining of those dear old days, before we learned that life has a coarser, flannel side, that must some time chafe our tender, sensitive spirits. What sport to try again that rainbow span that bridges the vista of fading years and find, at the farther end, memory's "pot of gold!" What rare treasures are hidden there! Pictures to grace any page, for time is a gracious mordant and has etched into this beautiful perspective only such tender lines as melt and blend into a tender retrospect.

To me, no scene of college life can ever be quite common-place because of its beautiful setting, some little bit of nature's exquisite carving, which goes to make up the artistic ensemble of Eureka and her environment.

The town itself, now taking on the bustling pretense of a callow city, but then a bright, cleanly little village on the banks of Walnut Creek, nestled in the hollow of its silver crescent, like a star floating in the slender shallop of the new moon; its outlying slopes of meadow and farm land, and its encircling army of trees, always beautiful, whether plumed and helmeted in soft old pinks and greens, the ensignia of spring, or trailing red banners wrested from the outposts of the advancing frosts, or standing like grim sentinels, clad in glittering mail, which seem to catch and shiver the keen lances of the furious winter.

With such a store-house from which to draw the shining threads, the weaving of a bit of personal recollection would be delightful. But, alas for human frailty; memory is a very treacherous line with which to drag up history from a receding past. That melancholy touch, effacement in the past, that is the real charm of retrospect, causes to vanish many of the clear-cut lines and incisive accentuating touches of reality that make the value of history. I realize that my memories have felt

18

this tendering, corrosive touch of time. The ruined
castles of the past are picturesque but treacherous.
The scenes that were once actually lived out on
the stage of earnest action have faded into shifting
panoramas,while even the personnel,once so sharp-
ly silhouetted on the retentive brain of youth, have
slipped down into the current of years, and now
their images elude the grasp and break into a con-
fusion of eddying waves which defy all attempts
to fix them in pen pictures on these pages. I realize that now, if never before, one must descend
from dreams and vain imaginings. We must un-
harness the muses and saddle the patient little
burro, that sure-footed but plodding beast that
stands ready to carry one safely over the difficult reaches of literary wanderings.

Of course, scattered here and there among my
college memories are strong personalities, with
loving hearts and kindly eyes, that were photo-
graphed in such intensely happy lights that they
sank into the impressionable brain of youth and
still form indelible vignettes on memory's pages.
With such an one I played at X, Y, Z, and strove
for championship in the game of numbers. In
life's strange processes of transposing and elimina-
tion, the value of his equation has far exceeded
mine. Whether the unknown quantity was souls
to be winnowed for his Master's harvest, or diplomatic honors to be wrested from under "The Star

and Crescent," the result was always the same—plus, never minus.

Another, with whom we measured triangles and calculated logarithms, seems to have reached renown by logarithmic methods, while his classmates—plodders—have lumbered on by slower steps.

There was the sweet girl friend with whom I spent so many hours in the luxurious shade on the old campus, while we made bold attempts upon the intricacies of Virgil and Horace. The sweep of years has carried us wide apart, but I know that lullabys have curved her lips into a sweeter mold, than when "Arma Virumque Cano" rippled over them like the words of a nun's "paternoster," and declensions like "beads" through her waxen fingers. And that other—but I hesitate to penetrate farther, with cold, dissecting pen, into the sacred domain of friendship. It seems unfair and makes one feel akin to that Prince of Boredom—the kodak fiend—who steals upon you unawares and fixes you *forever* in postures well enough for quiet moments of solitude and privacy, but to be handed down into posterity, *never.*

Perhaps of all the experiences of a student at Eureka, the most enjoyable related to his or her connection with one of the literary societies. Of the four societies which graced the earlier years of Eureka, but one admitted girls. In this one, dear old Excelsior, I held my membership throughout my college days, and until it ceased to be a society. And of this one alone will this brief retrospect have time to write.

Living always almost within the shadow of Alma Mater, my memory fails, at this long range, to fix the actual time when mere *impressions* of Excelsior became actual experiences, but my most vivid recollections, from earliest childhood, of gala days in Eureka, were of commencement and Excelsior's annual exhibitions.

Excelsior! a name to conjure by in the realm of pleasant memories.

Do you not recall it, in letters of living green, above the old brown pulpit of the little white church that once stood where now are silent streets and the narrow, crowded homes of our loved and sainted dead?

Somewhere, between, above, below the very happy Latin collocations, "Scientia tenebras lam‡ pade discutit," and "Bonis artibus gloriam quaeramus," your eyes eagerly sought and lingered upon that simple talismanic word, "Excelsior!"

What wonders it wrought. How its charm extended miles away and, like the strange music of the "Pied Piper," drew crowds of people, in every sort of conveyance, scrubbed, brushed, and in holiday attire, till they filled the church, and, windows having been removed, each aperture was rapidly filled with a sea of faces, eagerly alert, patiently listening, while simple ballads tinkled from the queer, old-fashioned, maple-boxed piano, and sweet, shy girls read "The Queen o' the May" or original effusions. At last came the *"piece de resistance"* of the evening—the "colloquy"—a kind of dessert after the solid feast, for which all had reserved an ample corner in their innermost capacity for enjoyment.

Simple? Yes, but mawkish, never. Oh, happy, laughing, innocent girlhood! How easy to win laurels when love fills the judge's seat. It was our girls who sang or read, looking as fresh and fragrant as the rosebuds in their hair. It was our girls who searched garret and closet for quaint dresses, indescribable bonnets and ridiculous reticule, which formed the only stage effects permitted in that sacred place. It was our mothers, whose toil hardened fingers sought to regain their cunning, and patted and coaxed and stacked and powdered refractory locks, till miniatures of themselves, when, southern belles, they dispensed the hospitality of the Old Dominion, or the happy Blue Grass region.

This in the evolution of the histrionic art in Eureka was the very earliest period, and it is by no means to be supposed that the development and higher demands of public taste were not satisfactorily met by the bright, ambitious girls who

felt upon their tender hearts the burden of keeping up the dignity of Excelsior. The colloquy
developed from what at first was not much more
than comic dialogue into real drama, and that at
length became classic drama. The enthusiam
with which we threw ourselves into the study of
mythology made abiding impressions of Greek
and Latin deities and heroes, which years of subsequent reading have scarcely deepened. Many
the earnest conferences held, diligent the research,
and cunning the ingenuity displayed to evolve the
necessary costumes from the rather scanty mate·
rial to be found in a country village. But no
Fairy god mother in metamorphosis of Ashenputet
into the splendid princess ever put such base
material to such noble uses. After a wave of the
magic wand, which somehow youth always pos-
sesses, anything was forthcoming, from the classic
drapery of statuesque Juno, to the purple buskins
of Venus, or the martial equipment of Minerva.
The Diana who poised above the Agricultural
palace in the vanished dream city by the lake
bathed in a stream of transforming light, was not
half so wonderful to my maturer vision as was
our girlhood's interpretation of the divine hun-
tress, even though, to those "behind the scenes,"
the fluttering drapery, the silver crescent and
bended bow were wonderfully suggestive of tissue
paper and tinsel.

Nor was classic lore the only bank of deposit those girls were providing against a future contingency. Within the sacred precincts of our dear old hall what brave discussions of serious questions waxed warm in debate or *conversazione.* Was not every chair and every stiff geometrial figure in the familiar carpet historic ground? For on every one of them was not some important battle fought, some victory gained, some dismal defeat suffered?

How often in later years, when lost in wonder at the dignity and skill of some old Eureka girl in presiding at conventions, handling measures and parrying unwelcome questions, have I said, she received her first training in Roberts' Rules in old Excelsior.

The dear old hall! how the thought of it opens the floodgates of happy memories.

Has ever sunlight, in recent years, gleamed across your pathway half so golden as once sifted in at those western windows, through the warp and woof of yellow damask? Every feature of that spacious hall seems knit into the very fiber of our heartstrings, and when the changes of advancing years seemed to demand the settlement of the question, "Shall Excelsior disband?" to one at least of the defeated minority the prevalence of the "ayes" was not only an inglorious Waterloo, it was a very Actium, for in the swollen pride of ambitious youth this hauling down of the old banner was not only *surrender*, but fancied *disgrace.*   ELLA MYERS HUFFMAN.

Prescott, Iowa.

SOME RECENT REMINISCENCES.

Being one of the youngest of the children of Eureka College, my memories have not yet been hallowed by the rare, ecstatic tone of "Auld Lang Syne." Reality stands so near that she almost deceives me into thinking that I am still responding to the summons of the bell, and living the monotonous yet ever-varied life of the student.

But even at this early day my college experiences are grouping themselves, at their own will, and defiantly fade or deepen the colors with which I formerly clothed them.

The "perfectly terrible" ordeals of hair-breadth escapes from exposing my ignorance of lessons, the smooth sarcasm or cold disgust of professors (for which we could conjure no cause), and the examinations, with their foretaste of the day of Judgment—these things, which we thought could never be forgotten, persistently withdraw from view, and, like the sun's spots, can only be seen with lenses and colored glasses. But memory keeps polishing the happy times, the friendships, the social gatherings, the walks, the growth of ambitions and fair ideals.

When I entered Eureka College in 1886 I was

at the formative age of fifteen, and my tastes and character were plastic.

I spent four busy and pleasant years there before graduation, and two years after.

So most truly has my Eureka College experience been "the fair seed-time" of my life.

My entrance to the school was co-incident with the presidency of Dr. Carl Johann, and my whole student life seemed tinged with the spirit of innovation which he brought with him.

During this time we celebrated the first Arbor Day with showers of eloquence which completely unnerved several trees and caused premature death. But grandly has our Edmund Burke tree flourished, which was rapturously cheered and exhorted by the poetry of Maud McDonald and the flowery words of T. A. Boyer.

During my junior year the Eureka College Pegasus spread forth its wings, with R. E. Hieronymus and O. W. Stewart as literary editors. We also started a successful lecture course, and the first oratorical contest was held.

The class of 1890, consisting of eight of "the finest and smartest" boys to be found, and myself, were also imbued with this spirit of innovation. We it was who unceremoniously were "fired" from Prof. Conklin's room one morning over a slight altercation concerning a problem in mechanics, who picked up our shattered dignity and withdrew to the chapel, organized our class, swooped down on the "Bon Ton Restaurant" that night and took out our spite on oysters. We were the first class to deliver a course of lectures in chapel, forty-five minutes long (their chief glory). We also set the example of wearing class colors. But that reminds me of the day when the presumptuous Calculus class challenged us to a game of base-ball. Of course we had to accept, being Seniors who were expected to carry courage on our sleeves. I was delegated to bear the colors, and when I appeared with them lusty cheers and dignified whoops went up from the diamond.

My pride, baloon-like, sought the ether—but alas! short-lived was my triumph. For——(But, of course, we were pre-eminently an intellectual class, rather than athletic).

My only experience with boarding halls was in 1888-89, when Lida's Wood was new. Many visions arise with the memory of that year which I must restrain. I have never heard that I was ever considered anything but a quiet, law-abiding student; but my consciousness is not without certain recollections of .larks and adventures, which, since the time of my graduation is not long past, and since I am still a resident of Eureka, prudence demands should be kept out of print.

But as an example of the *esprit de corps*, I will mention one incident. My room-mate and I had been the recipients of a barrel of nuts and apples from home. One evening we invited as large a number of girls as the room would accommodate to a feast. About bed-time we heard the ravishing symphonies of a band of serenaders, and scampered down stairs "to peep." After awhile we returned to the room and hastily retired. But immediate developments caused us to arise as hastily, only to discover beneath the sheets the hulls of the nuts we had so generously sacrificed.

Whether this was an expression of gratitude of the girls who had partaken, or the envy of those who were not invited, we have never discovered.

It was at Lida's Wood that we used to comfort those suffering with tooth-ache, measles or other prevalent fads, by singing, "Oh, turn you, oh, turn you, for why will you die?"

There also our landlady set aside the hours from two to four Sunday afternoons for "meditation hours," and we took turns fastening each other in the closet, deeming the seclusion and quiet of that place the most congenial to meditation.

An incident of my sophomore year which is indelibly stamped in memory, was my first experience in teaching. Prof. Herrick, at that time Professor of Mathematics, was obliged to be absent one day, and conferred upon me the honor of hearing the Geometry class. I had studied it the year before, and by a diligent furbishing again mastered the exercise. Being rather timid, I took my station in the rear of the room (ostensibly to see better the figures on the board). Everything was going smoothly until I called upon a noted college dunce for a demonstration. To my surprise he started out, but soon was in labyrinthian toils. I attempted to help him out, and continued until I had given the entire demonstration. I was congratulating myself on having made it very plain, when the moment my voice died away, he fastened a vacant gaze upon me and laconically uttered, "Mom?" A general explosion followed, and my self-possession had gone to the winds.

These and other oft-remembered experiences are only random threads which give light and color. But the ground-work of the tapestry of my college discipline I have not attempted to portray, nor have I sought to separate its closely woven figures.

No spot is so dear to me as Eureka. My happiest associations cluster about it. In rambles about its shady streets and neighboring rustic haunts, I have dreamed most pleasant dreams. Here is the birth-place and nourishing lap of ambitions and ideals, of happy friendships, of love's sweet dream and blest reality. My class-mates and associates are young in after-graduate life. Our future is yet to be unfolded. Our hopes and aspirations have not burned into cold, gray ashes on the hearth-stone of life's experience, but are still rainbow-tinted and dew-laden.

For the sake of our precious *Alma Mater* may all good purposes and high endeavors of her children come to bountiful fruition, and in adaptation of Rip Van Winkle's ever-ready toast, "May she live long and prosper."

ELLA SEASS STEWART.

MY MEMORIES.

In the getting up of a "History of Eureka College," I have been offered some space in its pages. But what shall I say? In my memory Eureka holds a sacred place. The young men and women with whom I was associated there will never be forgotten. At the same time, my whole life there seems a good deal like a dream —a something I have read about in books rather · than a something I have lived.

It has now been a third of a century since my connection with Eureka College was severed. Into that third of a century all the activities of my life have been crowded. A great war absorbed all my thoughts during the years immediately following my life at Eureka. It will not seem strange, perhaps, when I say that my college life is to me like a distant landscape, its details all obliterated.

Having led a very active life, it is not surprising that its struggles, successes and failures have crowded out of memory the lesser things of earlier life. Mine was not an easy lot while in college, and while I have no doubt that I enjoyed myself as well as the average student, and had my share of the fun and of the folly of student life, as I remember there is nothing in all of it worth writing about.

But I do remember Prof. Fisher. He was an earnest, conscientious, pains-taking teacher, the ideal drill-master of preparatory scholars. He was diffident as a girl, and could blush like one. I seldom saw him lose his temper or get discouraged in his efforts to bring his students forward in their work. Eureka owes a debt of gratitude to one who labored so faithfully for the college in the days of its struggles.

I remember to have assisted in taking care of him during a dangerous illness, and found him just as patient, just as considerate and uncomplaining in sickness as I had found him in the class-room. I do not think he inspired close friendships, or impressed his own characteristics upon his students to any great extent, but his quiet dignity and his conscientiousness made such impressions that long years afterward his students delighted to recall them.

Looking back to my college days, the scene at the old meeting-house, when the good people of Eureka bade us volunteer boys all good-bye as we were about to enter the army, is the one scene so effectively burned into my memory that it can never be obliterated.

Whenever I think of Eureka, I think of that parting, and of the home-coming three years later. I also think of sitting down behind an old elm tree in the evening of that home-coming, and of having a good cry at the thought that it was the last of my Eureka life. But these are not reminiscences of college life; they are rather the memories of meeting and parting.

J. HARVEY ROWELL.

19

MISCELLANEOUS.

THE CHURCH AT EUREKA.

The history of Eureka College would not be complete without some account of the church here, to serve as a sort of historic background.

Very many of the early settlers of Walnut Grove were members of the Christian Church. These soon began to meet regularly for worship, first in the several log cabin homes, or in groves, or barns, and later, when a schoolhouse had been built they met in that.

On an appointed day in April of 1832, thirteen of these met in the house of their preacher, John Oatman, and organized the church. These were, John Oatman, Nancy Oatman, Daniel Travis, Rhoda Travis, Joshua Woosley, Mary Woosley, Samuel Arnold, Rebecca Arnold, Eliza Oatman, Joseph Oatman, Clement Oatman, Jesse Oatman, Hardin Oatman.

John Oatman was chosen elder, and Daniel Travis and Joshua Woosley deacons. All these have fallen asleep except one; Hardin Oatman is still living in Missouri.

In a very short time the membership was more than doubled by other Disciples already in the community uniting with them. Converts were made also, and the numbers increased for several years. Then some disturbing influences arose that checked the growth for awhile. Meantime Elder Oatman moved away, and the church became somewhat disorganized.

During the years 1834, '35, '36, there came into the community with their families, William Davenport, a minister, B. J. Radford, Sr., Ben Major, Elijah Dickinson, E. B. Myers and A. M. Myers. These had all been active Christians before coming here, and of course continued active in church work.

About 1836 a partial re-organization of the church was made, and Ben Major elected elder. In 1837 Elijah Dickinson was also called to the eldership, and B. J. Radford, Sr., made one of the deacons.

Revival meetings were held from time to time, occasionally in some thick grove, but often on the broad threshing-floor of one of the few big barns of that time, temporary seats being provided. These, of course, were always held in the warm season. There was a forenoon and an afternoon service, daily, separated by about two hours for basket-dinner and recreation. At the close of the afternoon service, all returned to their farm homes to attend to the chores and prepare for the next

day's services, for there was no town here then, nor
for a long time after.

It was not till the summer of 1846 that the
church felt ready to provide for itself a house of
worship. Then "The Old Meeting House" was
built—the first in the community—a frame one,
facing the west, with two doors in front, and a
boxed-up black walnut pulpit between them. It
stood just within the north limit of the cemetery,
about where the Soldiers' Monument now stands,
the lot having been given for church and burial
uses by Elder Ben Major. Happy were those devoted people when at last they had a church house
of their own, built wholly by their own labor and
with their own means, earned with difficulty in
their pioneer poverty. The prevailing spirit of
the church from the first had been enterprising,
earnest, devout. Many were the meetings for devotion held within those consecrated walls, and
more than a few were held there to counsel together for devising ways and means for building up an
institution of learning much better than the common school.

And God's blessing rested upon these. The institution was established and developed year by
year. The church increased more and more. The
relation between the two was so close that their
interests were almost identical from the first, and
they have so continued.

With passing years other changes came. In 1856 the T. P. & W. railroad was built through and the village was laid out. Soon the congregation outgrew the house. Then a new church house had to be built, and built down town, and in 1863 the present brick structure was raised. " The Old Meeting House " about which had gathered so many sweet and tender memories, was sold, and passed to mercantile uses, and at present forms part of Vandyke's flour and feed store. The only part of it still in church use, so far as I know, is the cushioned walnut frame on which the Bible rested. This was transferred to the new house, and still crowns the pulpit and bears up before the people the Word of God. Long may its good service continue.

The church has grown until it now has about 850 members, and is prospering numerically and spiritually under the fostering care of its minister with the following board of officers.

ELDERS AND TRUSTEES: John Darst, E. W. Dickinson, D. R. Howe, C. B. Pickerill, N. B. Crawford, G. W. Hootman and W. T. Barnett.

DEACONS: W. S. Allen, D. P. Harber, Jo Major, F. M. Hoyt, J. A. McGuire, F. A. Musick, E. S. Cambe, S. W. Hall, F. M. Darst, H. N. Herrick, R. E. Hieronymus, W. H. Davis, W. W. Pratz, A. J. Mourer and A. W. Smith.

DEACONESSES: Mrs. Barbara Hamilton, Mrs. B.

D. Meek, Mrs. Jane C. Davidson, Mrs. W. S. Allen. MINISTER: W. H. Cannon.

It has again quite outgrown its house of worship, and is now considering what it would better do in the way of enlargement—whether add to the present building, or tear this one down and build a larger one.

It has ever been blessed with good preaching service, but never with what is known as pastoral work till the spring of 1868, when A. S. Hayden responded to a call to take charge of it. He remained three years. Then for a while there were several short pastorates, with periods of preaching only intervening between them. At the beginning of 1886, J. G. Waggoner, a graduate of Eureka College, was induced to undertake this ministry, and has just now, at the beginning of 1894, resigned, and W. H. Cannon, also a graduate of the College, has taken up the work.

AMOS SUTTON HAYDEN.

This genial, faithful minister of the gospel, was born in Youngstown, Ohio, September 17, 1813. He was the youngest of eight children, seven of whom were sons, and was also the father of eight children, seven of whom were sons. From early boyhood he was studious, and devoted much of his time to reading useful books. Was especially fond of religious works.

His religious convictions were early and deep. His parents were members of the Baptist Church, and he was brought up in that belief, but was never satisfied with the doctrines of that church. In his fifteenth year he heard the gospel preached by Walter Scott, by whom he was immersed, and soon after began to speak in public. In 1832 he began to hold protracted meetings. In 1840 he located with the church at Collamer, Ohio, as its pastor, and in 1850, when Western Reserve Eclectic Institute was founded, at Hiram, Ohio, he was unanimously elected its Principal. After seven years successfully devoted to that work, he resigned, and returned to his church work in Collamer·

(298)

Early in 1868 he accepted a call from the church at Eureka, Illinois, where he spent three years in earnest, faithful work in the congregation and among the college students. He was a man of refined nature and of fervent devotion, and his influence always and everywhere was excellent. He was much beloved for his work's sake.

In 1871 he again returned to Collamer, where he spent the remaining ten years of his beautiful, useful life, ministering to the church with which he had lived so long, then entered into his rest.

JOHN GARLAND WAGGONER.

The subject of this sketch, so intimately connected with our religious, missionary and educational work in Illinois for more than twenty years, was born in Moultrie county, Illinois, about eight miles west of Mattoon, April 22, 1844. His father, Edward M. Waggoner, of German extraction, was born in Rutherford county, North Carolina, and with his father's family, chiefly for their anti-slavery views, came to Illinois in 1829, settling in Moultrie county, about seven miles south of Sullivan. The older Waggoners were active in the war of 1812, and made enterprising pioneers for the new West. Susan Adaline Waggoner, the mother of J. G., was the daughter of Mr. Garland Simms, another pioneer, from Owen county, Kentucky. She died the spring after J. G. was born, and his father died a year later.

Before his father's death, the orphan boy had been committed to his aunt, Nancy M. Waggoner. In 1848 she was married to Mr. A. H. Edwards. In their happy, intelligent, industrious home he grew to manhood, in the enjoyment of every favor of an own son. Mr. Edwards was well

(300)

educated, and early inspired in all his family high and noble purposes for life. His only living son, Elder Thomas Edwards, is an able Christian minister of Gilroy, Cal.

During his childhood and youth J. G. attended the country school in winter and worked with his uncle in his tan-yard and on his little farm in summer. His early purpose to become a minister of the Gospel was ever his ruling purpose.

In the spring of '64 he formed the acquaintance of Elder J. W. Tyler, the father of the well-known Christian ministers, B. B. and J. Z Tyler. By father Tyler's counsel and the encouragement of his uncle Edwards, he entered Eureka College in the fall of '64. Want of means made his attendance somewhat irregular, but, by making fires, sawing wood, teaching school and preaching, he was enabled to graduate in the classical course June 6, '72. Three years later Eureka College conferred upon him the degree of Master of Arts.

Bro. Waggoner has been twice married; the first time to Miss Sarah E. Cox, of Mattoon, April 4, 1867; and the second time to Miss Ann A. Fouke, of Shelbyville, Illinois, January 28, '86. He feels inexpressible gratitude to God for such faithful, noble and true companions, who have shared so patiently his burdens, and added so much to his success. True, a minister's wife often has the harder lot, but her reward awaits her at her Master's hand.

Bro. Waggoner has four living children—William H., Edward F., Harvey G., and Susan M.—all of whom have obeyed the Gospel.

He was baptized by Elder B. W. Henry, August 18, 1859. His people generally were Predestinarian Baptists, but his uncle Edwards and wife were prominent pioneer Disciples. He began early to take some part in prayer-meetings and preached his first sermon in the spring of '65. He was formally ordained by authority of the church at Princeton, Illinois, April 16, 1868, Elders George McManis and G. W. Mapes officiating. This was during his first special work, which lasted but one year. During this year he held his first protracted meeting, when about fifteen became obedient to the faith.

From 1868 to 1870 he was at Lostant, Illinois, preaching and teaching school. He then re-entered Eureka College. Before his graduation the church at Harristown extended him a unanimous call to become its minister. During the following five years he served this church, which was about doubled in membership, its first young people's society was organized and several mission Sunday-schools were conducted.

His health giving way, he resigned, spent two months in the Rocky Mountains, and in the fall of

'77 was called to preach for the church in Shelby-ville, Illinois. During the following five years the church, notwithstanding many deaths and remov-als, about doubled its membership, and all the de-partments of the church were greatly strengthened. In the fall of '82 his wife's health induced him to resign and seek for her a milder climate. After ample provision for her in the home of a dear friend in Knoxville, Tenn., he took charge of the church at Greencastle, Ind. After fifteen months' work here, during which the church prospered, he returned to Illinois, locating at Pittsfield. He staid here a little less than two years, and in January, 1886, he yielded to the call of the church in Eureka, where he labored during the following eight years. This last pastorate he regards as the most fruitful that he has yet had, although his work has been uniformly successful and prosper-ous. He regarded the field in Eureka peculiar-ly favorable. Its removal from the temptations of city life, the intelligence of its citizens, drawn together by Eureka's rare educational facilities, the large company of young people gathered from our best homes, a willingness to work on the part of the people, an active and wise official board, and good evangelistic help, he regards as chief ele-ments in the church's prosperity. During the eight years there were about one hundred per-sons all the time on regular standing commit-

tees; the Christian Association, the Bible Workers, the Senior and Junior Christian Endeavor
Societies were formed; the two Auxiliary Missionary Societies, the Mission Band and the Ladies' Aid did their best work; the Sunday-school
greatly increased and about 1,035 persons were
added to the church. January 1st, '94, he resigned
in Eureka to take up the work in Buffalo, N.
Y. Besides his regular pastoral and pulpit duties he found time to foster many public enterprises, beyond the borders of the church, to which
his brethren called him.   He was active in the
Woodford County Christian Co-operation, serving
as its chairman, and one of the prime movers in
organizing the Ninth Congressional District for
missionary work, and in merging into it the
county work.

He was president of the State missionary convention in '85, and has served as one of its board
about seven years.   In the board he was regular at its meetings, and has served about four
years on the Permanent Fund Committee, and
seven years on its Students' Aid Committee.
Since the organization of the Illinois Christian
Encampment Association, he has been on its
board, several times president, and always active
in the preparation of its extensive program.   He
was one of the originators of the Bible Students'
Aid Fund, one of its most liberal contributors,

and he solicited in cash and pledges for its use more than $6,000.

He served on the Board of Trustees of Eureka College about six years. He has ever been one of its warmest friends, and is now president of its Alumni Association. To build and equip the Burgess Memorial Hall, he spent several weeks in the field, securing in cash and pledges about $9,000. He was a true brother to every professor and a warm friend of all the students.

He is a life director of the General Christian Missionary Convention, attends the annual meetings of the board and the convention, frequently serves on important committees, and for two years has been vice president of the convention. He is a life member of the Foreign Christian Missionary Society, and takes great interest in its work.

He has served several years on the State Sunday-school Board, and acted as president at some of its conventions. He has been the leading spirit in inaugurating and carrying forward Christian Normal Sunday-school Studies for teachers and Bible students among the Disciples.

He is a frequent contributor to our religious journals and to local papers. He has written several tracts; "What Must I do to be Save l?" and "A Plea for the Soul" having the largest circulation.

As a preacher Bro. Waggoner is clear, careful,
20

earnest and practical. Every sermon seems to inspire to better living or a clearer conception of the truth. His sermons are fresh without being sensational. He has held several very successful meetings, but has not worked much as an evangelist, his efforts being rather to keep the church for which he labors so full of life and warmth that the Lord may add to it daily the saved. In this he succeeds.

As a pastor he is regarded a model. His unusual freedom from favoritism, his large sympathy for the poor and afflicted, his knowledge of the temptations of the rich, his high appreciation of talent and his patience with ignorance, make him at once the trusted companion of all classes and ages. He spends much time among his people, not as a mere visitor, but as a true friend and brother, seeking to know, comfort, inspire and direct the spiritual life of all for the glory of the Lord.

Bro. Waggoner attributes his success and usefulness, whatever they are, to a happy combination of circumstances and influences far beyond his own ordering. The piety, industry and faith instilled in his childhood, in the home where the Lord cast his lot, lie at the foundation. He feels that he has always had the prayers of the church, and tries to live in close fellowship with the Father who has so mys-

1 A. S. Hayden.   3 W. H. Cannon.

       2 J. G. Waggoner.

teriously guarded, preserved and directed his life. The counsel of his brethren of experience and wisdom has been always most welcome and fruitful of good. For help and guidance in everything he looks to the Lord, believing that to be strong in the Lord and in the power of his might is the best of all strength.

WILLIAM H. CANNON.

W. H. Cannon is of German and Irish ancestry, and was born near Pittsfield, Ill., August 1, 1862. He attended the public schools of the community until he was eighteen years of age, when he entered Eureka College, where he completed the classical course in June, 1884. In 1889 he received from the same institution the degree of A. M. He attended the Bible department of Drake University for a little while, but lacked one year of graduation. From childhood he has had a desire to be a preacher, and his work in college had that aim constantly in view. December 31, 1882, he preached his first sermon, and was ordained by the church at Eureka in June, 1884. Immediately after leaving college he located at Sterling, Ill. Besides Sterling he has had pastorates at Illiopolis, Lincoln, Lexington, and now ministers to the church at Eureka.

In addition to his regular ministerial work he has been interested in Sunday-school work, and has been a member of the Executive Board of the Illinois Christian S. S. Association for four years, and is at present Corresponding Secretary and Treasurer of that organization.

ELDER H. D. PALMER.

Henry D. Palmer was a native of South Carolina, but early in life removed to Tennessee. He was a citizen of the latter State at the time of the *Louisiana Purchase*, and went as a volunteer to aid in the ceremony of unfurling the national flag at New Orleans.

As a Christian minister, he was an efficient worker with the early pioneers of the reformation headed by Barton W. Stone and Alexander Campbell.

In 1816 he removed to Illinois, locating near Vincennes, where he renounced all affiliation with American slavery by a formal emancipation of all his servants, believing the institution to be one of violence, unsupported by Christian principles.

About 1820 he removed to Indiana, and was a citizen of that State until 1835, when he removed to Illinois, locating in that portion of Putnam now included within the boundaries of Marshall county. In 1847 he represented his county in the convention called to revise the constitution of the State.

In 1849 he was nominated as one of the original

trustees of Walnut Grove Academy, but declined
to accept the appointment on account of his advanced age.

More than fifty years of his long life were zealously devoted to the work of the Christian ministry. At Cincinnati, Ohio, in 1849, he assisted in
organizing the first General Christian Missionary
Society. In 1850 he assisted in organizing the first
Christian Missionary Society of Illinois, and was
elected the first president of that body. Many
young men through his influence were induced to
enter the Christian ministry: About 1850 he became acquainted with O. A. Burgess, explained
to him the gospel of Christ as taught by the promoters of the Current Reformation, received his
confession, baptized him, induced him to become
a Christian preacher, and subsequently to enter
Bethany College. He died during the first year
of the great civil war, being eighty-one years old,
having long been known throughout all the Christian Churches of Illinois as " Old Father Palmer."

MRS. O. A. BURGESS.

MRS. O. A. BURGESS.

The journey of life was begun by Nannie J. Ledgerwood on a farm in Marshall county, Illinois, near the town of Washburn. Her parents were James and Polly (Palmer) Ledgerwood. Her national descent is English-French, with a trace of Scotch and Dutch. She obeyed the Gospel under the preaching of Elder John Lindsey in August, 1852, and immediately after went to Walnut Grove and became a member of the church there, and a student of the Academy, remaining one session, till July, 1853. Was married Oct. 17, 1854, to O A. Burgess. and during the more than twenty-seven years of their united lives she was his ever-sought and safe counselor and devoted help-meet in all his efforts to uplift humanity.

They were living in Indianapolis when the Christian Woman's Board of Missions was organized, in 1874, with headquarters in that city. She was chosen its treasurer at that time, and has been prominently connected with that work ever since. In October, 1880, she was elected president of the Board, but removing to Chicago the following spring, she resigned that office.

(311)

After the death of her husband, in 1882, she lived with her parents in Forest, Illinois, several years. In August, 1884, she was called by the Woman's Board of Illinois to be their State president, and was continued in that position till her removal to Indianapolis, in December, 1888.

She was chairman of a deputation sent by the Board in January, 1887, to visit its mission on the island of Jamaica, to inquire into its condition and needs, and to report on all phases of the work there. The trip occupied about three months, ten weeks having been spent on that luxuriant " Land of Springs." The report was published in the July number of the *Missionary Tidings* of that year.

Shortly after her return to Indianapolis, in 1888, she was elected vice-president of the C. W. B. M., and in October, 1890, was promoted to the presidency, which position she still occupies.

When the Christian Woman's Board of Missions was invited to participate in the Woman's Auxiliary Congress held in connection with the Columbian Exposition at Chicago, May 15-22, 1893, she was unanimously chosen as its representative, and by request of the Congress Committee gave a concise history of the organization, methods and work accomplished by the association.

She is the founder of Burgess Memorial Hall. Her noble husband, following his Master, went about doing good while he lived. When called to his rest, she nobly sought to build a monument to his memory better than bronze, more enduring than marble. As college professor and president, also as minister of the Gospel, his work was very largely among young people, leading them in wisdom's ·way and inspiring them with noblest purposes. Therefore it seemed fitting that the memorial should be in the interest of education— a continuance of his life work. And so. after several years of careful consideration as to where it would best be built, counseling from time to time with a number of her long-time, tried friends, Mrs. Burgess decided to make her offering to the Board of Trustees of Eureka College. This was accepted, the Board agreeing to furnish an equal amount for the building.

Thus we have Burgess Memorial Hall, where O. A. Burgess, being dead, yet speaks, by the wise action of his devoted Christian wife. May the young people gathering year by year within its walls be led to emulate the noble life and generous deeds of Mrs. Burgess.

ALUMNI REUNION.

B. J. RADFORD.

As the coolness of spring mid the glories of June
  Still lingers to temper its heat;
As the song of the morning still echoes at noon
  From the depths of some shady retreat;
As the breath of a garden o'er wearisome ways
  Comes wafted full many a mile;
So memory fragrant of dear olden days,
In the heart of *our* noontide still fondly delays,
  All our labor and care to beguile.

What an Eden indeed was our garden of youth
  As we gathered its fair trees about,
Plucking flowers of fancy and apples of truth
  Till destiny hustled us out,
Silly Adams and Eves, to a desolate place
  Of repentance and labor and pains,
Where we must, in the sweat of both body and face,
Root up brambles and thorns if we e'er get a place
  Upon which to raise apples or Cains.

What a queer brood of innocents were we, indeed!
  Not *abroad;* for the great field of life,
With its woodland and plain, with its mountain and mead,
  With its seasons of peace and of strife,
Was *terra incognita*, never a whit
  Like the one which our fancy portrayed,
Where all was romantic and happy and fit,
Where shadows for contrast would now and then flit,
  But the sunshine persistently stayed.

(314)

How we fed on the knowledge that puffeth men up
 Till our sphere became painfully small;
How we swigged at the wine in philosophy's cup
 Till we thought we had swallowed it all!
Undigested confections of Latin and Greek
 Swelled us out to an alderman's girth,
And we smile as we think of the whimsical freak
Of conceit, that in us a most marvelous streak
 Of good luck had o'ertaken the earth.

The embryo orator, gloomy and grand,
 Incarnation of all that was best
In Demosthenes, Webster and Burke, graced our band
 With an eloquence never suppressed;
For he tackled each theme of religion or state
 With a confidence born of—well, yes;
Of a large inexperience, plenty of prate,
And a roving phrenologist rubbing his pate
 With a fondly prophetic caress.

Where now are those tones that were destined to fill
 With their thunders the capitol's dome;
Whose echoes should waken a virtuous thrill
 From the palace to poverty's home?
O sad profanation of Mercury's powers!
 Even now, as the summer winds blow,
With the rustling of corn and the odor of flowers,
They bring the lost tones of that statesman of ours,—
 Stentorian "Gee!" "Haw!" "Wo-ho!"

Our philosopher, too; you remember him now,
 With his eye upon vacancy fixed,
And a skeptical air of importance; for how
 With his genius for getting things mixed,—
Always looking within for what should be without,
 Finding emptiness reigning supreme,—
Could he fail to be tangled in mazes of doubt

As to God or his wisdom, and loftily scout
Immortality's hope as a dream.

Not a secret of all of her intricate plan
  Could nature conceal from *his* gaze;
He could trace every step from the monad to man,
  And his hand could unerringly blaze
Through eternity's wilderness every road
  Evolution had taken or missed,
And forth in her footsteps he eagerly strode,
Unearthing of fossils and facts a huge load—
  For philosophy's mill a tough grist.

But look at him now, after labor-crowned years
  Have sobered ambition's wild pace;
No affected profundity ever appears
  In the lines of that strong, honest face; .
And those firmly-set lips never more repeat
  The old vaporing language of doubt;
For the skeptical pride and the shallow conceit—
Twin follies with mischief forever repletĕ—
  Like the measles, have worked themselves out.

And there was our scholar, as pale as a ghost,
  And as pulseless, and sombre, and dread;
For so long had he dwelt with the shadowy host
  Of earth's mighty and erudite dead,
That every blood-nurtured passion was gone,
  Even pedantry famished and died,
And our slow-creeping bookworm in solitude lone,
By some vermifuge law, had unconsciously grown
  To a chrysalis, withered and dried.

But a time of reviving the seasons brought round:—
  Some rich relative died, as he ought;
O, physiological secrets profound,
  What a metamorphosis was wrought!

By the magical breath of that life-giving spring
  The sealed fountains were opened again,
And out of that shriveled, unpromising thing,
Came fashion's gay butterfly, now on the wing
  In pleasure's fair summer domain.

Notwithstanding some poet has rhymingly said
  That along toward the evening of life
All approaching events cast their shadows ahead,
  'Tis not true of its morning of strife;
For our limb of the law had not even the germ
  Of that greatness to which he has grown;
But having served out his collegiate term,
  Seeking bread but receiving a stone,
When the father complained of the job that was done
In the polishing off of his favorite son,
The faculty pleaded in learning's behalf,
"We cast in the gold and there came out this calf."

But no matter just now who at first was to blame;
For he holds a first mortgage on honor and fame;
He has summoned the future, replevined the past,
And if cheated of honor and glory at last,
Will appeal to posterity's court, and compel
All the present to swear, and reluctantly tell
The whole truth, that for calibre never before
Had history known such a wonderful *bore*.

Our collegiate blue-stocking never, 'tis plain,
  Could have sprung from terrestrial mud;
Some etherial essence in every vein
  Took the place of our sin-tainted blood.
She would breakfast on Bacon—Lord Francis, I mean,—
  While at dinner-time Lamb was her food;
She could sup upon Sunset's evanishing scene,
When a Goldsmith enthroned her romance's fair queen,
  With a crown of the classical Hood.

But her heart was as frigid to love's gentle ray,—
  If indeed such a thing she could boast,—
As the heart of a polar-born iceberg, away
  In midwinter Labrador's coast.
Of the reprobate gods in mythology's list
  She thought Cupid decidedly worst;
While men were a sadly inferior grist,
Who would scarcely have been very grievously missed
  Had they never been made from the first.

Now search through the coveted tablets of fame,
  Or annals of commoner kind;
Not a lingering trace of her spinsterly name
  In the polyglot record you'll find.
By the magical "presto" of time's hidden art
  The old total depravity's gone;
Sincerity carries lost vanity's part;
Woman's sphere has been found in a motherly heart,—
  Love's proudest and peacefulest throne.

Our apprentice at high theological art,
  In his resolute struggle with sin,
Found so much of it lodged in his own wayward heart,
  That it kept him employed within;
So finding no time ammunition to glean,
  Nor cartridges make of his own,
He would load up from Spurgeon, or Beecher, or e'en
Any well-supplied secular truth magazine,
  When he thought it would never be known.

But the arduous labor of conning by rote,
  With its great intellectual strain,
Resulted at last in that dread sore throat,
  Which is ever the clergyman's bane.
But the practical point, whether physic or law,
  Should receive his illustrious aid,
He has never decided; for if he should draw

His conclusion in favor of one, he foresaw
    That the glory of tother must fade.

But that old-fashioned fellow who worked his way through,
    Who mended, and stitched and kept bach;
Whose clothes looked as if they had never been new,
    And his head like a weather-worn thatch;
Who made his own speeches, content with the pay
    Which duty unfailingly brings;
Respected his teachers, and studied away;
    Who was always in class, and was guilty, they say,
    Of a great many other odd things.

What of him? Well not much, I am bound to confess,
    In the eyes of the sycophant horde,
Who worship the man in another man's dress
    When it's better than they can afford;
But he makes a full hand in the vineyard of God,
    In a steady and every-day gait;
And pruning, or dressing, or turning the sod,
Or sent forth on errands of mercy to plod,
    He is learning to labor and wait.

But for Simon Pure greatness, or genuine gush,
    Our poet could discount them all.
And he soared aloft in his young fancy's flush
    Till the world seemed contemptibly small.
He affected the ways of the learned and great,
    Eccentricities, virtuous or vile;
A Shakespearean air and a Byronish gait;
And the nursery song to the star he'd inflate
    In hyper-Johnsonian style:—

" Coruscate, glow, and scintillate, O, Gem!
    Thou macrocosmic jewel in the diadem
Of umbral-robed, penumbral polonaised queen Night!
    The spectrum-painting, ether-propagated light,
When on the retina it thrills my optic nerve,

As in thy parabolic or elliptic curve
Thou sailest through the ultra-empyrean deep,—
Wakes wide-eyed wonder from her Rip Van Winkle sleep.

" When Phoebus with his phosphorescent photosphere
Of incandescent hydrogen doth disappear,
And yield his high chryselephantine throne to fair queen
    Night,
Whilst occidental splendors vanish from the sight;
When haughty exogens with inflorescence crowned,
And humble endogens low-bending to the ground,
Receive alike the sacrament of chrismal dew,
Whilst pageants of nocturnal glories pass in view,
Thy luminiferous vibrations kindly show
Itinerant pedestrians, their way below."

But he got safely off, somewhat limping and sore,
    From a fall from Parnassian heights,
And nothing could ever inveigle him more
    To venture such dangerous flights.
He has harnessed his runaway Pegasus now
    To a cart upon life's rugged way,
To help on with the burdens that cruelly bow
Us all down to earth, and he finds that, somehow
    It is better than fancy's wild play.

Our dandy, who doted on colors and clothes,
    Goes clad in the garments of toil,
While Rusticus, grown to a pedagogue, loathes
    To be known as a son of the soil.
Mr. Scapegrace, in folly so hopelessly lost,
    In an orthodox deacon is found;
But lament for our Sanctus, whose conscience was tossed
On the sea of conviction with foaming waves bossed,
    Till finally ship-wrecked and drowned.

Time disguises us all for the strange masquerades
We must enter as life falls to evening shades;

Raven ringlets and tresses are turning to gray,
 "The silver is tinting the gold ;"
Earth's beauty and loveliness hasten away,
And like mortals constructed of commonest clay,
 We are all growing ugly and old.

But the prophecies going before on us all,
 And our great expectations, were vain
As the mocking mirages that temptingly fall
 On the vision o'er wide desert plain ;
For our lives are as full of fantastical change
 As the ill-fated scenes of a dream,

Till we waken at last to the consciousness strange
 That none of us are what we seem ;
But are only the parts, without meaning beside,
 Of some infinite, wonderful whole,
As we mingle, and gleam in the light, and divide,
Till we fall in the shadow unheeded to hide,
 While the years their kaleidoscope roll.

But sometime, in the bounds of a new universe,
 From this fateful duality free,
Which compels every blessing to wed with a curse ;
 Where wide as eternity's sea,
Love is gladly divorced from the termagant hate,
 And pleasure from wan-visaged pain ;
Where Vice never more with Virtue shall mate,
 May we mingle our colors again,
Born of Beauty, the glorious bride of the light,
Of a day that shall never be wedded to night.
 21

HISTORICAL SKETCH OF ABINGDON COLLEGE.

P. H. Murphy and J. C. Reynolds opened a school in Abingdon, Ill., on the first Monday in April, 1853. They called it Abingdon Academy. Their purpose from the beginning was to make a first-class college of it. They were young men, full of zeal and the spirit of Bethany, both having sat at the feet of Alexander Campbell. Their ambition was high and holy. They earnestly desired to do a large thing for the good of humanity and for the glory of God. The school was conducted in the Christian Church, a plain frame building, until it was chartered and organized as Abingdon College.

The school grew rapidly, soon crowding the house and necessitating a third teacher. J. P. Roach was engaged, and taught for some time. He was a good man and very popular.

As soon as possible the first college building, a plain three-story brick, was erected at a cost of about $10,000, at that time a heavy burden for the people who furnished the money.

The Faculty, when the new building was occupied, consisted of P. H. Murphy, President; J. C. Reynolds, Professor of Languages; J. W. Butler, Professor of Mathematics; A. B. Murphy, Professor Natural Sciences.

J. W. Butler and A. B. Murphy were also young men and full of the spirit of Bethany, they too having been brought up at the feet of Alexander Campbell.

The first graduates of Abingdon College were two young ladies, Miss Meron Mahew and Miss Fannie Davis. They were good students and noble young women. The first class of young men receiving the degree of Bachelor of Arts were five in number: Adoniram Judson Thomson, William Decatur Stewart, Christopher Columbus Button, Francis Marion Button, and William Griffin. There were both brains and thorough scholarship in this class of Christian young men. A. J. Thompson is an eminent teacher and a fine preacher of the gospel. W. D. Stewart was an able and eloquent preacher. He died of consumption before reaching the meridian of life. C. C. Button and F. M. Button were both very superior teachers, but both fell victims to that fell destroyer, consumption, after a short, brilliant career. William Griffin is both preacher and teacher, and has filled the position of Superintendent of Schools in Hancock county, Ill., for many years. A college that can turn out such a class as that deserves a better fate than that which overtook Abingdon in after years.

J. C. Reynolds resigned his place in the school in 1859, having given six full years of the very best of his life to the Institution, A. B. Murphy having retired some time before that. Pres. Murphy died of consumption in the summer of 1860. He was loved and honored as a scholar, a teacher, an eloquent preacher, and a high-toned Christian gentleman.

J. W. Butler became President after the death of P. H. Murphy. Under his administration the College prospered until the new buildings, much larger and far more costly than the original one, had to be added to it, and were fully paid for.

J. P. Roach died recently in Iowa, and more recently A. B. Murphy died in Colorado. Both were worthy Christian men. J. W. Butler still lives, and with his son is engaged in the banking business in Fall River, Kansas. J. C. Reynolds is still living, and preaching in Callaway county, Mo.

Of the Alumni of Abingdon College there are several worthy of special mention, whom not to mention in this connection would be wrong. Geo. T. Carpenter, Chancellor of Drake University, Iowa, was an honored son of Abingdon College. Death lately claimed him also. But his name is an honor to his Alma Mater. James Monroe Martin, many years President of Hesperian College, California, is an honor to the Institution that trained him for his work. So also is Aaron Prince Aten, teacher, preacher, poet and Christian gentleman. Judge Durham, George E. Dew, J. T. Toof, Samuel P. Lucy, J. H. Smart and J. H. Garrison are all graduates of Abingdon. These all maintain high character for piety, learning, ability in the ministry, in literature, and in all that makes a man useful to his race.

Journalism also finds some of its brightest ornaments among the Alumni of Abingdon College. J. H. Garrison occupies the highest round as editor of "The New Christian Quarterly," and senior editor of "The Christian-Evangelist." He is also the author of several excellent and popular books.

Mrs. J. H. Smart, Mrs. J. H. Garrison, Mrs. J. M. Martin, Mrs. Judge Durham and other worthy women are graduates of Abingdon College. And now success and long life to Eureka College, to whose Alumni they now belong!

J. C. REYNOLDS.

ABINGDON COLLEGE AS I SAW IT.

I am asked for a reminiscence of "Abingdon College as I saw it." Am I becoming old, to be asked to pause and look back? Is J. H. Garrison an old-like man? Is he not now loving and courting Lizzie Garrett? Is he not her *garrison* as to the other boys? Is not J. H. Smart writing letters to her sister? Does he not now write short sentences and take the serious side of questions?

Who was it that last session, wrote that essay on "The White Wire Clothes Line?"

Where are Jim Dennis and Rob Heller, who, with another boy that loved the girls, made a plot to unite the Parthenian and the Philomathian societies?

Who does not rejoice that it succeeded, the faculty and public opinion to the contrary notwithstanding?

Thought continues to unfold. Men who accord or oppose die. Our dear Bro. Capt., who called another to the chair to speak against that union, has gone. I do not know where some of the others are, but the principle of co-education goes on.

(326)

Only yesterday a request was here from the old, staid University of Virginia, for arguments and facts which look toward co-education. Are the last strongholds of Protestant monkism beginning to prophesy?

Abingdon College was a pioneer in this blessed work of reform. Hers was genuine co-education, socially, religiously and through college work. It was accepted as a matter of course in all affairs of the school and the town. Some hurt may have come from it, but I have known of five times as much injury from one of the most conservative female schools in the south.

The man who refuses to masticate food because he may bite his tongue deserves to remain lean or starve. So of the institutions afraid of co-education.

I am glad to remember Abingdon College on this subject. In this field its work has been excellent. It did not hurt Smart, Carson, Garrison, Ingels, Lucy, John Moore and Dudly Barber to play games, recite and study with the girls, to walk with them to the cemetery, take them to the lectures and the concerts, read and talk with them; *it was an educational blessing.*

Did Thompson, Toof, Griffeth and a few other "honest fellows" get tangled in their love affairs? There is no better place this side of Heaven to learn to untangle social warp, or unfasten personal kinks, than in college life.

Yes, that September day in 1867 comes back to me. The old building. 40x60, three stories high, stood alone. As the assembly bell rang out, blooming and bashful, hopeful and manly faces, many strange to each other, but all seeking something each did not have, began answering its summons. How new it all was to me. I wandered through the day, listening to some explanations, talked with strangers here and there, went to Mrs. Crawford's and found board, to the college and enrolled. Paid one term's tuition, sixteen weeks, $16, and $2 contingent fee. At 7 P. M. another bell rang, and soon we were assembling in the old college chapel. The song was sung. Quiet came. A tall, somewhat slender, straight man, with dark skin, black eyes and well shaped forehead, and sleek, combed hair, came to the platform. That was President Butler, who welcomed us. His talk was plain, his tone was flat, his manner angular, but the feeling left was respectful.

Then came a man of slender stature, young, but shoulders drooped, full forehead, dark eyes, black hair, broad mouth with a natural smile and a pleasant voice. His manner was easy, thoughts cheery, and we all felt well. That was Professor A. J. Thomson.

Then came Professor Judge Durham. Plain

goodness, in looks, speech, style, and college work. It is true that afterwards, in primary Astronomy, first period afternoon, he did not always keep ns all wide awake, but it did us good to love him.

Then Prof. Lucy, the man whom we afterwards found studied teaching as a fine art, appeared before us. He was interested in us then, there, and always afterward, but, though his love was real, he never could get wholly away from the man in the mirror. In the home to which he has gone we can all indeed be brothers.

But here is Prof. Linn, brush-heap head, hairy face, shaggy eyebrows, thick lips and broad, smiling mouth. Of course he told a joke. He had not learned the modern humorous reference or allusion to introduce a speaker. Most of us were like him, from the joking class, so we laughed, and when he told his experience in carrying his possessions on his back as he came to Abingdon College, many boys of that class felt at home, and from the frank earnestness of the dear man all the others respected him. He has gone; we can see him no more until the great day. I do not remember certainly the old students who followed in the short speeches to welcome us green ones to this *reunion*, but think most of them were from that large class of 1868.

But this reunion brings us to another interesting

feature of "Abingdon College as I saw it." We
were introduced ; our hands were cordially grasp-
ed ; our eyes met with smiles ; our ears heard gladness and welcome. Our hearts felt warmed ; we
were loved—we loved. Thus began a student's
new life at Abingdon College.

This same kindly spirit continued in class and
village, in literary society and chapel. It had a
good influence on students. It could have been
more finished, more intellectual, if more of the
students had grown to the higher phases before
coming there. But this feature, as it was growing
partly out of co-education and partly out of the
influence of genial spirits in the early history of
the school and early settlement of the country,
increased by the manly ingathering just after
the war, made a social life which was *another
educational blessing*.

During the years from '67 to '73 the Faculty as
a body stood before us, not brilliant, not superior
in natural force, but as plain, honest workmen.

There was some lack of suggestiveness. They
sprang but few general questions, they started too
few inquiries and did not sufficiently awaken the
spirt of reading and *individual investigation*.

A higher appreciation of such subjects would
have much preferred a $30,000 house and $10,000
to establish and aid in conducting a library to a
$40,000 house and no library.

Again, as I saw Abingdon College, neither the teaching nor the general conduct of the work was vital enough. There was too much form of recitation and not enough *zest* in hunting thoughts as pioneers hunt foxes.

I was sometimes thirsty for fresh, clear thought from the well-springs of the teacher's own experience and original sources of investigation.

A very happy feature of Abingdon College, which in part supplemented this want, was the LITERARY SOCIETIES. After very many visits and a tolerably wide observation and inquiry as to this kind of work, for the facilities afforded, I have never known more cheerful and prompt efforts. The societies were open, not secret. The rivalry was as a rule healthy, not bitter. Nearly all the members would take part weekly, not quarterly. There was a general expectation that each one would, and a fair understanding that he should, try to act his part well. There was a union of criticism and encouragement rarely excelled.

Bronson's old Elocution for the whole school the last period in the evening of each day, and the literary societies on Friday night, made a *distinctive educational blessing.* Many hearts will thrill with joy, some eyes fill with tears, as those scenes and days are recalled.

As we go up the old steps and reach the third floor, I see the small man of quick step, the taller

one of grace, the stiff, tall man, the low, stocky
man with long sandy whiskers. There are Ab
Lovett and John Huston, George Brokaw and
George Dew, John Hopwood and Will Garrison.
There is Sam Hungate, the artist, returning with
his present—a portrait of Washington. I see his
pleased face and hear that broken, short prayer
the last night we ever passed together. He is
dead. My first thought on hearing of his death
was of that last prayer. We all loved him.

There are the two gentle but self-reliant women,
Rachel Rose and Mattie Morris,' the memory of
whose patience and works in educating themselves
has been a continued blessing to others. They
have left us to unite with God's Alumni. The
memory of their lives will 'make others willing to
follow on. Now from this third floor the two hall
doors open, Newtonia on the south, Philomathian
on the north. The assembling ones divide, while
others, T. H. Good-night, Tom Odenweller, Emma
Crawford, John McClure, Ella Mozier, Bell Price
and a host more come on until with members and
visitors the rooms are well filled, and the evening
work begins. Each meeting left its impress for
life and eternity.

To me the most important feature of the school
was the Religion. I came to Abingdon College a
member of the Methodist Episcopal Church. The
spirit of religion with students and teachers was

not officious. The young man was left to look on and hear. Sometimes I would go up to Heading College and hear Methodist brethren preach. When the debate between President Butler and Rev. Smith in Abingdon College chapel came off I took pretty full notes of part of it. So the growth went on until Bro. Franklin held the great meeting, March, 1869. No one could have met my case better than he. He was plain, honest and strong. He was manly, and appealed to the law and the testimony in such a manner as to make all feel that exactly the right thing to do was to accept its evidence.

There was no fawning about the matter, that we could take the Word of God if we liked it better than what we had; but, here is truth, there is tradition; here is liberty, there is bondage; obedience brings life, refusal is death.

It had been for years that as I read the Bible it seemed immersion was required. I would then go to the preacher, or read Watts or Clark or especially Rice, and be re-established.

Then Bible reading would break the rest, and the contest would be gone over again. But the night Dr. Yonkin walked with me into that old chapel baptistry settled the question of baptism.

The religious training at Abingdon was not so well done as many churches and schools have since learned to do. It did not take hold of the young people to make them active workers, but President Butler's morning lectures called attention to the Bible, gave outlines for study, and were without question of much value to students, especially for the first two or three years of college life. They furnished a religious frame-work. They gave a religious tone to the school.

In conclusion, this reminiscence has carried me back to the old chapel of '67, with its two rows of wooden columns, with its south end platform pulpit, on which President Butler stands giving the morning Bible lecture ; it leads us to the second story recitation-rooms, where Durham and Linn and Lucy meet us to honestly act their parts. It leads us to face Professor Thomson in the northwest corner on the third floor, to inflect *amo* while boys and girls reflect to each other *amabo* and *ames*. It has brought us to the public entertainments, even to when M. Ingles played "Black Eyed Susan" and repeated it the next week; back to the spring-time of 1868 when a declaimer, an essayist, and orator and a debater were chosen from each of the two societies for that notable battle of the senior giants to come off commencement week. It brings us to the union of winter and spring, 1869, and we hear Bro. Franklin, with his full voice and strong arguments, followed by the one hundred and twenty-five good confessions.

Years pass. I am in other halls and other

places, and return to Abingdon in 1872, to find the
new and the changed, the larger, and, in some
ways, better affairs. The gentle Aten is here. The
manly, strong Linn has gone hence.

We are going to Galesburg to hear John B.
Gough. We are going, again, to the inter-colle-
giate contest between representatives of Monmouth,
Lombard, Knox and Abingdon Colleges.

Spring is coming. Love and flowers are about
us; commencement is here. Seven classics and
fifteen of the other courses are accounted ready for
the rostrum. June 3rd, 1873, we said our pieces
and bowed ourselves out of college into the working world. And now I am told that we are Eure-
kans, that we have found a new mother, that we
have lost none, but found many noble brothers and
sisters.

So let wisdom go on with love and the spirit of
united work, until all our race have been freed
from the hand of strange children, and until, as
President Baccalaureate in 1873, said, "Our sons
have become as plants grown up in their youth,
our daughters as corner-stones, polished after the
similitude of a palace, and we are all a happy people, whose God is the Lord?

J. HOPWOOD.

Milligan, Tenn.

RECOLLECTIONS OF ABINGDON COLLEGE.

Abingdon College? Yes, the very name recalls many tender memories of the past, and "may my right hand forget its cunning, and my tongue cleave to the roof of my mouth," if I forget thee, O Abingdon!

It was in May, in the eventful year of 1865, when the sulphurous war-cloud was rolling away, and the last sullen roar of cannon and musketry was dying in faint echoes in the far Southland, that I received my first furlough from the army, during a service of four years, and, taking passage on a Mississippi River steamer, came up the Father of Waters to Quincy, Ill., and thence, after a few hours' ride by rail, I landed in the town of Abingdon. I came unannounced and unexpected. I had come to visit two of my sisters, whom I had sent there to attend the college. I can recall yet some of the strange emotions which I felt as I stepped upon the platform, a stranger in a strange land, among civilians, clad in the uniform of an officer of the United States Army. The experience was

(336)

new to me, and I noted with surprise that there were then those, in the great and patriotic State of Illinois, who regarded me with a suspicious look because of my uniform, and because of the black crape around my right arm, worn by order of the War Department in honor of the martyred President.

My visit was a short one. Seeing from the papers orders concerning the movements of the army, I returned to my post before the expiration of my furlough. But when, in the following August, our regiment was mustered out of service in St. Louis, I again visited Abingdon, this time in company with a brother. We went by way of Springfield, Ill., visited the home and grave of Lincoln, for whom the nation was mourning, and thence, by way of Peoria and Galesburg, to the little town which was destined to play so important a part in my life.

It was vacation, on our arrival, and, of course most of the students were away, and the little town at first wore a very dull, uninviting aspect to one who had just arrived from the exciting scenes of the war. I had been there but a few weeks, however, when I decided to remain and take a course in the college. I had not gone there with my mind made up to pursue that course, but there was something in the social atmosphere of the place, in the friendliness of the people, and

22

in the character of the few teachers and students
I met, that caused me to make this decision.
Whether it was wise or unwise, I have never yet
had occasion to regret it.

The chain of events that brought me to Abingdon College affords a good illustration of how
our lives are often moulded by apparently trivial
circumstances. Having been wounded in the
battle of Pea Ridge, in March, 1862, I was sent
to Springfield, Mo., for medical treatment. While
there I was brought in contact with a young man
who was a soldier in an Illinois regiment, and we
became intimate friends. On inquiry of him for
a suitable school somewhere north beyond the
range of musket and cannon, to which I could
send my two sisters, he recommended Abingdon
College, having himself been a student there.
Thither they were sent, thither I went to visit
them, and then, to become a student; and there
I was caught in the current of a religious reform from which I have never made the slight-
est effort to escape! How much that minnie
ball had to do in changing my whole course
of life, I dare not say; but it is reasonably
certain that had my friend in gray aimed his
musket a little differently my aim in life would
have been different also.

There was nothing in the location of Abingdon
nor in the town itself, to make it especially at-

tractive. It is like a hundred other Illinois towns, made up of frame cottages, built on a flat surface of black soil, with board sidewalks and surrounded by a rich farming country. It was simply the fact that there was a college there, where young men and women had assembled to train their minds and hearts for life's duties, that made it a place of interest. There was, too, an air of sociability, good will and fraternity in the community, which, during the three years from 1865 to 1868 that I remained there, were the characteristic features of Abingdon life. The college was a family. The President was its head, the professors were its elder brothers, and the rest of us were the boys and girls— brothers and sisters all. There was no class feeling, no high nor low, no social distinctions. All occupied the same level, religiously and socially. The professors were not very learned men, it is true, but they understood fairly well the branches they taught. and had ardent love for the students, and seemed personally interested in the success of each one of them. This is a large compensating feature in Western college life. There was, as I remember, during my stay at Abingdon, no library, no apparatus for illustrating the various sciences, and the old building in those days had few facilities for college work. And yet, in spite of all these drawbacks,

I look back to-day across the intervening years to the scenes and associations of Abingdon College with the tenderest emotions. The friendship which bound teachers and students together, the contact of mind with mind in the class-room and in our literary societies, and the religious quality which dominated all, made it an exceedingly healthful and stimulating training-school for young men and women.

The years I spent at Abingdon were full of hard mental toil, relieved by few outside diversions. I recall, however, a day now and then, in the glad spring time, when a few of us went into the woods botanizing—some boys, some girls, about an equal number of each. We gathered wild flowers, sang snatches of favorite school songs, and sometimes, it must be confessed, the conversation dropped into low, sweet tones—and botany was not the theme. And then again, on bright, starry nights, the astronomy class went out, sometimes, to trace the constellations in the heavens. The boys hardly ever cared to go alone, the girls *could* not, and we generally went together. What went we out for to see? Not the stars alone, but eyes which shone with a warmer glow than far away Orion and Pleiades and Arcturus. The "morning class" with its hearty singing, the elocution class, "running the gauntlet," the exhibitions, the discussions in the literary societies, the political feeling that ran high when young patriots on each side panted to save the country, but above all, commencement day, with crowded chapel, decorated platform, fair girls in white muslin dresses, roses, joyous anthems by the chorus, the speeches that laid bare the history, condition and needs of the world in general, and the American Republic in particular, the valedictory, the diplomas, the alumni supper, and the farewells—how it all comes back to me, especially the commencement of '68. O the tuneful bells of memory. What sweet melodies they bring to us across the chasm of the years.

If at times I have felt a momentary regret that the years spent at Abingdon had not been spent in one of our Eastern colleges, I have always on reflection, decided that I would not exchange what I received at Abingdon for all the superior advantages I could have secured elsewhere. I cannot forget that it was at Abingdon that I first became acquainted with the principles and aims of the Reformation, to which I at once gave my heart and pledged the services of my life. This change in the current of my religious life, I recognize as of more value than the knowledge of many sciences. Nor can I forget that it was among the daughters of Abingdon College that I found one who has been the partner of all my toils, my sorrows and my joys, and an unceasing inspiration in all my work. These two considerations, if there were none other, would always make Abingdon College a green place in my memory. In its day and time it wrought a good work, and made its impression on the life of the world, even though in an humble degree. That its period of unity, fraternity and prosperity was succeeded by a period of division and strife which terminated its existence as a separate institution, is a matter of profound regret to all of us who cherished the memory of its better days. But as an offset to this regret we have reason to rejoice that its life and history have been blended with those of Eureka College, whose adopted children we have all become. We rejoice, also, in this unification of our educational interests in Illinois, and in the brightening prospects and increasing power and usefulness of our new Alma Mater.

Tears for the Abingdon College that was; cheers for the Eureka College that is, and blessings on the heads of the old boys and girls who gathered in the halls of the former, more than thirty years ago.

J. H. GARRISON.

THE COLLEGE BELL.

A. S. FISHER.

The loyal graduate who went forth from his Alma Mater, during the early sessions of our beloved college, returns to the old campus, laden with laurels from the field of adventure, and, reclining upon the green sward, beneath the cooling shade of a favorite old tree, hears once more the *College Bell*.

THAT *Grand Old Bell* suspended there,
Transmitting calls on waves of air,
For many years, in " Long ago,"
We honored, as it bade us go
To *Chapel-hour*, for prayer and praise,
Through all along our college days,
By sending forth its rumbling call,
For teachers and for students all.

How joyful were those days, now gone,
And floating with the current down—
A-down that stream without an end,
That parallels eternal trend—
Those joyful, buoyant, college days,
Made pleasant by the classic ways
Of patient teachers, while they sought
To guide us in the ways of thought;
To lead us forth in Wisdom's realm,
To give us compass, chart and helm—
And thus equipped, to cheer us on
Toward the distant far *beyond*.

That *Grand Old Bell*—it did us good,
To hear its rumblings through the wood.

(343)

And now we stand, as days of yore,
To hear it sounding out once more.

Of college times and youthful ways,
And of those solemn morning lays,
There's nought can say *so much* and *well*
To cheer us up as that *Old Bell.*

Then pull the rope and turn it o'er,
And let it rumble as before—
Yes, let it sound—we love it well—
The rumblings of that *Grand Old Bell.*

Kansas City, Mo.

TO ALMA MATER.

B. J. RADFORD.

O, *Alma Mater*, well beloved, thou
Hast fealty sworn to Beauty, Love and Truth ;
Hast laid thy hand upon the three-fold cord,
Religion, Science, Art, not quickly broke,
To do thy part in drawing back the race
From death. We bid thee in this holiest work
God-speed, and pray thee to thy sacred trust
Be true; for ever as each child shall take
Its upward way to that sublimer height,
Where God meets lofty spirits face to face,
Another star shall glisten in thy crown.
    The seeds thou sowest shall not ripen all
In time; nor should thy patient husbandry
Spend all its strength upon the transient fruits
That ripe and rot within a season's round.
To teach thy children how to see and name ;
To gather meaning from an ancient tongue ;
To follow nature's vestiges through all
Her ancient ways; or give them power against the foes
Of mortal life, and set them in the way
Of earthly gain, is but the meaner part
Of all thy ministry. All earthly light
Must darken into gloom, and every star
That blazes in the firmament of time
Must set; but teach thy children how to shape
Their course upon the stormy sea of life
By that pole-star of all the universe—
The Cynosure of God's Incarnate Truth.

(345)

TEACHERS OF EUREKA COLLEGE.

The following is an alphabetical list of all the teachers employed by Walnut Grove Academy and Eureka College from the beginning to the present time. The dates after the name indicate the years in which they taught. One single date indicates that the teacher was employed only one year. Two dates thus, 1860-1870, indicate that the teacher taught from 1860 to 1870 without interruption. The teachers whose last date is 1894 are still teaching in the College:

Allen, J. M., 1856-69 and 71-86.
Atwater, J. M., 1891.
Blair, D. M., 1874-76.
Bruner, H. L., 1885-86.
Bruner, F. M., 1885-89.
Burgess, O. A., 1855.
Callender, Geo., 1858-62.
Chalmers, James, 1887-89.
Clark, Mollie G., 1861.
Conklin, R. E., 1888-90 & 92-94.
Conover, R. A., 1855.
Coombs, J. V., 1882-84.
Deweese, B. C., 1889-94.
Dickinson, E. W., 1876-78.
Dickinson, Elmira J., 1853-55, and 1858-60, and 1867-70.
Errett, W. S., 1884.
Everest, H. W., 1863-71 & 77-81.
Ewing, Jane, 1858.
Fisher, A. S., 1848-75 & 78-86.
Fisher, Sarah, 1853.
Goodspeed, Emma, 1885.
Hay, O. P., 1869-73.
Herrick, H. N., 1886-88 & 90-94.
Hieronymus, R. E., 1889-94.
Hittle, Laura, 1863.
Jackson, W. T., 1891-93.

Johann, Carl, 1876-94.
Johnson, B. W., 1857-63 & 1866.
Johnson, R. H., 1860-63.
Jones, Annie J., 1891-94.
Jones, Sue E., 1850.
Kirk, James, 1876-84.
Laupheare, Sarah, 1860.
Lindsey, John, 1850-52.
Loos, C. L., 1856-57.
Meek, S. E., 1886-88.
Miller, G. A., 1888-93.
Minassian, H. A., 1888-93.
Mitchell, W. T., 1888.
Myers, M. Josephine, 1857.
Neville, John H., 1852-57.
Newcomb, H. O., 1863-65 and 1867-70.
Pearre, S. E., 1857.
Radford, B. J., 1869-80 & 1883-85 & 1892-94.
Robinson, Harriet A., 1866.
Rowell, J. H., 1855-57 & 1860-64.
Stickel, Sina A., 1888-91.
Thompson, M. J., 1884.
Vawter, S. D., 1894.
Weston, A. M., 1869-76.
Youngblood, A. J., 1881-91.

(347)

TEACHERS OF MUSIC.

Allen, Annie, 1889-90.
Alvey, Millie, 1889-94.
Blitz, E. F., 1882-84.
Bruner, Lettie, 1885.
Buckley, Mrs. M. E., 1857.
Depue, John, 1883.
Franklin, Estelle, 1887-89.
Gray, John R., 1886.
Hersey, L. E., 1885-88.
Hootman, Mrs. G. W., 1888.
Johnson, Belle, 1863-64 and 66.
Johnson, Mrs. S. S., 1862.
Lauder, W. W., 1885-86.

Mason, Miss O. M., 1865.
Meek, Miss Julia, 1861.
Meek, Mrs. S. E., 1887.
Metcalf, J. W., 1875-77 and 81-85.
Miller, Phene, 1867-69.
Page, Emma J., 1879-81.
Plowe, F. H., 1871-73 and 74.
Plowe, Harold, 1884.
Smith, Sue S., 1858-61.
Taylor, Ella F., 1878.
True, Miss E. F., 1855-57.
Vandervort, Janie, 1889-93.
Wright, Eva, 1877.

ART DEPARTMENT.

Bruner, Lettie, 1884.
Burrows, May I., 1886.
Campbell, C. W., 1876.
Garrett, Sarah J., 1881 and 84-86.
Hatch, Clara J., 1882-84.

Holder, Sarah E., 1880.
Major, Cora, 1889-91.
Minassian, Jessie, 1891-93.
Naramore, Mattie, 1894.
Patrick, Latina, 1865.
Vandervort, Mina, 1887-89.

COMMERCIAL DEPARTMENT.

Allison, J. T., 1894.
Buzick, F. M., 1891-93.
Burnham, F. W., 1891-94.
Eggert, Belle, 1891-94.
Hager, Carrie, 1890.
Hootman, G. W., 1887-94.

Page, O. J., 1891-93.
Perry, W. S., 1889-91.
Reynolds, G. W., 1876.
Richmond, N. L., 1882-87.
Smalley, R. O., 1891.

NAMES OF THE PRESIDENTS

IN THE ORDER IN WHICH THEY SERVED.

W. M. Brown, 1855-56.
C. L. Loos, 1856-58.
George Callender, 1858-62.
B. W. Johnson, 1862-63.
H. W. Everest, 1863-71.

A. M. Weston, 1871-75.
B. J. Radford, 1875-77.
H. W. Everest, 1877-81.
J. M. Allen, 1881-87.
Carl Johann, 1887—

THE ALUMNI.

The star (*) indicates that the parties graduated in Abingdon College, which has been united with Eureka College, they becoming thereby Alumni of the latter institution of learning.

A. M., means Master of Arts.

M. A., means Mistress of Arts.

A. B., means Bachelor of Arts.

B. S., means Bachelor of Science.

M. E. L., means Master or Mistress of English Literature.

B. E. L., means Bachelor of English Literature.

OFFICERS OF THE ASSOCIATION.

President, Prof. B. J. Radford.
Vice-President, O. W. Stewart.
Secretary, Miss Clara Davidson.
Treasurer, Pres. Carl Johann.

The officers are also the Executive Committee.

1893.

H. B. Boone, A. B. Student of Medicine, Chicago, Ill.
Zua I. Briggs, B. S., Music Teacher, Eureka, Ill.
Frank Culp, B. S., Student of Medicine, Chicago, Ill.
J. P. Lichtenberger, A. B., Minister, Greenview, Ill.
C. C. Maxwell, B. S., Student of Law, Lincoln, Ill.
J. P. McKnight, A. B., Minister, Harristown, Ill.
W. S. Perry, A. B., Teacher, Cornell, Ill.
F. E. Pope, B. S., Merchant, DuQuoin, Ill.
J. M. Shepherd, B. S., Banker, Lovington, Ill.
W. W. Sniff, A. B., Minister, Watseka, Ill.
H. W. Wohlgemuth, A. M., Teacher, Washington, Ill.

1892.

Mabel Atwater, B. S., Prof. Oskaloosa College, Oskaloosa, Iowa.
J. W. Carpenter, A. B., Minister, Augusta, Ill.
J. R. Crank, A. B., Minister, Iroquois, Ill.
L. F. Davis, A. B., Minister, Nunda, Ill.
W. E. Garrison, A. B., Student in Yale Univ'sity, New Haven, Ct.
J. C. Hall, A. B., Minister, Albion, Ill.
Charles Hamilton, B. S., Medical Student, Chicago, Ill.
Edna Hamilton, A. B., Teacher, Harristown, Ill.
Howard Hamilton, B. S., Medical Student, Chicago, Ill.
Mary S. Hedrick, B. S., Teacher, Taylorville, Ill.
Silas Jones, A. B., Student Harvard University, Cambridge,
    Mass.
B. B. Melton, A. B., Teacher, St. Joseph, Ill.
R. D. Pope, B. S., Student of Medicine, Washington, D. C.
L. Mabel Riddle (Carlock), B. S., Peoria, Ill.
K. C. Ventress, A. B., Minister, LaHarpe, Ill,
W. H. Waggoner, Student Yale University, New Haven, Conn.
J. C. Watson, A. B., Student Harvard Univ'ty, Cambridge, Mass.

1891.

Lizzie Dickirson, B. S., Lawrenceville, Ill.
Ella Ferry, M. A., Teacher, Geneseo, Ill.
Annie J. Jones, M. A., Teacher of Elocution, Eureka, Ill.
W. T. Brownlie, B. S., Merchant, Cherokee, Iowa.
L. J. Carlock, A. B., Attorney-at-Law, Peoria, Ill.
C. C. Rowlison, A. B., Student Harvard Unv'ty, Cambridge, Mass.
R. D. Smith, Jr., A. B., Minister, Robinson, Ill.

1890.

J. M. Allen, Jr., B. S., Merchant, Tollhouse, Cal.
J. W. Eichinger, A. B., Teacher, Decatur, Ill.
T. W. Mavity, A. B., Minister, Onarga, Ill.
G. A. Miller, A. B., Minister, Covington, Ky.
W. M. Roberts, A. B., Physician, Macomb, Ill.
O. W. Stewart, A. B., State Evangelist, Eureka, Ill.
Elvira J. Seass (Stewart) A. B., Eureka, Ill.
R. E. Thomas, A. B., Minister, Batavia, Ill.
L. G. Whitmer, B. S., Bank Clerk, Bloomington, Ill.

1889.

W. W. Chalmers, A. M., Superintendent of Schools, Grand
    Rapids, Mich.
Thomas Chalmers, A. B., Minister, Port Huron, Mich.
Andrew B. Chalmers, A. B., Minister, Cleveland, Ohio.
E. A. Gilliland, A. B., Minister, Lexington, Ill.
R. E. Hieronymus, A. M., Professor English Literature, Eureka,
    Ill.

W. T. Jackson, A. M., Student Harvard University, Cambridge, Mass.
H. A. Minassian, A. M., M. D., Physician, Des Moines, Ia.
Maude McDonald, M. A., Teacher, Arthur, Ill.
Mary Musick (Herrick), M. A., Eureka, Ill.
C. T. Radford, B. S., Editor, Eureka, Ill.
I. S. Whitmer, B. S., Bloomington, Ill.

1888.

Amber, Amsler, M. A., Bloomington, Ill.
T. A. Boyer, A. M , Evangelist, Eureka, Ill.
James Chalmers, Ph. D., Professor Ohio State University, Columbus, Ohio.
C. B. Dabney, A. M., Minister, Mt. Pulaski, Ill.
Effie Gepford (Pritchett), M. A., Niantic, Ill.
Minnie Hobbs, A. M., Teacher, Eureka, Ill.
Myra Henderson, M. A., Virden, Ill.
T. H. Haney, A. M., Principal of Schools, Richland Center, Wis.
N. L. Kiser, B. S., Merchant, Mechanicsburg, Ill.
W. T. Mitchell, A. M., Nebraska.
Carrie McClun, A. M., West Liberty, Iowa.
Eva McDonald, M. A., Teacher, Arthur, Ill.
J. T. Ogle, A. M., Minister, Cameron, Mo.
E. A. Riddle, A. M., Deceased.
Nannie Taylor, M. A., South Omaha, Neb.
Marcie Waughop, M. A., Teacher, Eureka, Ill.

1887.

May E. Edwards (Wright), M. A., Denver, Col.
S. A. Ennefer, A. B., Minister, Toulon, Ill.
J. W. Kern, A. M., Lawyer, Watseka, Ill.
Fannie Lampton (Craver), M. A., Minneapolis, Minn.
Lucy Major, M. A., Eureka, Ill.
L. C. McPherson, B. S., Minister, Buffalo, N. Y.
Mamie H. Richardson (Thrapp), M. A., Gibson City, Ill.
W. G. Smith, B. S., Minister, State Line, Ind.
J. N. Swartz, A. B., Lawyer, Chicago, Ill.
H. M. Shafer, M. S., Teacher, Lafayette, Ill.
R. F. Thrapp, A. M., Minister, Gibson City, Ill.
C. R. Vandervort, A. M., Principal of Schools, Peoria, Ill.

1886.

E. V. Aten, A. B., Editor, Houston, Texas.
R. E. Conklin, A. M., Professor Natural Sciences, Eureka, Ill.
H. N. Herrick, A. M., Professor Eureka College, Eureka, Ill.
L. C. Spooner, A. B., Lawyer, Armourdale, Kan.

1885.

George E. Goodin, A. B., Farmer, Pittsfield, Ill.
Perry B. Hobbs, A. B., Editor, Roanoke, Ill.
Penelope B. Hobbs, M. A., deceased.
Harry C. Hawk, B. S., Merchant, Bloomington, Ill.
Rosa A. Rhodes, (Btrd), M. A., Mechanicsburg, Ill.
S. D. Vawter, B. S., Professor of Mathematics, Eureka, Ill.
Cora Ma jor,M. A., Eureka, Ill.

1884.

W. H. Cannon, A. B., Minister, Eureka, Ill.
W. D. Deweese, A. B., Minister, Buffalo, Ill.
L. D. Hickman, B. S., Clerk in Music Store, Wichita, Kan.
Anna McClure (Banta), M. A., Eureka, Ill.
Clara B. Roberts (Cannon), M. A., Eureka, Ill.
W. E. Shastid, A. B., Physician, Wichita, Kan.
*Frank Bruner, B. E. L., Physician, El Paso, Tex.
*Jessie Bruner (Minassian), M. E. L., Des Moines, Iowa.
*Minnie Younkin (Hall), M. E. L., Monmouth, Ill.
*H. B. Scheitlin, B. E. L., Bank Cashier, Abingdon, Ill.

1883.

Maggie Baird (Roberts), M. A., Eureka, Ill.
J. Clarence Lindsey, A. B., Physician, Chicago, Ill.
Ola Moore, M. A., Eureka, Ill.
Emma Neal (Walker), M. A.; Springfield, Ill.
Ollie Whitmer (Wilson), M. A., Bloomington, Ill.
*Fannie Bruner (Jeffrey), M. E. L., Terre Haute, Ind.
*Anna Givens (Thomas), M. E. L., Oklahoma. *_
*Nettie Gallaspie, M. E. L., Beatrice, Neb.
*T. F. Weaver, B. E. L., Minister, Chatham, Ill.
*R. E. Conklin, B. E. L., Professor, Eureka, Ill.
*J. Hopwood, A. M., Pres. Mulligan College. Johnson City, Tenn.
*J. D. Graham, B. S., Prof. of Telegraphy, State Agricultural College, Manhattan, Kan.

1882.

J. D. Dabney, A. M., Minister, Hastings, Neb.
J. F. Ghormley, A. M., Minister, Bozeman, Mont.
L. E. Hedrick, A. B., Teacher, Chicago, Ill.
L. C. Hickman, B. S., Merchant, Wichita, Kan.
W. H. Kern. A. B., Minister, St. Louis, Mo.
J. M. Smoot, A. B., Attorney-at-Law, Kingman, Kan.

1881.

Millie Brooks (Smoot), M. A., Kingman, Kan.
John C. Eldridge, A. M., Gainsville, Texas.
Louis C. de Guibert, A. B., Lawyer, Sioux City, Iowa.

Ermine L. Huston (Henry), M. A., Ouray, Col.
E. Grace Moss, M. A., Teacher, Lebanon, Mo.
Geo. W. Ross, A. B., Minister, Spokane, Wash.
Frank G. Willson, A. B., deceased.
J. Oscar Willson, A. B., Banker, Bloomington, Ill.

1880.

John D. Allen, A. B., deceased.
Anna E. Davidson, M. A., Eureka, Ill.
James H. Gilliland, A. M., Minister, Bloomington, Ill.
Metta Hart (Barton), M. A., deceased.
Minnie Harlan (Eyman), M. A., Galesburg, Ill.
Cora L. Lindsey (Lauder), M. A., Chicago, Ill.
Charity E. Munsell (Davidson), M. A., Eureka, Ill.
Clay C. Price, A. B., Eureka, Ill.
Joseph H. Sutherland, B. S., Minister, Monte Vista, Cal.
Arabel Trumbo (Megredy,) M. A., Laomi, Ill.
*W. H. Clark, A. B., Editor of the *Argus*, Abingdon, Ill.
*J. M. Morris, A. B., Minister, Abingdon, Ill.
*J. B. Campbell, A. B., deceased.
*H. L. Bruner, A. B., Prof. in Butler University, Irvington, Ind.
*Lloyd Kirkland, B. E. L., Lawyer, Chicago, Ill.
*W. H. Smith, B. E. L.
*Effie Marshall, M. E. L., Abingdon, Ill.

1879.

B. O. Aylesworth, A. M., LL. D., Pres. Drake University, Des
    Moines, Ia.
John D. Clark, A. B., Editor *Enterprise*, Mackinaw, Ill.
E. O. Eyman, A. B., Banker, Galesburg, Ill.
P. A. Fetter, A. B., Farmer, Eureka, Ill.
Clay Willcoxson, B. S., Teacher, New City, Ill.
*Lettie Bruner (Givens), Des Moines, Ia.
*Edgar Hawes, B. E. L., deceased.

1878.

Harvey O. Breeden, A. M., Minister, Des Moines, Ia.
Abner P. Cobb, A. M., Minister, Springfield, Ill.
George Carlock, A. M., deceased.
DeWitt C. Pixley, A. B., Merchant, Orange, Cal.
*C. C. Pierce, B. E. L., Minister, Kansas.
*Henry C. Cox, A. M., Teacher, Chicago, Ill.
*A. G. Lucas, A. M.

1877.

Sallie M. Carson, M. A., deceased.
*D. F. Givens, A. B., Manufacturer, Des Moines, Iowa.
23

1876.

Millard F. Anderson, B. S., Farmer, Colfax, Ill.
Hiram K. Coleson, A. B., Editor, De Funiak Springs, Fla.
Leora Emerson (Richardson), M. A., Denver, Col.
Eva Howe (Leeper), M. A., Virginia, Ill.
Orson Q. Oviatt, A. M., Minister, Greenwood, Ind.
Lovell B. Pickerell, A. B., Minister, Clinton, Ill.
W. Frank Richardson, A. M., Minister, Denver, Col.
Belle Sharp (Van Volkenburg), M. A., Livermore, Cal.
George Shirley, A. B., Lawyer, Chicago, Ill.
*H. E. Allen, B. S., Indianapolis, Ind.
*C. S. Nesbitt, B. S., County Surveyor, Chase Co., Kansas.
*J. C. Snyder, B. S., Farmer, Constant, Kan.
*Sadie B. Harris, Mrs., B. S., Burlington, Colo.
·*C. H. Craig, B. S., deceased.
*D. V. Hampton, B. S., deceased.
*Lou Bailey, B. S., Teacher, Bryant, Ill.

1875.

Emma Hodgson (Pickerell), M. A., Clinton, Ill.
Charles Sharp, A. B., Hanford, Cal.
*J. H. Gilliland, B. S., Minister, Bloomington, Ill.
*J. S. Huey, A. B., Lawyer, Chicago, Ill.
*Myra Patrick (Huey), A. B. Chicago, Ill.
Theda Dodge, (Gill), B. S., McPherson, Kansas.
*J. B. Ingels, A. B., Physician, Des Moines, Iowa.
*H. Knappenberger, B. S., Physician, Sciota, Ill.
*Minnie Newcomer (Townley), B. S., Macomb, Ill.
*Ella Rice, B. S.
*C. Robbins, B. S., Principal Business College, Sedalia, Mo.

1874.

Lucinda Carson (Heiss), M. A., Oregon.
Annabel Clark (Livingston , M. A., deceased.
Arthur A. Leeper, B. S., Lawyer, Virginia, Ill.
George L. Warlow, B. S., Lawyer, Fresno, Cal.
*E. C. Bonham, B. S., deceased.
*W. D. Williams, B. S., Banker, Seguin, Texas.
*D. S. Harris, B. S., Banker, Burlington, Col.

1873.

Georgina Callender (Johann), M. A., Eureka, Ill.
Ammon Coombs, A. B., Druggist, Paxton, Ill.
J. E. Harris, A. M., Minister, Talmage, Neb.
Janet E. Murray (Darst), M. A., Wataga, Ill.
Charles A. Shirley, B. S., Minister, Chicago, Ill.

Geo. R. Shirley, B. S., Lawyer, Chicago, Ill.
*D. C. Barber, A. M., Druggist, Denver, Ill.
*J. S. Griffin, A. M., Adamsville, Tenn.
*J. W. Hopwood, A. M., Teacher, Snowville, Va.
*M. Ingels, A. M., Sunday-School Evangelist, Topeka, Kan.
*J. W. McClure, A. M., Minister, Preston, Ia.
*Ada Byram (Morris), B. S., deceased.
*Carrie Byram, B. S., Abingdon, Ill.
*G. W. Oldfather, B. S., Teacher, Knox Co., Ill.
*A. A. Gingrich, B. S., Lawyer, Toulon, Ill.
*Mrs. Libbie Ingels, B. S., Topeka, Kan.
*Susie Latimer (Vandervoort), B. S., Shenandoah, Ia.
*Mollie Scott (Morris), B. S., deceased.
*G. L. Brokaw, A.M., Minister, State Evangelist, Des Moines, Ia.
*C. W. Domback, B. S., Merchant, Des Moines, Iowa.
*E. B. Dixon, B. S. Baders, Ill.
*J. W. Moore, B. S., Mound Station, Ill.
*J. W. F. Scott, B. S., deceased.
*A. H. Turner, B. S., Merchant, Austin, Kan.
*W. Taylor, B. S., Summit, Ill.
*C. L. Neall, B. S., Merchant, Rushville, Ill.

1872.

M. Leona Boggs (Dale), M. A., Delevan, Ill.
Charles W. Campbell, A. B., Topeka, Kan.
W. H. Crow, A. M., Lawyer, Pittsfield, Ill.
Albert W. Carson, B. S., Physician, Dover, Kan.
E. J. Hart, A. M., Minister, New Philadelphia, Ohio.
Edward Litchfield, B. S., Banker, Flanagan, Ill.
T. L. Trowbridge, B. S., Teacher, Wymore, Neb.
J. G. Waggoner, A. M., Minister, Buffalo, N. Y.
J. M. Willard, A. B., Decatur, Ill.
*S. B. Campbell, A. B., Teacher, Industry, Ill.
*C. W. Hardesty, B. S., Montana.

1871.

John I. Barnett, A. B., Teacher, Hallville, Ill.
J. K. Breeden, A. M., Lawyer, Tuscola, Ill.
Clara S. Davidson, M. A., Eureka, Ill.
Joel Dunn, B. S., Lawyer, Bement, Ill.
Jas. Kirk, A. M., Assistant State Superintendent of Public Instruction, Springfield, Ill.
Charles Wilson, B. S., Lawyer, Peoria, Ill.
*Wm. Adcock, B. S., Farmer, Utah.
*E. Adcock, B. S., Lawyer, Chicago, Ill.
*G. W. Armstrong, B. S., Teacher, Kansas City, Mo.
*J. Boyd, Agent, Sedalia, Mo.

*W. H. Berry, B. S., Blandinsville, Ill.
*S. H. Butler, Banker, Fall River, Kan.
*Emma Crawford (Aten), Owensboro, Ky.
*F. M. Gideon, B. S., Lawyer, Kokomo, Ind.
*S. C. Hungate, B. S., deceased.
*G. W. Hustead, B. S., Fort Madison, Iowa.
*J. C. Jackson, B. S., Teacher, Iowa.
*W. H. Kern, B. S., Minister, St. Louis, Mo.
*W. H. Lovitt, B. S., Music Teacher, Blandinsville, Ill.
*T. F. Odenweller, B. S., Pastor, Kellogg, Iowa.
*George Sharp, B. S., Billings, Mo.
*Florence Givens (Hatchett), B. S., Abingdon, Ill.
*Nettie Murray, B. S., Morning Sun, Ohio.
*Anna E. Quinn (Price), B. S., Toulon, Ill.
*E. M. Dew, deceased.
*Mary Stockton, B. S., Augusta, Ill.
*J. M. Morris, Minister, Abingdon, Ill.
*T. H. Goodnight, Minister, Cameron, Ill.

1870.

O. P. Hay, A. M., Ph. D., Chicago University, Chicago, Ill.
Ella M. Myers (Huffman), M. A., Prescott, Ill.
Hattie Orton (Longfellow), M. A., Longmont, Colo.
*J. H. Bacon, B. S., Farmer, Weaver, Iowa.
*J. M. Butler, B. S., Teacher, Tennessee.
*D. C. Chipman, B. S., State's Attorney, Minneapolis, Kan.
*J. B. Shawgo, B. S., Physician, Quincy, Ill.
Emerson Wood, B. S., Napa, Cal.

1869.

Cicero Buchanan, A. M., Lawyer, Evansville, Ind.
W. T. Cussins, A. B., Lawyer, Decatur, Ill.
E. R. Eldridge, A. M., Lawyer, Chicago, Ill.
Geo. W. Sweeney, A. M., Minister, Oakland, Cal.
*G. E. Dew, A. B., Pastor, Albany, Mo.
*Emma Veach (Lomar), M. E. L., Abingdon, Ill.
*O. J. Beam, B. S., Merchant, Avon, Ill.
*J. F. Long, B. S., deceased.
*A. B. Price, B. S., College Professor, Canton, Mo.
M. Ingels, B. S., Topeka, Kan.

1868.

John Bain, A. B., Minister, Marysville, Kansas.
Minnie I. Callender, M. A., deceased.
Emma A. Clark (Crow), M. A., Pittsfield, Ill.
H. U. Dale, A. M., Minister, Delevan, Ill.
S. F. Davidson, Editor, Chicago, Ill.

Laura F. Fisher (Gibson), M. A., Teacher of Music, Kansas
   City, Mo.
W. J. Longfellow, B. S., Farmer, Longmont, Colo.
Maria J. McCorkle (Poynter), M. A., Albion, Neb.
Edwin Rogers, A. B., Minister, Mankato, Minn.
Eliza F. Rodgers, A. B., deceased.
*A. D. Butler, A. M., Farmer, Napa, Cal.
*J. W. Carson, A. M., Wakeeney, Kansas.
*J. H. Garrison, A. M., Minister, Editor Christian-Evangelist,
   St. Louis, Mo.
*R. E. Hiller, A. M., Lawyer, Topeka, Kans.
*J. H. Smart, A. M., Minister, Colfax, Ill.
*Lizzie Dodge (Carson), M. E. L., Wakeeney, Kan.
*Lizzie Garrett (Garrison), M. E. L., St. Louis, Mo.
*Jennie Hamilton, (Jacobs), M. E. L., West Branch, Wash.
*Rinda Hamilton (Chesney), M. E. L., Topeka, Kans.
*F. G. Johnson (Allen), M. E. L., Santa Rosa, Cal.
*Mattie Morris (Shawgo), M. E. L., deceased.
*Ella Mosher (Price), M. E. L., deceased.
*Rachel R. Rose, (Garrison), M. E. L., deceased.
*William Garrison, B. S., Sharon, Kansas.
*A. N. Norris, B. S., deceased
*R. A. Lovitt, B. S., Lawyer, Salina, Kan.
*A. N. Miller, B. S., Miller, Roseville, Ill.
*J. T. Toof, B. S., Minister, New Haven, Conn.
A. E. Thompson, B. S., Pueblo, Colo.

1867.

John W. Allen, A. M., Minister, Chicago, Ill.
N. S. Haynes, A. M., Englewood, Ill.
Jennie H. Neville (Campbell), M. A., Topeka, Kansas.
James H. Nutting, A. B., Minister, Woonsocket, R. I.
W. A. Poynter, A. B., Farmer, Albion, Neb.
Eliza F. Rogers, M. A., deceased.
*S. E. Garrett (Smart), M. E. L., Colfax, Ill.
*G. S. Smith, B. S., Lawyer, Omaha, Neb.

1866.

Emma Campbell (Ewing), M. A., Jacksonville, Ill.
W. W. W. Jones, A. M., Supt. Neb. Schools, Lincoln, Neb.
J. H. McDonald, A. B., Lawyer, Springfield, Ill.
B. J. Radford, A. M., Professor, Eureka, Ill.
Peter Vogel, A. M., Minister, Somerset, Pa.
Carrie V. Wright (Dixon), M. A., La Hogue, Ill.
*Mary Harris (Thompson), M. E. L., California.
*W. H. Clark, B. S., Editor, Abingdon, Ill.
*O. P. Nicholas, B. S., San Francisco, Cal.
*Maggie Thompson (Harris), M. E. L., Macomb, Ill.

1865.

*A. Linn, A. M., deceased.
*M. N. Parker, B. S., Teacher, Sabetha, Kan.

1864.

*S. P. Lucy, A. M., deceased.
*C. S. Woodmansee, A. B., Mississippi.
*J. Hyde, B. S., deceased.
*Bettie Davis (Lucy), M. E. L., Teacher, Wichita, Kansas.
*Lizzie Lyon (Linn), M. E. L., Hastinos, Neb.

1863.

Eli Fisher, A. M., Minister, State Evangelist, Oregon.
Belle Johnson, M. A., deceased.
Leroy Skelton, A. B., Minister, deceased.
*L. M. Butler (Ground), M. E. L., Monmouth, Ill.
*A. Linn, B. S., deceased.

1862.

Samuel K. Hallam, A. M., Minister, Belton, Tex.
*S. M. Charles, A. M., Aurora, Ill.
*Judge Durham, A. M., College President, Irvington, California.
*G. H. Laughlin, A. M., Prof. in State Normal School, Kirksville, Mo.
*W. S. Ross, A. M., Farmer, Alma, Ill.
*H. A. Coffeen, Editor, Danville, Ill.
*S. P. Harris (Reed), M. E. L., Sheffield, Ill.
*D. S. Ross (Laughlin), M. E. L., Kirksville, Mo.

1861.

T. R. Bryan, A. B., Kansas City, Mo.
W. J. Carpenter, A. M., College President, Colusa, Cal.
H. D. Clark, A. M., Minister, Mt. Sterling, Ky.
Mollie G. Clark (Hawk), M. A., Mt. Carroll, Ill.
Sallie J. Davidson (Crawford), M. A., Eureka, Ill.
Rutilia Gillum (Hoyt), M. A., Forrest, Ill.
J. F. Davidson, A. M., Lawyer, Hannibal, Mo.
D. V. B. Hallam, A. B., Merchant, Los Angeles, Cal.
Nellie R. Jones (Bryan), M. A., Kansas City, Mo.
A. H. Smith, A. B., Teacher, Eureka, Ill.
J. H. Rowell, A. M., Lawyer, Bloomington, Ill.
Lizzie A. Waughop (Wilmot), M. A., Sparland, Ill.

1860.

E. W. Dickinson, A. M., Eureka, Ill.
*A. P. Aten, A. M., Minister, Owensborough, Ky.

*J. H. Black, A. M., Farmer, Ridgefield, Ill.
*J. H. Freeman, A. B., Deceased.
*C. E. Price, A. M., Surgeon U. S. A., Fort Custar, Mont.
*J. A. Dawson, B. S., deceased.
*H. C. Maxwell, B. S., deceased.
*W. S. Ross, B. S.
*Fannie Charles, M. E. L., deceased.

1859.

*G. T. Carpenter, A. M., deceased.
*A. M. Coffeen, A. M., Champaign, Ill.
*J. M. Martin, A. M., Santa Rosa, California.
*A. P. Bennett (Martin), M. E. L., Santa Rosa, California.
*E. L. Covey (Tickner), M. E. L.
*M. A. Gaines (Coffeen), M. E. L., Champaign, Ill.

1858.

*C. C. Button, A. B., deceased.
*M. F. Button, A. M., deceased.
*W. F. Griffin, A. M., Carthage, Ill.
*W. D. Steward, A. B., deceased.
*A. J. Thompson, A. M., Minister, Louisville, Ky.
*G. H. Field, B. S., Physician, St. Louis, Mo.
*M. C. Murphy (Hallam), M. E. L., Galesburg, Ill.
*A. L. Upham (Wood), M. E. L., Virginia, Ill.
*E. J. Whitman (Durham), M. E. L., Irvington, Cal.

1857.

*Fannie Davis (Smith), M. E. L., Abingdon, Ill.
*M. G. Mahew (Lonsdale), M. E. L.. Columbia, Mo.

HONORARY DEGREES.

George Callender, A. M., Eureka, Ill., 1869.
Elmira J. Dickinson, M. A., Eureka, Ill., 1869.
O. S. Reed, A. M., Springfield, Ill., 1869.
J. B. Crane, A. M., Baltimore, Md., 1872.
R. C. Norton, A. M., Ash Grove, Mo., 1873.
Carl Johann, A. M., Eureka, Ill., 1879, LL. D., 1887.
H. W. Everest, LL. D., Irvington, Ind., 1881.
B. J. Radford, LL. D., Eureka, Ills., 1893.

www.ingramcontent.com/pod-product-compliance
Lightning Source LLC
Chambersburg PA
CBHW021341110726
47900CB00005B/1561